COLD
FUSION

The Apocalypse Series
Book Two

Patrick Astre

Cover and Book design by eBook Prep
 www.ebookprep.com

February, 2016
ISBN: 978-1-61417-829-3

ePublishing Works!
www.epublishingworks.com

CHAPTER 1

I was headed toward the Wickenburg-Prescott area, driving one of those desert roads that eventually hooks-up with US 60, when I saw her in my side mirror. She passed me as if my SUV with beefed-up 380 LIP engine was merely parked on the side of the road and not doing eighty. She drove some kind of Japanese sports job, bearing down on the horn and gas as she passed. Her features and long dark hair flashed by, giving me barely enough time to identify her as female. Before I could figure out what the hell was wrong with her, another vehicle blew past me as if some demon tied both cars together in a madcap steeplechase.

The second car was a Plain Jane four door Crown Victoria, the kind favored by law enforcement throughout the country. I saw the outline of two men in the front seat.

I have a well-developed nose for trouble. Through my years growing up in Brooklyn, New York, followed by four years with the Army Rangers and twelve with ATF, this sort of sixth sense always warns me when something is about to go down.

I nailed the gas, and followed them. We drove that way for probably five minutes as she opened the gap between her car and the slower, bulkier Crown Vic.

I saw her problem coming, probably before she even realized it. The road twisted into a sort of S turn to avoid a huge boulder on one side and culvert on the other. Her brake lights flashed as she slowed frantically, but it was too late. She weaved around the first bend and completely lost it on the second one. I saw her car bounce up as it hit the raised shoulder of the road, coming down hard in the packed desert sand, slewing sideways until it rolled twice and came to rest on its side.

Moments later, the Crown Vic pulled over on the opposite side of the road and the two men got out. They looked to be in their mid-thirties, dressed in light conservative gray suits, like someone's idea of what an FBI agent should wear. I would have pulled right behind them, but as they emerged from their car, I saw they both had their weapons drawn.

If they were chasing some dangerous perp, it was the right thing to do. Even after rolling over twice, you couldn't take the chance a desperate individual wouldn't emerge from the wreck with just cuts and bruises and a .45 in their hands.

But still, something didn't feel right, and my hackles jumped when one of the men crossed the road, heading for the wreck, while his partner walked toward me, gun in hand.

I stopped about fifty yards away and got out of the car holding up my shield, yelling, "Federal officer."

I saw that slight twitch of the arm a split second before he raised his weapon. I dropped to the ground and the shot whined above my head, passing through the sheet metal of my open door with a dull plunk.

I rolled out of sight behind the SUV. The fall had taken my breath away and purple flashing spots danced in my eyes. I felt the coarse dirt and pebbles of the desert against my body, smelled the dust and heat of the place. I shook my head, had to get my breath back, meanwhile the shooter started crossing the distance toward me. I reached under my vest and pulled out one of my best friends since Amy died: A nine millimeter custom built H&K with a two-inch extra length barrel, rifled for competition accuracy and equipped with a modified eighteen round clip. I fired a quick shot, deliberately off by a few inches, saw dust kicking up at the target's feet. The guy backed up to his car. From the corner of my eye I saw his partner stopped a few feet from the wreck, and looking toward me. The shooter let off two more rounds that kicked up some dirt, inches from my face, trying to blow my head off. No warning shots there. I rolled, sighted down the barrel and squeezed off two rounds. At least one hit the guy. He spun around and crumpled with a yelping noise. His partner ran back, stopped in the middle of the road, held out his gun in a classic Weaver combat stance and fired twice into the wreck.

I've seen lots of evil shit in my career with ATF, and this was one of those truly repulsive events. I suddenly hated that guy with a killing rage. It takes a real mutt to fire at a woman lying there, most likely already hurt from the accident. I shot at the guy twice as he moved. I missed, but must have come close enough for him to hear the rounds singing just a few inches away. He ran back to the Crown Vic, firing as he went, forcing me to stay down. He threw his partner through the open door, pushed him to the passenger seat and jumped behind the wheel. The car took off in a cloud of road dust and screeching tires.

I stood and leaned against the SUV, closed my eyes for a moment, letting my heartbeat slowly return to something more normal. Out of instinct I looked at my watch, marking the event timeline. The digital read out fixed on 11:52 and the temperature approached one hundred. Undulating heat waves rose from the macadam surface of the road and I felt the desert sun like a blowtorch. No breeze stirred and the smell of cordite from the gunshots hung in the air. In the distance the Crown Vic disappeared to a fuzzy dot. I put the gun back in the holster and walked across the road to the wrecked car. Every step brought a lance of pain in my side and I struggled to stop panting as I walked. I felt like I had just gone the distance with Mike Tyson.

Nearly a year ago, at the hospital, they nicknamed me Lazarus, said I was one of a handful of people who took a direct hit from a .357 Magnum, full-load Talon munitions, and lived to wonder why. Usually the hydrostatic shock to the body alone would seize vital organs, shatter bone and rupture arteries. The bullet entered my right side, leaving an entry wound the size of a quarter and did a through-and-through, taking out part of the rib that deflected it, blowing out an exit hole in my back. Now, it's pretty much healed into a mass of angry red and purple scar tissue that never stops talking to me.

I crossed the road and walked the few feet to the wreck. The sports car rested on its side and the occupant lay half out of the sunroof. She was a slender, middle-aged woman who had probably been quite attractive until a few moments ago. She must have been in the process of crawling out of the overturned car, when the bastard fired those two shots, and both found their mark. A good chunk of her lower jaw had been blasted away and a wide stain, spreading red across her halter-top told me where the other round hit.

I knelt down and moved my hand toward her throat, feeling for a pulse, when she opened her eyes. Her light green orbs held panic, and something else, a mixture of resignation with a tinge of hope. She moved the part of her jaw that remained intact and a noise came out like something scrapping against her vocal chords.

"Don't," I said softly. "It's okay, you'll be all right."

I lied and I knew it, but worst of all, I was certain she knew it also, yet she tried again. I leaned forward.

"Key…take…Stan…chalk…please…"

I found myself making useless soothing noises, the kind you make when there's nothing else you can possibly do. I saw her left hand jerk upward in a move that morphed into a spasm. Something white and stained with her blood fell from her hand: An envelope.

"Don't…" she said.

"No, I'll hold it for you. I'll make sure you get it back. Help's on the way, you'll be okay."

"Don't…let…"

"Shh, don't try to talk."

"Let…them…get it."

A soft rattling noise came from deep within her and the light went from her eyes as her life force evaporated while I held her.

I gently laid her head on the ground and stood. I leaned against the wreck and thought of Amy, her face never far from my thoughts and now floating in my consciousness against the backdrop of the desert. A sob escaped my throat, and I felt the wetness rolling down my cheeks to be immediately evaporated by the voracious dryness and heat of the Arizona air.

I don't really know how long I stayed there in the suffocating stillness. It could have been a moment or it could have been an hour. I felt something small and hard in the envelope. I didn't open it, just folded it and placed it in my pocket.

I took out my cell phone and dialed 911.

CHAPTER 2

Albuquerque, New Mexico, bus terminal.

Nathan Ragowski, PhD, took a small pair of scissors he had purchased for just that purpose and cut up his driver's license, flushing the small laminated pieces down the toilet of the men's room in the Albuquerque bus terminal. He did the same with his credit cards, library card and every piece of ID carrying his name.

He removed a small bundle from his pocket, unwrapped it, and placed his new ID, Pennsylvania driver's license and two credit cards in his wallet.

His hands shook and he dropped the card and license twice before he got them into the little slots. Outside the stall, travelers moved about in the crowded men's room. At one point someone rattled the door to his stall. He barely managed to croak out a pitiful, "Just a minute." His throat felt clogged, as if he had swallowed a mouthful of dust.

He stepped out of the stall, holding the briefcase in one hand and the carry-on bag in the other. His fists were clenched tight enough to hurt and suppress the shakes he felt throughout his body. He was now officially Shelby Morgan, the name on the fake ID Sergei had given him.

He rubbed his new mustache. He could see the top of the bushy thing when he looked down his nose. It seemed strange and itched all the time from the theatrical glue holding it in place. At least the black-rimmed, clear, non-prescription glasses didn't bother him. As he exited the men's room he saw himself in the bathroom and wondered if his friends would have recognized him.

"Does not take too much to cause a change," Sergei had told him. "You never wear a hat and your hairline has receded, so you wear this cap, low on your forehead. There, now you look distinguished, the mustache and glasses, you are different person, *da?*" Sergei snapped a series of photos with a digital camera, and returned the next day with the license, credit card, and social security card.

"But how…"

"These things are from my world. Do not worry," Sergei had replied.

Indeed he was right. Nathan belonged to the world of science, the predictable environment of nuclear physics with clear rules and dependable cause and effects. He was thoroughly frightened in this new arena he had been thrust into, a domain of hidden power and deadly influence where nothing appeared as it really was.

He purchased a ticket for Kansas City, paid cash and got on the bus at the last minute. This early in the morning the bus was only about two thirds full. He walked down the center aisle, trying not to be obvious as he looked at each face. Two soldiers sitting together near the front, a young couple, his arm around her, more people sitting together, or single with that little aloof posture of those who traveled alone. A tall black man wearing rough work clothes seemed to stare at him a little too long. Nathan looked away as he sat down, briefcase on his lap. He felt awkward, holding this satchel, but it represented his only chance, perhaps his life. Sergei had been adamant about that.

Nathan placed the briefcase on the empty seat next to him. After a few moments he put it back on his lap. He wished he had one of those little chains that would fasten the case to his wrist.

Nathan spent a miserable five hours until the bus finally

reached the Amarillo depot. He was sure that black man stared at him constantly, watching him. He sat in his seat, not daring to move, while the passengers got off to stretch their legs or leave the bus. The black man didn't leave his seat.

When the driver returned and started the engine, Nathan suddenly stood and exited. He heard the driver calling after him, "Hey, we leave in five minutes, should'a taken a break before."

He ignored the driver and walked away rapidly, clutching his briefcase, until he reached one of the wide beams on the walkway and ducked behind it. He continued watching the bus as it left, right on time. No one had gotten off after him. He realized he had left his overnight bag on the bus, but it just wasn't important. Only the briefcase mattered.

Nathan purchased a new ticket, this time to Little Rock, Arkansas. From there he could chance a flight to New York. Once he landed at JFK, it was only a taxi ride to Brighton Beach in Brooklyn, and the safety of Sergei's people in that famous Russian enclave. He thought about Mary Orlowsky and wondered how she was doing. Had she made it to her destination, Los Angeles, to lose herself in that huge city, among her connections?

"They are more powerful than you can imagine," Sergei had said. "They are everywhere and will stop at nothing."

He liked Mary Orlowsky. He hoped she'd make it okay.

CHAPTER 3

One hundred miles outside of Phoenix, Arizona.

I stayed on the line with the 911 operator for at least ten minutes, giving her all the information. At the end she patched me through to the Sheriff's office and I repeated the story. This time a woman's voice came on the line.

"This is Shirley Case. I'm the Sheriff of Desert Spring County."

Desert Spring is a small county squeezed between Phoenix and adjoining Mariposa. The small wedge is mostly retirement communities of folks who prefer to avoid the sprawl of Phoenix yet not be engulfed by the vast stretches of desert that was Mariposa County.

Swell, I thought, now a small town Podunk sheriff's office would have jurisdiction over this murder.

"Sheriff, my name is Gaston Duval," I answered. "I'm an ATF agent. I gave your dispatcher my ID and badge number."

"I know, Lieutenant Duval. We're confirming it now."

"Look Sheriff, I'm on a side road that hooks up to Highway 60, about fifty miles from Morristown. I shot one of those guys, and they took off in a Ford Crown Victoria, 00 or 01. I gave you the Oklahoma tag number. They're headed north, you can nail them before they hit US 60."

"We're on it, sir. Are you okay?"

"Yeah, as fine as I'll ever be."

"Good. Please remain on the scene. We're ETA to your location in about twenty."

She sounded like a no-bullshit kind of person, possibly former military, which I liked. I tend to be leery of Sheriffs because it's an elected position. Sometimes they're more concerned about politics than law enforcement.

I put away the cell phone and leaned against the overturned car, looking down at the woman's body. Her eyes remained open, lifeless but still conveying some message I could almost feel. I thought of Amy, what she would say or do in this situation. Sadness enfolded me for this stranger, slaughtered for whatever senseless reason possessed her killers. She was well dressed with manicured nails and light makeup well applied. What went on in her life? What unwitting act caused her violent end on this desert road? Were loved ones waiting somewhere, listening for the noise of her automobile in the driveway? I could hear Amy as if she stood right there in the desert beside me.

C'mon, sport. Isn't that why you're in law enforcement, to speak for the victims, to do what others can't?

I knelt by the dead woman and closed her eyes.

"I will speak for you," I said softly, to her, and to myself.

I wrote her last words down in the small notepad I always carried.

Key—take—Stan, or maybe Dan—*chalk—please*—and finally*: Don't let them get it.* I felt the weight of the envelope in my pocket.

I walked back to my car and took a pair of latex gloves out of a canvas bag, what I call my "crime kit."

I put the gloves on and squatted next to her, facing the open sunroof of the overturned car. Only the lower part of her legs remained inside the vehicle. I had enough room to work the upper part of my body through the opening. I moved cautiously to avoid contaminating the site. A spider-work of cracks latticed the windshield, and the sun poured through, adding to the rays coming in the side windows, now facing directly upward. I started sweating in the intense heat of the cramped space.

I saw it jammed between the seat and the door, a small pocket book. I took it, got out of the stifling interior, and sat next to the wreck to examine the contents.

Her photo peered at me from the lamination, dismal as only a driver's license snapshot can be. I jotted down the information in my note pad.

Mary Orlowsky
27 Sunburst Drive, Unit #16A
Pojoacque, New Mexico
License Number 437789044

Okay Mary Orlowsky, I have your name and address, that's a start. Then I found her other ID and stared at it for a few moments. On that photo her smile radiated out at me, all flashing white teeth, short blond hair and bright eyes.

Los Alamos National Laboratory
Department of Energy
Employee—followed by a series of bar codes.
Special Division-CF Section

She worked at the nation's leading nuclear laboratory. That alone made it a national security issue. I wrote the information down, put the ID back and went through the rest of the purse. Everything else was standard stuff, lipstick, compact, tissue, but for one major exception: A Palm Pilot.

I held the device and stared at it a moment as a jumble of thoughts flashed through my mind. I couldn't extract the information and copy it before the local Sheriff's Department arrived, and when they got here, I sure wouldn't be part of the investigation and would not be privy to the information inside. I had all ready decided I would follow this. I wouldn't let these murdering bastards get away just because a small town Sheriff Department bungled it, or didn't care enough to see it through. Although I had no experience with local law enforcement in this part of the country, I instinctively didn't trust them to have the resources for something like this.

What do you think, Amy?

Go for it, Sport!

I made a snap decision and stashed the woman's Palm Pilot in my pocket. If I was satisfied with the investigation, I could always say I found it outside the car and in the heat of the moment, had forgotten it. What could they do?

I did another quick search of the car and found nothing. I replaced everything the way I had found it, and settled down to wait for the sheriff's people to arrive.

The heat continued, relentless. They say it's a dry heat out in the desert, not as bad as a humid hot day. I don't think they know what the hell they're talking about. I kept thinking about those classic desert pictures of cattle's skulls, bleached white and dead as could be. How do you think they got that way?

The scars in my side blazed with pain and the heat bore down on me. I stood, stretched and walked to the road. I was seriously thinking about getting in my Suburban and turning on the AC when I spotted the flashing red and blue lights of an approaching emergency vehicle. I waited at the side of the road and a Sheriff's Department cruiser pulled next to me.

The driver got out of the car and walked around to my side. She managed to convey authority yet maintained a feminine presence. She wore a Smokie hat with wide brim, a necessity in the desert sun, doubly so for her fair skin. Strands of blond hair peeked out from under the rim, complimented by two small gold earrings. She wore little make up and classic features framed deep blue eyes. A narrow scar ran a couple of inches along the bottom of her chin. She was pretty in a no-nonsense way, and the small scar highlighted it like a beauty mark.

I held out my ID, she took it, read it, passed it back to me, and held her hand out.

"Lieutenant, I'm Sheriff Shirley Case."

"Gaston Duval, good meeting you."

She nodded and asked me what happened.

"Are you taking my statement?"

"No, I just want to know how you saw it while it's fresh in your mind."

I told her, leaving out the part about the envelope and palm pilot.

"It was an execution," I stated at the end of my story. She stared at the body for a moment then returned her gaze to me.

"If it was, then they botched it. She may have spotted them, and tried to escape."

"Possible."

"Likely."

I shrugged, okay, if you say so, but I knew she was right.

CHAPTER 4

—————◆—————

Little Rock, Arkansas.

Nathan remembered reading somewhere that Little Rock, the State Capital, was probably the least interesting city in Arkansas. Well that didn't matter, he thought, he'd be out of there by tomorrow morning.

He started to feel a little better as soon as the Greyhound pulled out of the bus terminal. He dozed in fitful moments during the long trip from Amarillo, but he hadn't really slept in two days. Weariness lay over him like a prickly blanket. Things seemed a little better because he was pretty sure at this point that he had not been followed. He'd gotten off the bus, taken a taxi immediately outside the terminal, got out after three blocks and doubled back. He walked two blocks in the opposite direction until he reached a small indoor mall that included a travel agency.

Nathan purchased a ticket to JFK, an early flight the next morning, paid in cash and used his new ID.

"Will there be anything else Mister Morgan?" the travel agent asked.

He looked at her blankly, couldn't put his thoughts together until he realized she had used his new name. He shook his head to clear it, tried to put on a smile.

"Uh no, I mean yes. I'm sorry. I've been traveling all day.

I'm just beat."

"I understand Mister Morgan," she replied. "There's a nice Marriott across the river in the Convention Center. Would you like me to call for a reservation for you?"

"Please."

It was dark when he left the travel agency, and in spite of the lights, he felt vaguely threatened. Somewhere out there some very nasty people wanted him dead. A middle-aged, well-dressed woman passed opposite him and their eyes met. She turned away and he realized he must not look very good, unshaven, rumpled, carrying this briefcase and nothing else.

The air had that city smell of dusty concrete, automobile traffic and people. Nathan hailed a cab to the Convention Center but made the driver let him out at the pedestrian walkway to the bridge. The Arkansas River split the city in two with the Convention Center rising on the other side, just over the bridge. The sidewalk was almost deserted. He felt a little more secure than in traffic. He'd felt trapped inside the cab, but now his fear subsided a bit. He saw the Convention Center from this side of the river. A short walk across and he'd be in the Marriott. There were shops in there and he would buy some fresh clothes, toiletries and a carry on bag to replace the one he had left on the bus in Amarillo. A quick ride to the airport early next morning and by the end of tomorrow he'd be safe in Brighton Beach with Sergei's people.

He'd walked halfway across when he noticed the jogger approaching from the opposite side. It wasn't exactly a jogger, rather a race walker, moving with that comical fast gait using exaggerated hip and arm movements. The man appeared older, at least in his sixties with a shock of white hair. Somebody's grandpa was trying to stay in shape for the grandkids.

When the old man was a bare ten feet away, he stopped for a moment, unhooked a water bottle from his belt and raised it to his mouth.

Nathan heard a soft whoosh and felt a sting in his neck.

He reached with his free hand and grasped something soft protruding from his flesh. He pulled and it came loose. He looked at it, but couldn't seem to get his thoughts together. The small dart-like thing had a feather at the end and a thin needle that had embedded in his neck.

He knew something was very wrong, yet he felt at peace. The briefcase slipped out of his hand and it didn't seem to matter. All sensations ebbed out of his body and his sight dimmed. He was barely aware of the jogger coming level with him and reaching under. Then the world seemed to tilt, the ground became the sky, the sky the darkness of the river below as the jogger flipped Nathan over the side of the bridge railing.

When his body smashed into the water, it lost what little consciousness remained. He didn't feel a thing as he drowned beneath the dark, muddy waters of the Arkansas River.

CHAPTER 5

One hundred miles outside of Phoenix Arizona.

Three deputies arrived in two cruisers. I think it must have been half the police force of Desert Spring County. One of them quickly erected a small shade tent while the other strung yellow crime-scene tape around Mary Orlowsky's overturned automobile. Her spirit haunted me, having left her savaged body as it lay there, half on the desert floor—half out of her car, it hovered over me, spoke to me. *Find justice for me*, it said, *help me, speak for me.*

I sat in a folding chair under the shade tent while one of the deputies took my statement via a small digital recorder. I felt dazed and the tender scar tissue in my side throbbed, so I popped a couple of Demerols and a Codeine. I knew I would have to deal with that growing dependency, but first I had to get stronger.

The deputy finished. I walked over to where Shirley Case leaned against her cruiser, writing in a notebook. She looked up as I approached and gave me a tiny smile.

"Hey," she said. "You okay, Lieutenant?"

"Call me Gast, and yeah, I'm as okay as I'll be for a while."

She nodded and looked at me. I liked her face and especially her eyes, a mixture of gray and blue framed by beautiful lashes. They looked natural, but who could tell?

"Any luck with the perp's auto?" I asked, getting my thoughts back onto Mary Orlowsky's killers.

She took off her hat, releasing a mass of shoulder length blond hair. She wiped her forehead, and in one smooth gesture swept her hair to the top of her head and put the "Smokie" hat back on.

"No, not a sign, but they can't go anywhere," she said. "I notified Mariposa County Sheriff and Arizona Highway Patrol. Roads are blocked and there are a dozen units out there now. Problem is, we've got lots of little canyons, culverts and rock formations they can get behind, you know, just pull off the road and hide. They must have done that, because we've covered all the exits."

"Do you have detectives in your department?"

"You gotta be kidding Lieut...uh, Gast. My entire department is fourteen people, including clerical and dispatch. Phoenix Homicide will handle it. I've notified them, along with the Bureau."

"I think the Bureau's going to take it and Phoenix will let it go."

"You're probably right," she replied. "With the victim's New Mexico plates and Los Alamos ID and the perps' Oklahoma tags you reported, that definitely makes it interstate and the Lab connection gives it a potential national security issue."

"Coroner?"

"Phoenix."

She opened the back door of her cruiser, reached inside and pulled out a quart plastic bottle of water.

"Here," she said, handing me the bottle. "Keep drinking water. You don't realize how quickly you dehydrate here."

I nodded, took a long pull and handed the bottle back to her.

"You keep it," she said. "You sure you're okay? You look kind of pale."

She was right, I felt dizzy and my side throbbed. No exertion, the doctors had said. Right.

I walked under the shade tent and sat heavily on one of the folding chairs the deputy had placed next to the field table.

It's a sound etched in the backdrop of my life, the kind of unique noise that brings memories filled with adventures, bone chilling anxieties and terrors, the steady thumping noise of big rotors beating the heated, thick desert air.

I saw it while it was barely a dot, then as it approached at its cruising speed of 160 mph, a Blackhawk helicopter, running low, about a hundred feet above deck. The big machine flared, and dropped to a smooth landing across the road from the crime scene. The rotors created a dust storm that covered the deputies' cars and scattered the crime scene tape meticulously placed by Sheriff Shirley Case's little police force.

I stood turning my head away as I heard Shirley mutter, "Asshole."

The machine was painted a dull gray, adorned with a round FBI seal and just below that, a strange logo with the letters I.R.D. and the legend "Investigative Research Division."

The door of the Blackhawk opened and two men got out. One crossed the road and stopped facing the wrecked auto. He topped out at least six feet four on a thick frame, and wore a dark blue jump suit devoid of any insignias. The man following him had on a dark tee shirt with FBI stenciled on the back. Behind them six more men got out of the helicopter and started lugging equipment toward the crash site. I followed Sheriff Case as she approached the two men. She had a bit of a pissed off expression on her face and I could see her rapidly building an attitude.

"Tell your people to back off. This is my crime scene, I have jurisdiction."

The big guy turned and looked at her for a moment, then reached in his pocket and placed an ID attached to a chain, around his neck. He held it out to Sheriff Case.

"Dallas Wilson, director of Investigative Research Division. We're a new agency under the Justice Department, created by the Enhanced Patriot Act. Your jurisdiction is superseded, Sheriff. This agent will give you the details," he said, waving to another guy wearing an FBI tee shirt.

"You're the witness?" he asked turning to me.

"Yup," I said.

"Gaston Duval, from ATF?"

"Yup."

I didn't like this guy's attitude and my Gary Cooper impersonation tends to irritate people like him, which I find very gratifying, if not always productive. It didn't seem to work on Dallas Wilson. He nodded then walked toward the overturned car, ignoring me.

Shirley Case looked like she was seriously contemplating shooting the guy. Her mouth opened but before she could say anything her cell phone rang. She listened for a few minutes, gave a few brief okays, yes sirs, and one I understand then flicked the cell phone closed and put it back on her belt clip. Now she looked really pissed.

"Takes care of that," she said. "It was the County Executive on the phone. He got a call from the Governor. We're to turn over the entire investigation to the FBI and their new investigative group, lock stock and barrel."

She called off her deputies as the IRD men swarmed over the wreck. One of them examined Mary Orlowsky's body and made some notes in a pad. They took a body bag, placed the corpse inside, and zipped it up. Others scoured every inch of the car, removing items and placing them in evidence bags.

The FBI man came over and asked to speak to Shirley and me.

"I'm agent Orlando Guttieres, liaison for IRD. You are the witness?" He asked, nodding in my direction.

"That's right," I replied. "My name is Lieutenant Gaston Duval, Alcohol, Tobacco and Firearms, also a federal agency. I never heard of IRD. Why is the FBI acting as runners for this group?"

Agent Guttieres managed to look annoyed and embarrassed at the same time.

"Look, Mister Duval, IRD is a newly created special division charged with investigating and closing only cases of national security. Under EPA, Enhanced Patriot Act, the FBI is to provide all assistance requested. That's my job with this team."

"You're required to wait for a coroner," Shirley Case said, waving toward the two men busy placing Mary Orlowsky in the body bag.

"One of those men is a federally licensed coroner. This team is fully equipped and authorized to investigate and control any crime scene."

"They're good with the control part, but as far as investigating, it looks to me like they're just tagging and bagging everything."

"Mister Duval, you and the Sheriff here have no idea what goes on with this case so you cannot possibly make any judgments. However, the important thing here is that both of you fall under Enhanced Patriot Act-Title 18-07. Anything you have seen or have information about involving this crime, you are required to report immediately. You are also prohibited from revealing any information you have knowledge of to any source except the FBI or an IRD investigator. Do you understand?"

We both replied that we understood.

"Good. Sheriff, will you inform your deputies of this?"

"Yeah."

"Very well, it behooves you to take this matter very seriously," Agent Guttieres said as he walked away.

"Prick," Shirley muttered.

CHAPTER 6

As I walked to my car, the heat poured out of the ground, and each step was a chore. It was closing in on evening and the sun gave me one last furnace blast for good measure. I reached my car and leaned against the hot metal surface a moment. My side ached and the world spun. I was getting ready to pop a Codeine when I saw Sheriff Case approaching.

"Where you going? You don't look too good."

"I don't feel too great either. Where's the nearest motel?"

"'Fraid it's about forty miles away, at the end of this road. Can I give you a ride there? I'll have one of my deputies drive your car down."

"I'll take you up on that," I said.

I finished the water bottle while she drove, and closed my eyes for a few minutes until things steadied down a bit.

"I really do appreciate this, Sheriff."

"My pleasure, and you can call me Shirley. What's wrong anyway, touch of a virus?"

"I wish. Got shot in a raid near Wichita, nasty combination of terrorists and drug runners."

"I heard about that. Happened last year, some fatalities too, weren't there?"

"Yeah, good friends of mine."

"Shit, I'm sorry. Didn't you guys wear armor? Was it a head shot?"

"Yeah we had armor and helmets. Problem is they had those new Full-Point Teflon munitions. That stuff is designed to go right through body armor, and it does. There wasn't supposed to be any in the country. The Habu Hassan cell brought it in, gave it to that Mexican crew we raided. I got hit in the side, but..." I stopped at that point, didn't want to explain. I bit my lip and looked out the window.

"I'm so sorry," I heard her say.

"It's okay Sheriff, nothing to do but go on."

"How long until...I mean is it permanent?"

"No. I should be fully recovered in a couple of months. I'm on line of duty convalescent leave."

"Will you be going back?"

C'mon, sport. You ain't giving up that easy.

Yeah, right. Thanks, Amy.

"Probably. I guess, shit, I don't really know," I replied and looked out the window again.

I saw what she meant when she said there were all kinds of places to hide a car. Even in the growing darkness, culvers and hills of boulders sporadically lined the road, interspaced by outcroppings of land and rocks from some archeological upheavals millions of years ago. Shirley had the scanner on in the cruiser and checked periodically with the other police units, but so far nothing. My perpetrators seemed to have vanished.

"So what'd you think of that whole setup back there?" I asked her.

"Something's wrong, that's for sure, never seen anything like it, and I've worked with Feds before."

"You have? Here in Desert Spring County?"

"No," she replied. "In Boston. I was a homicide detective with BPD, North Side. We did lots of work with the FBI."

"So how'd you get from a bitch of a job like that, to Arizona?"

It took her a moment to answer. When she did, I felt the strain in her voice.

"That job almost ate me alive. Cost me my marriage and dammed near took a bite out of my soul. My own partner swallowed his gun and I never saw it coming. I mean, you step everyday in the sewers of humanity, get down to the lowest denominator, and pretty soon it just carries you along. I had to leave, answered an ad for a deputy sheriff out here and a year later ran for the office and got elected. I hit it off with the retirees that make up the biggest block of votes in this county."

She paused for a minute, looked at me and smiled, "So you see Gast, I've got lots of investigative experience for a hick country sheriff."

I tried to picture her toe-to-toe with some low life on the North Side, and yeah, I could see it, she had a certain undeniable toughness about her.

"I see five things wrong," I said. "Tell me if you agree on them. One: the speed of that response. I mean an entire team in a Blackhawk within three hours of notification? When does that happen?"

"Never that I know of," she replied. "Although, that by itself isn't a problem, because maybe it's that new agency, or whatever it is, this IRD section."

"Okay." I said. "How about for number two, no crime-scene work, none of those guys did anything technical. No prints, no fiber searches, nothing. Number three, which is the biggest as far as I'm concerned, they didn't seem to give a shit about catching the perps. If I'd been in charge of that team I would have dropped off a couple of bozos to search the scene, then jumped back in that Blackhawk, coordinate with ground units and caught those bastards. They didn't do any of that. Four, no cooperation, they cut you right out of the loop and sent us all to take a hike."

"You have no idea how much that pisses me off," she said. "I mean how'd they get to the Governor so fast and get him on the county executive's ass to pull me from the case? All right, so both the Governor and County Executive are political toadies, hacks, but still, it should take longer than a couple of hours. Whoever yanked the strings must have some pull."

"And fifth and last, most disturbing to me," I said, "Those guys weren't investigating the scene. They were *cleaning* it, getting everything in bags, taking it away. I'm willing to bet that stuff will never be seen again, even with a court order."

She nodded and we rode quietly with our thoughts for a while until the lights of a motel appeared, followed by a string of businesses marking the end of that desolate stretch of road.

Shirley pulled into the parking spot near the office. I got out with my bag and walked around to her side.

"You going to be okay?" she asked. "Need a doctor or anything?"

"No, I'll be fine, a good night's rest will do the trick, but you know what I really need?"

"What?"

"I need to know that something's being done about Mary Orlowsky, that she didn't just get killed in front of me, a federal officer, and have her murder ignored or swept under a carpet as some bastard's idea of something good for national security. Can you work with me on that Shirley?"

The briefest hint of a smile lit her face, and quickly disappeared as something surfaced in the electric blue of her eyes.

"Oh yeah Gast, that I can do. Why don't you use your ATF connections to find out what you can about this case and that IRD outfit with this Dallas Wilson guy, and I'll track down information on Mary Orlowsky."

We exchanged cards and cell phone numbers and agreed to touch base in a day or two.

I checked into the motel, told the clerk a deputy would drop off my car and went to my room where I took a couple of pain killers, laid down on the bed, and basically, passed out.

CHAPTER 7

————◆————

I felt a hell of a lot better the next morning and started the day with just one Demerol, determined that it would have to last 24 hours. I sensed the dependency growing and knew I had a tough fight ahead.

After getting my car from the office clerk, I paid the bill and drove to the first diner for breakfast. Nine in the morning and the temperature had already reached the eighties. I got back in the car, turned on the AC, took out my cell phone and dialed the Oklahoma City ATF office. I identified myself, asked for information services and got Latoya Billings.

Latoya is a hefty African-American woman who's always been a little sweet on me since I helped her out of a bad situation with an ex boyfriend.

"Hey Latoya, it's Gast."

"Gast! How's my favorite white boy? Great to hear from you sweetie! How you doing?"

"Getting better Latoya, getting better."

"So you ready to come by sweetie, let me take you for a ride."

"I don't know if I could survive it Latoya, all that black sensuality."

"Listen Gast, I never got a chance to tell you, I mean they

kept all visitors away, and then they moved you, but I knew you'd call sooner or later. What I mean, shit Gast, I just don't know how to say it. I'm real sorry about everything."

The color washed out of the world and the bright sunshine disappeared from my vision, turning the day into an oily glow. I stayed very still and felt a sharp pain as I bit my lip.

"Gast?"

Sometimes it works that way. I can pass a spell of time and everything is cool, like soft background music. But suddenly, something sets it off and reality hits me like a studded two by four and gnaws on the sore edges of my soul.

"Gast?"

I open my mouth and I'm surprised at my voice, hoarse, dry as fried dust.

"I'm here Latoya."

"Oh God sweetie, I'm so sorry, I didn't mean...I had to say it, you know?"

"No, it's okay Latoya. In a way, you were involved too, you know?"

"Oh sweetie," she said, and we were both silent, tied together by friendship and memories. A long moment passed, maybe an hour, maybe a minute. I really didn't know, until the image of another woman appeared in front of my eyes: Mary Orlowsky.

"Latoya?"

"Yeah, sweetie."

"I need a little help."

"Name it, baby."

I told her the whole story of Mary Orlowsky's death, meeting Sheriff Shirley Case, running into IRD and being chased off the scene. I also related to her that Shirley and I agreed we would continue to dig into this strange murder.

"Could you use your resources Latoya? I need to know more about this IRD outfit, I never heard of them. Also, what's happening with this case? Who is Mary Orlowsky? Anything at all you can find out."

"Sweetie I've been running the information services division for the last twelve years. Whatever's out there that can be found, I'll find it for you."

"Be discreet Latoya, I've been warned off by this Dallas Wilson guy and his Bureau agent sidekick, Miller. Don't let on what you're up to."

"You think I just got here from the backwoods of Alabama yesterday? I know my way around the system Gast."

"Yeah, I know you do. Just be careful, you hear? I got a feeling about this one."

"Okay, I got it," she said.

"Thanks Latoya, you're a sweetheart," and I sent her a kiss over the wire.

"Ooh," she said. "I'll take a rain check for that one in person."

CHAPTER 8

———◆———

Hotel De Ville Louis XIV, Bordeaux, France.

Overlooking the *Place De L'opera,* and beyond that the Gironde River fronting the busy Port of Bordeaux, the Louis XIV is quite probably Europe's most opulent and newest hotel. Although the latest technology was used to build the structure, the interior brings the visitor back to the extravagant age of the Sun King, Louis XIV who lent the hotel its name. No cost had been spared in the wealth of exotic imported materials and decors. A highly trained staff, the best in Europe it was said, catered to every whim a wealthy visitor could have. It was common knowledge among moneyed circles world wide, that if you wanted to visit the south of France, the Louis XIV in Bordeaux was the only place to stay.

Sir Hubert Montrose III didn't think too much about the Louis XIV. To him it was merely a place to conduct some very special business. Opulence therefore, was *de rigueur.*

Montrose stepped outside his villa and paused, taking in the magnificent panorama.

He'd had the house built on top of a low bluff strategically designed for the view. Toward the West a series of dunes some five kilometers away marked the beginning of vast beaches fronting the Atlantic Ocean. The

North side faced the waters of the Bay of Arcachon, and since the floor of the Bay only rose a few inches above sea level, it emptied itself twice daily with the falling tide, revealing vast stretches of tidal mud flats.

Facing east, the resort city of Arcachon backed by stretches of pine forests, bordered the Bay. Following the *Nationale* road from Arcachon, the city of Bordeaux lay a bare fifty kilometers away.

Montrose believed he had found one of the most beautiful places on earth and spent as much time as he could here, as opposed to any of his dozen or so luxury homes around the world.

Sir Hubert Montrose was the majority shareholder and chairman of the board of BPC Inc., the second largest petroleum conglomerate in the world. During the nineties and the decade following, Montrose quietly accumulated vast holdings in British Royal Petroleum and Conoco Oil until he managed to broker a merger between the two giants creating British Petroleum-ConocoOil: BPCO.

Montrose's chauffeur/bodyguard pulled the big Citroen DS limo to the front of the house, got out and opened the door for his boss.

Although it was mid morning, traffic still jammed the streets of Bordeaux so it took the better part of an hour to reach the Louis XIV. When he walked into the lobby, accompanied by formally dressed, solicitous concierges, he went directly to a small alcove behind the spacious front desk. A single plain door stood recessed into the burnished copper of the decorative fascia surrounding the alcove, affixed to the door, porcelain letters spelled out *Prive-Defense de Rentrer;* Private-Entry Forbidden. Montrose pushed buttons on the keypad located where a knob would normally be, and the door opened. He walked in, letting the door shut behind him and it latched itself in a soft whirl of electronic gears.

He stood in a small private elevator lobby that the public would never see. The elevator led to the 13th floor reserved secretly for the exclusive use of the *Commite Des Cinq.*

The name *Commite Des Cinq*, Committee of Five, would never be found anywhere, yet it had provided financing for the Louis XIV and owned it outright. The 13th floor did not show on any floor plans or map of the hotel, but it was the most luxuriously appointed floor, serving as the *Commite's* global meeting place.

Sir Hubert Montrose III, with his vast BPCO holdings served as the unofficial chairman of the *Commite*. An associate of Montrose and next member of the *Commite,* was Nicholas Petrovsky, a ruthless Muscovite who used the fall of the Soviet Union to hire former KGB officers and Russian mobsters to consolidate Petrovskaya Eastern Resources: P.E.R. Petrovsky ruled the giant conglomerate like Stalin did Russia in the forties. P.E.R. extended tentacles throughout the republics that had constituted the old Soviet Union, and deep into Asian oil, energy and manufacturing corporations.

Richard Vandermere, representing Energy Sources Ltd, was the third member of the *Commite Des Cinq*. Once dubbed by Worth Magazine as "The wealthiest Recluse on Earth." Vandermere liked it that way. Having parlayed into one of the largest dotcom fortunes ever recorded, his obscure company held controlling interests in three multinational oil corporations whose names were known to all automobile-owning households.

Burt Wells Jr., the fourth member of the *commite,* had surprised everyone since he reached his 21st birthday. Heir to a vast Texas fortune going back to coal and railroads at the turn of the century, Burt had lived the life of the spoiled playboy heir to the hilt. His uncle, trustee to the family trust fund, and the family attorneys expected to keep Burt content on his large stipend while they happily went about running the family business. Instead, Burt Wells Jr. instinctively grasped business opportunities, and took control of the family fortune. In just a few years, he'd expanded it into vast manufacturing empires serving the global needs of the petroleum, natural gas and coal industries.

The fifth member of the *Commite,* Sylvie Papadapeoulos, last heiress to a legendary shipping empire, had transformed it into a global monopolistic enterprise that shipped and transported 90% of the world's petroleum, natural gas and coal.

Montrose walked into the meeting room and nodded a curt greeting to the members gathered around a mahogany table nearly the size of a tennis court. A waiter materialized at his side, placed a cup of strong black coffee, just the way he liked it, at his side and promptly vanished. No one said a word, for this was far from a social gathering.

Montrose raised a hand toward a technician at a computer console in the far side of the room. The man activated some commands through the keyboard. A foggy glow materialized from an unseen aperture in the ceiling. A beam of light descended in a transparent shiny column until it reached the surface of the table. The technician tapped a few more keys, and quickly left. No one would enter the meeting room until the five members were done. The room itself was one of the most secure places on earth, "swept" daily for any listening devices. Continuously updated arrays of the most sophisticated electronic anti-spying devices protected the sanctity of conversations held within.

A face appeared in the center of the column of light. From each of the five members' seats, the face appeared to look at them directly. It was a state-of-the-art holographic live conferencing system connected to an encrypted satellite hook up. The electronically disembodied face of Dallas Wilson spoke first.

"Good morning sir. Am I coming through clear?"

"You are, Mister Wilson. Progress report if you please."

"Yes sir. I am happy to say that we have eliminated the second target, Doctor Nathan Ragowski, in Little Rock, Arkansas. Doctor Mary Orlowsky was neutralized the day before."

"And the third one Mister Wilson? Doctor Yakov Katamay? He is after all the key player and the final link, is he not?"

The holographic representation of Dallas Wilson held such quality of details that even the small wrinkles around the corners of his eyes clearly showed as he frowned.

"Doctor Katamay has proven to be more difficult. We believe he has connections within the Russian expatriate community and they are sheltering him."

"I will send someone to turn those miserable bastards upside down. His shelter will evaporate," Nicholas Petrovsky growled.

"That may be useful," Wilson's holographic figure replied, "providing the right people are sent with all due discretion."

"There is a time-limit here Dallas," Montrose cut in. "The window is closing for effective suppression. If you do not succeed, there will be no choice but to activate the Tinia Protocol."

"We will stay on it. Hopefully I will have good news on my next report."

"See that you do," Montrose replied, and severed the connection. The holograph vanished instantly. He turned his gaze to the other four seated around the table as he spoke.

"Gentlemen, Miss Papadapeoulos, I intend to stay at my suite in the Louis XIV until this matter is resolved one way or another. I want a reaffirmation by verbal vote that we are all in agreement as to the use of the Tinia Protocol. Your vote is now being recorded. Mister Petrovsky?"

"Yes. Whatever is needed."

"Mister Vandermere?"

"Yes."

"Mister Wells?"

Burt Wells Jr. slowly shook his head and his voice when it came, sounded like the whisper of silk across a rough surface.

"For heaven's sake man, this will mean the death of millions of people."

"Yes Mister Wells. You knew this might be a possibility when you voted for this course of action, and funded one fifth of it, as well as using your influence. It's too late to back out at this stage. To do so would end our way of life, change the world for the worse."

"Perhaps I may have erred. Perhaps I never thought the day might come when…" He looked around him, his face flushed and a haunted look came in his eyes as he stood.

"Look," he said. "You have my word, you may be assured of my silence, but I simply cannot continue to participate in this monstrous scheme."

"You are a fool." Sylvie Papadapeoulos whispered between clenched teeth.

"All right, Mister Wells. As long as we may be assured of your discretion, you are free to go."

The slightest tic animated the corner of Burt Wells Jr's mouth and his hands shook perceptibly as he left the room.

"Sylvie Papadapeoulos?"

"I vote yes, of course. Are we really going to let that idiot walk away from this?"

"I assure you he will be silent," Sir Hubert Montrose III replied.

CHAPTER 9

I felt its presence. Somewhere up in those hills, or the outcropping of huge boulders that composed this part of the Arizona desert, less than fifty miles from Scottsdale. I sensed the crosshairs of a military sniper rifle targeting the silhouette of my head behind the windshield.

I passed the sign bearing the legend "Private-No Entry Without Prior Approval." Well I certainly had prior approval, yet I knew that in spite of it, anyone approaching the Consoli estate would automatically be in the crosshairs of something powerful enough to bring instant death to those attempting a move against them. This kind of caution was the reason Vito Consoli had reached his eighties, the only big-time mobster to retire to Arizona since Joseph "Joe Bananas" Bonnano.

I continued, slowing down to negotiate the continuous serpentine turns, just like the designers had intended. After another ninety-degree turn, I stopped the car directly in front of the security gate. Even though I had visited a number of times before, the sudden emergence of the security stop never failed to surprise me. I shut off the car, got out and walked to the gate. It looked deceptively flimsy, but I knew it would take an armored personnel carrier to pass through. Stainless steel bars deployed on

Patrick Astre

pivots held in a track system anchored to the bedrock surrounding the road, and backed by titanium mesh, all painted and decorated to resemble the portal of some Renaissance country palace. A few feet behind the gate, four apertures peered out of the ground like air vents, but were actually a high tech version of powerful land mines. That was in case someone really came with an armored personnel carrier.

Twenty feet past the gate, a guard post stood. Built to blend in with its surroundings, it looked like a miniature southwestern adobe condo. Two guards were outside holding AR-15's. The gate slid open. One of the guards waved me inside. I got back in the car, drove up to the gate and stopped.

A man came out of the guardhouse. His olive complexion, burnished by the desert sun, gave his skin a youthful appearance that belied his true age. I figured that he had to be in his seventies by now. His face was handsome with the long, slightly hooked nose and classic features found in ancient Roman sculptures. His hair was dark. It had been salt and pepper last time I saw him. He must have been hitting the old Grecian Formula. One thing hadn't changed: The muscles of his arms stretched the golf shirt he wore and not a trace of a potbelly rounded the waist of his tan slacks.

I stepped toward him. He grabbed me in a bear hug that sent flashes of pain from my side. He pushed me back and held my shoulders at arms length the way he had always done for the last twenty or so years whenever we met. His voice resonated, the timbre strong and confident, as if he took voice lessons.

"Gast, you look good. How you feeling, boy?"

"Good Franco, I'm good, getting my strength back."

"Glad to hear it. You'll be staying with us a few days?"

"Yeah, one or two, not sure."

"Well I don't hafta tell you, ya got an open ticket here."

"Thanks Franco, you look great too. Did something with the gray eh?" I said, pointing to his temple.

"Nah wise ass, it's the desert air, darkens your hair. Betcha didn't know that, college and all."

I smiled at him. I couldn't remember a time when Franco hadn't been around like a wise old uncle, dispensing tough love to Anthony and me as we grew up in the rough sections of New Lots and Canarsie, in Brooklyn, NY. One of his duties was watching out for us since we were seven or eight. His other duties had included running Vito Consoli's most prosperous crew as *Capo*, chief enforcer, and eventually, *Consiglieri* of the Consoli family.

"Leave your car here, the boys will bring it to the house. Get in," he said, motioning toward a golf cart with overhanging sunshade. I sat beside him as he drove the cart up the road.

"So when did you break down, Franco? Started taking up golf, I mean."

"What are you, a wise ass now? You know what the problem is in Arizona? There ain't enough Guineas around. This place is packed with fucking Wasps and Jews, retired accountants and lawyers, walk around all day in their stupid shorts and fucking flower shirts playing golf. White shirts and white shoes, what kinda outfits are these anyway? You know what we call'em?"

"What?"

"Fuckin Q-Tips."

I grinned as he laughed and I replied, "That's why you got shoe polish on your hair now?"

"Hey, fuck you kid. I shoulda stepped on your oxygen hose when they had you hooked up to all that shit in the hospital."

That was another of my memories from my months in the hospital. Whenever I opened my eyes, someone from the Consolis would be there. Sometimes Anthony, or Maria, Anthony's wife, other times it would be Franco, even the old man himself, or at least one of the old timers, "made men" who had followed Vito into his retirement in Arizona. When I gained enough consciousness to receive the news about Amy, it was Vito, Franco, Anthony and

Maria who held up my spirit, willed me to live, to keep going. My parents are both dead, and my sister lives in New Jersey with her husband and three little kids. She visited twice, but it was the Consolis who provided the strength. In spite of his terrible reputation and the things he was supposed to have done, I always felt affection for Franco, and it was never stronger than at this moment.

"Hey kid," he said, his voice now soft, "listen, I mean I said it a couple of times, but I want to say it again. I'm sorry, what happened, broke our hearts, ya know?"

I looked away and remembered what Amy had told me.

You're a mess of contradictions, sport. I mean your best friends are all Mafia hoods and you're ATF. How'd that happen?

One's got nothing to do with the other, Amy. They practically raised me.

Still don't make sense. Good thing I love you, Gast.

"I know Franco. Thanks," I replied and squeezed his arm, feeling the muscles like stones wrapped in leather.

We approached the main house, a great Tudors style mansion forming a wide U fronted by a circular driveway and flanked by gardens and graveled paths. About a hundred yards to the right stood a grove of trees, a swimming pool and a cabana the size of a suburban track house. It looked as if a grand magician had transported a chunk of some English royalty's palace and plunked it down in this part of Arizona.

Franco drove the golf cart past the house and took the path heading toward the grove of trees and the pool. I heard something yapping excitedly and turned to see a little Jack Russell, its tiny paws barely touching the graveled path as it fairly flew toward the golf cart. Franco stopped and the little dog jumped on his lap, stood on its hind legs and started licking his face.

"Hey, hey, good boy Killie."

"Killie?"

"Yeah, stands for little killer."

"You been out here too long Franco. You're turning into a pussy."

"Yeah? You wanna put the gloves on with me again? We'll see who's the pussy."

Putting on the gloves with Franco had become a family legend with the Duvals and the Consolis.

I had just turned eighteen and Anthony was a few months behind me. I topped out at 6'2" a good four inches above Anthony. We pumped iron, boxed and made the school wrestling team. It sounded good and wholesome, but in reality we had launched a reign of terror among the teenagers in the neighborhood. It wasn't just that we were strong, and as we believed, tough as nails. Since Anthony was Vito Consoli's son, we were also "connected." We had begun stealing cars and extorting other kids for money, getting them to steal from their parents for us under threats of beatings. We had turned into the neighborhood low-lifes when under Don Vito Consoli's direction, Franco intervened.

One Saturday afternoon Anthony and I parked in front of the old candy store off New Lots Avenue. The store constituted our social club. We wanted to get a few cronies and build a crew like the one that worked out of the Bergen Fish & Hunt Club for John Gotti. We were headed toward being the worst kind of punks.

The car was "borrowed" from a transit worker whose petrified son had gotten us the keys, and the moment we got out, Franco's black Cadillac double-parked next to us.

He didn't look like he had good intentions that morning, and I suddenly understood his position as the Consoli family's enforcer.

"Get in," he said. There could be no question of doing anything else. We got in the back seat, and as he drove I wondered how many other men had sat in the back seat of Franco's car, driven someplace to meet a fearsome beating for some underworld infraction, or worse.

Without a word, Franco drove down Linden Boulevard to Pennsylvania Avenue and into Canarsie. Anthony and I looked at each other, not daring to break the silence. Franco's sudden and palpable hostility enveloped us, and the air in the Cadillac seemed thick and oppressive.

Franco turned down a side street into a neighborhood of decrepit buildings and empty lots brimming with weeds and trash. A couple of junkies were lighting up a crack pipe on the stoop of a boarded up brownstone. A homeless man made his way down the street pushing a shopping cart filled with rags and empty bottles. A vague stench of decay filled the air.

At the end of the block a long one story structure stood as if someone had decided to throw together a building out of rejected construction materials. Part brick-part wood, the building's masonry looked slick with mold and long strips of peeling oxidized paint hung in tatters from what passed as trim. A single steel door marked the entrance and all the windows were boarded up. A wooden, hand-painted sign above the door proclaimed the place as "Coogan's Westside Gym."

Franco parked directly in front of the fire hydrant, didn't even look at us as he said, "Let's go, mutts."

We walked into the place behind Franco. The steel door swung shut behind us with a dull thud. The place smelled of old sweat and liniment. Cheap neon lights set inside rusting reflectors, hung from a ceiling pocked with watermarks, provided a dim illumination that highlighted the overall dinginess of the place. Two boxing rings on either side of the cavernous room were the centerpieces, and the only place under bright lights. Throughout the room, a dozen men worked out on speed bags or heavy bags hanging from chains fastened in the ceilings. Others skipped ropes or pumped free weights. Coogan's obviously wasn't a gym for sculpting lean bodies or promoting health. It was a place of bent noses and scared faces, where the sheer brutality practiced there wiped out any pretensions to nobility the sport of boxing might ever claim.

Suddenly we weren't so tough, Anthony and I, we understood how a minnow might feel before being fed to predators.

Franco led us to one of the rings and motioned to an old man with stringy arms filled with prison tattoos and a face that seemed to have imploded.

"Hey Dusty, get some gloves and helmets for these punks, we're gonna do some sparring."

Dusty looked at us, cackled and pulled gloves and helmets from a footlocker under the ring.

"You first," Franco said, removing his shirt and pointing at Anthony.

We were strong young Turks. I had the height, four inches over Anthony, but he was built like the stump of an oak tree, and we were both fast with our hands. Maybe this might turn out to be fun, I remembered thinking for a brief moment. Then, Anthony took off his shirt and got in the ring with Franco.

Anthony got in a good couple of punches, but he might as well have been hitting the plaster walls of the gym. Franco just shrugged them off, taunting Anthony, "C'mon punk, whatta you a fag? I'm twice your age. Knock me on my ass."

It lasted three rounds. Every two minutes Dusty would ring the bell signifying the end of a round, but there were no breaks, and the relentless thudding of Franco's punches hammering Anthony's body and helmet-covered head continued without mercy.

After the third bell Anthony staggered off the ring on wobbly legs. His eyes had a hint of a glaze and he winced as he walked.

"It ain't like picking on fucking high school kids, is it?" Franco yelled after Anthony. Then he turned to me, "You're next sport."

I climbed in the ring, and it was the last thing I would remember distinctly for the next six minutes. Franco didn't wear a helmet and I cold-cocked him, a fast punch that hit him square on the side of his head.

I felt like a man who tugged at something furry sticking out of a bush, and discovers it's the tail of a very pissed off grizzly. I didn't even feel Franco's head move. His grin made the lining of my stomach want to disappear. He responded with a hook to the body that shook me down to my toes. For the next six minutes Franco pounded me with hooks, jabs, roundhouses, uppercuts and a few hits that just aren't in the book. Stars danced in front of my eyes, my breath came in ragged pulls. In spite of the helmet, I tasted blood in my mouth. As I left the ring every step brought a flash of pain from my battered chest and bruised ribs.

Franco jumped from the ring and faced us. He didn't look like he even broke a sweat.

"Both of you listen to me. Your old man and me," he said, nodding at Anthony. "We know everything that goes on in the neighborhood. You can't even fart in Brooklyn that we don't know about it. You stop the shit youse are doing, right now. You become Mary fucking Poppins model citizens right the fuck now or we're gonna do this every day until youse are both a pile of bloody rags. You unnerstand?"

"Yes Franco." We mumbled.

"Good. Now walk your asses home."

It took two weeks for the various blacks and blues and contusions to disappear and by that time we became the model citizens Franco demanded. The neighborhood reign of terror ended leaving our contemporaries extremely happy about our sudden conversion to good guys.

Two years later we joined the Army under a buddy program. After basic training we both volunteered for the Rangers and made it through the grueling selection and training program. Shortly after that, in early 2002, we found ourselves with a Rangers Special Ops company in Afghanistan. I guess we turned out okay, Anthony and I, and that session with Franco at Coogan's Gym had a lot to do with it. Brutal, yet packed with surprisingly effective old-world wisdom, the lesson took very well.

I looked over at him and smiled. "No Franco, I don't want to put the gloves on with you, ever." And I meant it.

CHAPTER 10

"How's the old man?" I asked Franco as we approached the cabana.

"Mean as always, and that's good."

Franco stopped the golf cart. We got out and walked toward the pool. Vito Consoli sat on a lounge chair dozing under wide sunglasses. Next to the chair a plastic coffee table held an empty espresso cup, a cell phone and folded newspaper. A thin-screen plasma television set tuned to CNN rested on a movable stand, and an older woman in a maid's uniform sat further away in the shade of the cabana. When she saw us approaching she stood and walked toward us. Vito Consoli took his sunglasses off, rubbed his eyes, stood and hugged me. He seemed a curious combination of strength and frailty, as if the two could exist in one body.

"How ya feeling Gast?"

"A little weak Mister Consoli, but getting better. Should be back to a hundred percent in a few months."

He pointed to his empty cup, and the maid nodded and left. We sat at a table by the pool and it felt good. The water seemed to suck some of the heat from the air and the sunshade over the table kept us cool. A slow breeze drifted over us from the desert and the late morning sky was a brilliant blue background for the Sierra Ancha Mountains behind us.

The maid brought three espressos as we talked about old times, and it felt just fine. Anthony's wife Maria was in nearby Scottsdale, shopping and the kids were in school. Anthony was due back around noon. A small airstrip bordered the property and Anthony commuted to wherever the Consoli family's now legitimate business took him, in a fast private aircraft.

Vito Consoli held up his hand, said "quiet" and pointed at the TV. We stopped and listened. The CNN anchor spoke about the mysterious crash of a private airplane, a Lear jet, over the Atlantic Ocean, a hundred miles west of England. The plane's owner had been on his way back to the US from Bordeaux France. He was presumed killed along with the crew of three. A picture of the man appeared in the upper corner of the screen. He was a wealthy industrialist from Texas, and I had read about him several times.

His name was Burt Wells Jr.

CHAPTER 11

Moscow, Russia.

The last thing Victor Zurinov resembled was a stone cold killer, because at first glance he wasn't physically imposing. He stood taller than most Russians, but not overly so. His features had the bland, pale complexion of one who spends his winters in Moscow. He was well groomed with sandy hair that had begun to thin as he approached his forties. His clothes were expensive slacks, and a light turtle neck sweater covered by a fine cut brown sport jacket. He could have been any one of the newly minted Russian millionaire businessmen who rose out of the twisted economic agonies of the former Soviet Union, or one of the upper echelon Mafia leaders, succeeding through cunning, using others to handle the brutality and treachery. In America he would have been taken for a lawyer or accountant. But there was something about the eyes, a vast glacial quality that recognized no human emotions and gave no quarter. Under the clothing, his body hinted at Victor Zurinov's true history. Tight ropy muscles danced on a frame as devoid of fat as an oak tree. Dozens of scars, almost iridescent white against the paleness of his skin dotted his body. Calcified scar tissue covering his knuckles told of the continuing hours of martial arts training, and there was a predatory grace to his step, like a lean jungle cat about to explode on a hapless prey.

He participated weekly in that unique Russian activity, which to a westerner seemed certifiably insane; a five-minute swim in a narrow channel cut from two-foot thick lake ice. The regulars who met for this ritual, instinctively knew there was something dangerous in this man, and wanted no part of him.

Zurinov sat in a spotless, new café-restaurant fronting a wide boulevard running off the Sparrow Hill district. These trendy new places sprouted throughout Moscow along with Pizza Huts, Burger Kings and other icons of American capitalism, now adopted enthusiastically by Russians.

He sipped his tea while reading the newspaper, a rite that preceded each mission. When he looked out the large plate glass window fronting the boulevard, he saw a black Mercedes with glass tinted so dark, it hid the driver and passengers. A Cadillac SUV, equally dark, had been trailing the Mercedes and now parked alongside. *That would be the security team,* Zurinov thought. Actually, Moscow was safer now than it had been for many years and chase cars were mainly for form, like an entourage. The most aggressive businessmen had killed each other off and the uneasy truce between Mafia factions seemed to be holding.

Two men in jogging suits got out of the Mercedes and headed into the restaurant. Both men were tall and bulky with rough faces and small eyes that hinted at barely restrained brutality, the marks of some Mafia clan. They walked with a rolling aggressive gait, as if to tell the world they were the top predators, the apex of Moscow's human food chain.

They walked in the restaurant in a swirl of cigarette smoke and loud voices, heading toward the best table in the house: Zurinov's.

The first man stopped in front of Zurinov and ground his cigarette out on the bare surface of the table.

"Get the hell out. You're in our spot." He growled at Zurinov.

Zurinov stared at him, and leaned forward, both arms

resting on the table. As he extended his arms, the sleeves rolled back revealing a tattoo the size of an American half-dollar on the front of his right forearm.

The tattoo was a meticulous representation of the head of a black bear. Gleaming white teeth filled the bear's maw and the slightly elongated canines held the hint of a curve, giving the animal head a ferocious, vampire look against a background the color of bright arterial blood.

The second man's gaze fell on the tattoo, and he grasped his companion's arm. "Leave it Pasha," he said, and turned to Zurinov.

"Excuse us please, we did not know," he said, "Your bill is paid, our pleasure."

Zurinov said nothing, and continued to stare at them as the man pulled his companion to another table, whispering fiercely. When Zurinov finished, he rose, left his paper on the table and walked out of the restaurant. At the curb, a BMW sedan waited for him, chauffeured by a dour-looking old man. Zurinov got in.

"Sheremetyevo?" The old man said, naming the Moscow International Airport as he looked at him in the rear view mirror.

Zurinov held up a hand. "Wait," he said. He punched numbers on a cell phone. He looked at the resulting confirmation message scrolling across the phone's screen. Half a million dollars, US, had been deposited in his Swiss numbered account. When he succeeded—no question of "if" existed—an additional one million would be added. He liked working for Nicholas Petrovsky, chief executive and shareholder of Eastern Resources, the largest conglomerate in Russia and Asia. The man didn't have a single molecule of bullshit. The mission was on.

"Yes, the airport," he told the chauffeur. A direct flight to Charles DeGaulle International in Paris, switch from Aeroflot to Air France, and he'd be in New York by tomorrow morning.

CHAPTER 12

I dialed Sheriff Shirley Case's number on my cell. She answered on the first ring. I felt strangely happy to hear her voice even though it was just business.

"Hey Shirley, its Gast. How you doing?"

"Good, you?"

"Fine, any word on our poor friend, Mary Orlowsky?"

"Yeah, but it's not good. The more I dig into it, the more convinced I get there's something going on. What'd you come up with?"

"Nothing yet Shirley, but I have a well placed friend at ATF in Oklahoma City. I set her loose on the Federal end. She's tenacious as hell. I know she'll come up with something."

"Good enough. Here's what I've got on my end," Shirley said. "They took the victim's car to the Phoenix police impound lot. That's where the Bureau sends cars involved in their cases. They have an arrangement with Phoenix PD. Now here's the thing, nobody looked at the car yet. No crime scene technicians, no forensic experts, no one. They found the perp's car yesterday, early in the morning. Took it to the impound lot also, and still haven't looked at it. Now that's big time strange, I mean that's the car the killers drove, they should be on that thing like an army of ants at a picnic."

"Unless they all ready know who the perps are," I replied.

"There is that, but here's something else: Did you know Mary Orlowsky doesn't exist?"

"What are you talking about Shirley? Did you run her driver's license?"

"Oh yeah, and that's what I'm talking about. According to the New Mexico DMV, that license number belongs to someone named Arthur Tremmell, deceased over a year ago. There is no Mary Orlowsky recorded as having a New Mexico driver's license."

"It could be a fake, not the hardest thing to get."

"Yess…but then we have the problem of sequence."

"Sequence?"

"That's right, New Mexico issues driver's licenses in numerical sequential order. Mister Tremmell's had his license far longer then DMV records indicate. He was 81 when he died. The sequence of his license number doesn't fit."

"Maybe he got his license late in life."

"Wrong. I found his insurance companies. He's been driving since 1948. Somebody with the ability to tamper with New Mexico DMV records, wiped out Mary Orlowsky's and put her number on a dead person."

I gave a low whistle. "Good work Shirley. You must have been hell on wheels as a Boston PD detective."

"You haven't seen the half of it. Tomorrow I'm taking a commuter hop to Albuquerque where they keep the original DMV applications on microfiche. You want to bet dinner I come across an application from Mary Orlowsky that doesn't correspond to any existing license?"

"You're on," I said. Some bets I just love to lose.

"Oh yeah, and there's another thing. I got a call from the Governor's office first thing this morning."

"He's looking for a new running mate?"

"Not exactly. I didn't speak to the man himself. It was one of his flunkies. Somebody in Phoenix found out I was asking about the status of the cars and the investigations. They warned me off, said it was out of my jurisdiction, in

Federal hands. Gast, I'm as patriotic as they come, but goddammit somebody got murdered on one of my roads and last I looked, the star on our flag that represents Arizona wasn't replaced by a fucking swastika."

I liked this woman more every day.

"Okay, keep going, but be careful. I'm staying over at some friends near Scottsdale. Soon as I hear from my sources I'll start digging also."

"All right," she said, "call me soon as you have something."

I put away my cell phone and returned to the table. Vito Consoli placed a wide brimmed hat on his head, grabbed his cane, well, you couldn't really call it a cane, more like a walking stick. Straight as could be, with a carved rendition of a wolverine's head, it tapered down to a narrow rubber-tipped end. I wondered if it was the kind of thing that hides a sword. He waived me over. "Walk with me a bit," He said.

There must have been three or four miles of neatly tended graveled paths on the estate. They connected the various parts, the gardens, pool and cabana, the garages, tennis and shuffleboard courts, and on the far edge of the property, the hangar at the end of the runway. The air smelled of lilacs and roses from the gardens, stirred by a light desert breeze. If you could stand the heat, this had to be one of the best places on earth.

"I walk two miles in the morning and one in the afternoon," Vito told me, "After this walk, I'm going to take a nap. That's the secret to growing old, exercise and rest, and one more thing: Keep your family near you."

"The way you're going, Mister Consoli, the only problem we're going to have is getting a hundred candles to fit on your cake."

He stopped and looked at me, his eyes serious, appraising me under the shade of the wide-brimmed hat.

"Look around you, Gast. There's everything an old man could ever want. But you know what? It don't mean shit," he said, the Brooklyn accent of his roots taking over, as if to emphasize the deep meaning of every word.

"It don't mean shit if'n you aint got your family, know what I mean? I knew both your parents very well, Gast, wonderful people and they felt the same way about our family. When my Louisa died, all I had left was Anthony. I started making my plans to retire, gave all the pieces to the Capos, made sure they were apportioned among the remaining New York families, took enough with me to build this life, but it only works because of what you did seven years ago."

"Mister Consoli, that's not…"

"Quiet, you don't interrupt me, ever."

I knew what he was going to say. He had told me once before, six years ago.

It happened early in 2002 in the mountains surrounding Kandahar. Anthony and I were part of a Ranger company on a special ops ambush against a particularly wily Taliban chief. They knew the terrain cold and managed to turn the ambush against us. The first RPG exploded near Anthony. I carried him as we retreated into a natural redoubt of boulders and craggy volcanic rocks. We got separated from the rest of the platoon, but some remained within range, enough to help with covering fire. I stayed with Anthony, alternately giving him first aid and firing at the enemy. An adrenaline-filled eternity passed, that in reality had been about four hours, until air strikes and two Ranger companies drove away the remaining Taliban. I carried Anthony down to where the Medevac chopper could reach us. He had a variety of concussions, shrapnel wounds and lacerations, and I was credited with saving his life, at least that's what it said on the letter that accompanied the Silver Star I received a month later.

"Don't say it, Gast. Don't tell me how Rangers never leave anyone behind. I don't give a shit about your military slogans. You did it because my son is your friend, that's the real reason."

The old man paused, looked up at the sky as if some hidden meaning of life was inscribed there, and turned back to me.

"Now go get a drink or something, I got a mile to go and you're in no shape for this walk."

I headed back toward the pool thinking how I've got to recuperate, get back to my old self. He's eighty-four and I'm thirty, and *I'm* in no shape for this walk?

I reached the pool area and sat down. Franco had gone somewhere, and the maid brought me an iced glass of Pelligrini mineral water just as my cell phone rang. It was LaToya:

"Gast, can you talk?"

"Yeah, what's up?"

"I'm getting a little scared, Gast."

I sat up. That got my attention, Latoya saying she was getting scared?

"What about, your cell phone bill?"

I heard her chuckle on the other end. "There's some kinda shit going on Gast, and it's big, way too big for this lady. You gotta come here Gast, we gotta talk. Can you meet me tomorrow night?"

"I can do that. I'll touch base with you tomorrow."

"And Gast, there's one more thing you should know."

"What?"

"I don't know how to say it, it's about Amy."

I felt myself gripping the little phone as if I could remold it like a piece of putty.

"What about Amy?"

"She was involved in it, in this thing. You didn't know it, none of us did, but she was involved."

CHAPTER 13

———◆———

It's hard to believe how fast the character and noise level of the estate had changed since three-thirty PM. That's when a yellow school bus stopped at the gate and disgorged five boisterous kids. Two were Anthony's, a nine-year old boy and his seven-year old sister. The other three belonged to the Mexican maid and her husband, one of the caretakers. The family lived on the estate in a cottage attached to the main house by a brick walkway.

Maria, Anthony's wife arrived a few minutes later from her shopping spree in Scottsdale. She squealed when she saw me, hugging and kissing me on both cheeks. I've known Maria my whole life. As far back as I can remember, it was always me, Anthony and Maria, growing up inseparable in Brooklyn, through grade school and high school, until life sent us on different paths. Well, me anyway. Maria married Anthony, and I could see they were expecting their third child.

"So," I said, "you're determined to populate this section of Arizona, are you?"

She grinned. Her face had a slightly hooked nose that only served to emphasize her dark, beauty. She was tall, topping Anthony by about an inch, coming in just under my height.

"Yeah, why not? We love kids. Look at that, is there anything better in the whole world?" she said, pointing toward the pool, where all five kids jumped and ran through the water like aquatic gazelles, amidst a noise level that must have jumped off the scales.

At that moment, a deep buzzing washed over the area as a twin engine plane passed overhead, no more than a couple of hundred feet high. The plane banked away and climbed, gaining altitude as it lined itself up with the runway. Anthony had come home.

It took a good hour for things to settle down, the kids out of the pool, dried and off to their homework, and Maria supervising a special dinner for my visit. Anthony and I remained at poolside, seated at a table under a wide umbrella while tubes built into the steel latticework emitted a fog of fine droplets, a drizzle that cooled the desert air by at least ten degrees. A mix of fragrances filled the early evening with scents of hyacinth and magnolias mixed with clear mountain air and desert breezes.

"So how you coming along with that?" Anthony said, nodding toward my side.

"Another six months of physical therapy and should be about 90% recovered. I'm told that the other 10% may never come."

"The hell do they know, eh? So what'd you decide about your job?"

"I don't know," I answered, shaking my head.

"Think about what I told you before, Gast. I could use the help. We're 100% legit now. My business is a chunk of South-West Water. An entire district we own, plus the hotels, the catering halls and the two casinos. The money's terrific and you'd get equity over the years, stock options and all. What do you say Gast? I can't think of anything better than having you work with me. We'd kick ass together, just like old times."

"Before I can think seriously about all that, I've got to get to the bottom of this thing with that murder."

"That Mary, what's her name?"

"Orlowsky," I had told him the story of the murder, and the apparent stonewalling of the investigation.

"But there's more, Anthony. Remember I told you about this friend of mine in ATF information services, LaToya?"

"That's the one who said she dug up information that Amy was involved somehow?"

"Yeah, and I was pretty rattled when she told me that. I mean, how the hell could Amy be involved? She worked hostage rescues, SWAT equivalent, when would she have time for something like this? And besides, I would have known."

Anthony looked away toward the mountains. A pair of hawks floated on lazy currents of heated air rising from the desert floor. One of the raptors dropped its wings into a plummeting dive toward some hapless prey invisible to us.

Anthony took a sip of his Margarita, and spoke softly, "Sometimes Gast, you don't always know what's going on in a person's life. It's not necessarily a bad thing."

"Well it got me bugged pretty badly, so I decided to check something out. That Palm Pilot I told you I took from the woman's purse, I checked her address and phone number data base, and found some strange shit."

"Like what?"

"Well every listing's got a regular name, first and last, middle initial, address, email, phone and fax. She kept perfect records in that little device, except for three items: the first one had only one name: Izgoi."

"Izgoi? What the hell is that?"

"I looked it up on Google. It's Russian, means "The Lost Ones," What it signifies beats the shit out of me, but it's a 212 area code though."

"Brooklyn, Queens."

"Yeah, including parts of Manhattan nowadays. Anyway, I called it."

"And?"

"Somebody answered it, and not in English. Sounded like Eastern European, you know, Polish, Slav, Russian. I didn't want to scare them off, so I said wrong number and hung up. Gives me a chance to track it down later, but that's not the strange part, it's the other two names and numbers that really threw me off so badly. I just don't know what to make of it, but I've got to find out, there's no choice now, if there ever was one."

"Okay, what were the other names and numbers that got you spooked, Gast?"

"Amy's number is in there. Just think about this, Anthony. Here's this woman, a complete stranger to me, who gets murdered in the middle of nowhere, right in front of me, and she's got a Palm Pilot with my fiancée's phone number in it."

Anthony whistled softly, "Shit," he said, "what's the other name and number?"

"Mine."

CHAPTER 14

JFK Airport, International Arrival Building

Zurinov passed through the security and customs check just like any other passenger. He traveled on a tourist visa to the US from Moscow, showing visits in Rome, Madrid and Paris.

He scanned the crowd of limo drivers and tour operators holding up little signs with the names of their customers. He spotted one that read: Ivanov Smith-Welkomen. The man holding it wore a long coat over a dark suit and tie, identical to scores of other livery drivers roaming JFK. A close look would have revealed a hard edge, something more than the average limo driver. The man was built like a ladder-all hard angles and straight lines. Two small scars ran from the upper part of his neck and disappeared inside his collar beneath squashed features reminiscent of an aging prizefighter. He stood very still as Zurinov approached and spoke a single word, *"Shatun."*

The driver reached in the pocket of his coat, took out an iPod and handed it to Zurinov, who looked at the illuminated face. *Je Ne Regrette Rien,* by Edith Piaf, was displayed on the face of the device. Zurinov nodded, identification was authenticated and he followed the man to the parking lot where he handed him a key and pointed to a gray Toyota Camry.

"That is yours. It is registered to a rental agency in Brooklyn. Records will show this rental was arranged three weeks ago for your visit as a tourist. I have been told you are familiar with New York. You have been on missions here before?"

"Yes," Zurinov replied.

"Good. Should you need to call me, here is a number. I will be within minutes of your location wherever you are in New York. I assume it is improbable that you will need my help?"

"Yes."

"Very well. Here is the name and address of your target. Call me once you have the information, and we will arrange for the next stage."

Zurinov nodded, took the folded piece of paper and put it in his pocket. The man disappeared as Zurinov got in the Camry, started it, and took the Belt Parkway exit toward Brooklyn.

CHAPTER 15

10,000 feet above Arizona, the next morning.

We reached cruising altitude in Anthony's plane. It felt good to have him along. Last night I had told him about meeting LaToya in Oklahoma City the following evening, and from there on, I couldn't keep him away. Although, I had to admit to myself, I didn't try very hard.

"Anthony, I'm a Federal Agent, remember?" I had said. "You don't have reason to get mixed up in this. It's something I've got to do. You have your own business."

"Yeah, at least a half dozen by last count, and they'll all run fine without me for a while, but how many friends do I have? I mean real friends? You tell me, eh?"

"You got a family, Anthony, that's worth more than friends."

"No, not worth more, just requires a higher level of allegiance and a set of different skills. Friends still friends, and Maria wanted me to go too, you know."

"Well, thanks. I'm glad you came. I just don't know where this will lead to."

"What's your take on it Gast, what do you think?"

"About as strange as it can get, I guess. I've been in the hospital four months, rehab another five, haven't been involved in any cases since I got shot. Now, dammed near a year later, this Mary Orlowski passes me on a road, chased by some people who wind up killing her. I've never seen her before, never heard of her, yet she carries my number and that of Amy, in her Palm Pilot. Now, the night before I forgot to charge my cell phone, so it was shut off that day. There were four calls recorded to my cell from the same number, no messages."

The plane jolted, dropped a couple of yards, and resumed cruising. Anthony sat up and looked at the controls.

"Everything okay?" I asked.

"Yeah, just an air pocket, can't see them coming. So what'd you make of all that?"

"The only logical thing I can come up with," I continued, "is that she must have known Amy, maybe asked for her help with some problem. Amy must have been working on it. For whatever reason she didn't tell me. She must have given Mary Orlowski my number for a backup. Four months later those people are after Orlowski. Orlowski can't reach Amy so she calls me instead. She can't reach me, but found out where I'd be going and tries to catch up with me. Instead, she gets killed in front of me."

"Sounds logical, just leaves about a million questions to be answered."

"Yeah, tell me about it."

The plane seemed suspended in the clear air. The only sign of movement came when looking down at the ground below, the passage of roads, towns and deserts at a seemingly slow crawl, but an actual ground speed of about 400 MPH. The engines hummed away, and the whisper of air moving over the fuselage was downright hypnotic. No wonder Anthony loved flying this thing. He looked like a kid at a movie, hands behind his head, taking it all in.

"Hey, shouldn't you have your hands on the wheel or something?" I asked him.

"Nope, automatic pilot, I just keep an eye on things. We'll be in Oklahoma City by four this afternoon."

Anthony was off by about seven minutes. By the time we landed, arranged for securing the aircraft and got a rental car, it was past six o'clock. We would be late for our dinner meeting with LaToya.

The Soulful Rib was one of Oklahoma City's unique restaurants. The place attracted primarily an African-American clientele, mostly Federal employees stationed far from their native homes in the Northeast and Southern states. I'd been there often with Amy, double-dating with LaToya and one of her numerous boyfriends.

The noise level of clanking silverware and plates floated above the hubbub of conversations and orders shouted back from waitresses and kitchen staff. The rough-planked walls were decorated with amateur paintings and photos, all with the motif of the Old South. The floor was covered with sawdust and the tables were Formica. That made for easy cleaning since just about nothing served at the Soulful Rib could be eaten without making a mess. Wispy clouds of steam floated above the half wall that separated the kitchen from the dining area, and the bittersweet aroma of tangy barbecue sauce filled the air.

I stopped for a moment at the entrance, taking it all in, imagining Amy waiting for me, as she had so often. A tall, black waitress walked up to us and smiled.

"Hiya," she said. "Table for dinner?"

"Yes, we're meeting someone here. We're a bit late."

"Her name LaToya?"

"That's it."

The waitress led us through the crowded dining room to a rear table. LaToya stood when she saw us, let out a whooping holler and grabbed me in a bear hug. She's a large rambunctious woman, and the strength of her two-armed grip brought a flash of pain from my side.

"Easy LaToya, things aren't all healed up yet."

"Oh man, it's so good to see you, up and all, getting better. I worried about you, you know."

"I know, LaToya, I know," I said, kissing her and returning the hug warily. "This is my friend, Anthony

Consoli. Hope you don't mind I brought him along."

"Honey, I don't mind at all. Hoowhee, you better believe them tongues are gonna wag, me having a date with two cute white boys."

We sat down and ordered a pitcher of beer. The waitress brought the menus. There's really only one plate to have at the Soulful Rib, but it's the best in the world: The Southern Barbeque Special, a combination of chicken, ribs and shrimp smothered in a barbecue sauce whose ingredients had been kept secret since before the Civil War. It's the kind of dinner where you need a towel-size napkin wrapped around your neck and shoulders. We ate and talked, and when the plates were cleared, I asked LaToya what she found out. And her face got serious.

"It's a little scary, Gast. I mean I ain't run into nothing like that in all my years in information services."

"Is it that IRD thing the Bureau is all knuckling under?"

"Yeah that's part of it. Here's the thing about IRD: It was created by Senator McLaughlin, you know, the Texas oil senator?"

I read about Senator McLaughlin often enough. Immensely popular and charismatic, the Senator came from a wealthy family so heavily involved in petroleum, the press nicknamed him "Senator Oil."

"Well this here Senator is chairman of the Senate Homeland Security Committee. He founded IRD as a special investigative agency that would be small enough to get results where a large organization like the FBI wouldn't work. IRD has access to full FBI resources, so they can really kick-ass. Also, they got full authority over any other agencies."

"Yeah, and they exercise that authority, kicked that Sheriff right off that case, warned us all off. How come we never heard of this outfit before?"

"Well, that's part of the strangeness," LaToya replied. "They're small. Only about thirty people in all, and as far as I can tell, the only work they've done is around Los Alamos and the surrounding states. And here's another strange thing, the way they're funded."

"Lots of government money?" Anthony asked.

"No, that's just it, original funding voted and approved was twelve million. That's a drop of piss in a windstorm. The government spent more than that studying crabgrass. There's a provision in the bill that allows funding by interested parties, which means anyone having an interest in effective antiterrorism investigations can contribute."

"Isn't there precedent for that?" I asked, "I mean there's even a mechanism for individuals to contribute to the US treasury to help relieve the national debt. What's wrong with antiterrorism?"

"Nothing wrong with it, except no one contributes to stuff like that, except for Investigative Research Division, apparently. IRD so far this year has received over three hundred million in funding."

"From whom?"

"Don't know. Privileged information."

"Wait, all contributions have to be made public, its IRS regulations."

"Wrong, Gast. That applies only to certain things, like charitable contributions that you deduct on your income taxes, what the IRS calls 501© organizations, or political contributions. Private, non-deductible donations to a minor agency of the US government requires no disclosures."

"Okay LaToya, so we've got this minor agency getting private funding, taking over the Orlowski murder investigation on the grounds of national security, and not really doing anything to solve it..."

"Yo dawg, hold on, there's more," LaToya interrupted. "They also seem to have eyes all over the place and they sure ain't happy about someone like me asking questions about them."

"You heard from them?"

"Indirectly. My supervisor—you remember that monkey-ass, Al Meyers?"

I remembered him, had a few run-ins with him myself. Uptight, uncooperative pain in the ass, he was one of the things wrong with the federal bureaucracy. The overwhelming majority of federal employees are honest, hard-working civil servants, but it only takes a handful of Al Meyers to screw up the system. Whatever competence he had, was long ago gobbled up by pompous bureaucratic nonsense, mostly aimed at keeping his own little fiefdom intact.

"Yeah, I remember him, how could you forget an asshole like that?"

"Well he called me in his office, specifically to forbid me to inquire into IRD background, or anything to do with them. Obviously someone higher up delegated that to him, knowing he's a little shit-toady and wouldn't question why a legitimate federal employee like me wanted information that is supposed to be public."

"What'd you tell him?"

"I told that whitebread-shithead I'm acting at the request of an ATF officer, that's you Gast, working an undercover investigation. I think that jarred him a bit, but he still ordered me off. I said I'd have to think about it." LaToya pursed her lips, crossed her eyes and said in a whiny, exaggerated mid-west drawl, "See that you do."

"What are you going to do?" I asked.

"Fuck him," she said.

"He'd probably like that," Anthony grinned at her.

"Not even with your dick," she replied with a wider grin. "Anyway, I don't think that boy likes sex with anybody who's got to sit down to pee, know what I mean?"

"So you're going to keep on digging."

"Bet your ass I will, this is America, remember? I know my rights, and if they fuck with me, there's plenty I can do. Since I'm black I can play the discrimination card. I know its bullshit, but it's for a good cause, and I can also do something that will knock him four ways from Sunday: claim sexual harassment. I'm female in case you hadn't noticed."

"We noticed."

"Maybe not enough, sweetie."

"Okay, but what makes you think Amy's involved?"

"She wasn't doing anything wrong, Gast, she loved you so much," LaToya replied, her voice soft, yet husky, "She told me a few days before, you know…She thought about joining this new IRD division. They were actively recruiting and screening. She was looking into some of their cases, how they worked, why they did certain things, and I don't think she liked what she found."

"How do you know all this?"

"She told me, Gast. She was looking into one of their investigations at Los Alamos, on something called the CF Project. She said she thought something illegal was being done by IRD and it might even involve murder."

I didn't reply. I was there, yet I wasn't.

We can't do this all our lives, you know, sport?

Do what, Amy?

Hostage rescue, this Wild West bullshit, I want to settle down a bit.

You want to be Suzy homemaker?

She'd looked at me then, her eyes kinda faraway. She'd leaned over and kissed me, and whispered.

Maybe

"Gast?"

CHAPTER 16

Brooklyn, New York.

Steven Colin took a sip of his beer and remembered a distant time when he had been Stefan Colonov, literally another life away. Sitting at the bar stool of a gin mill on Avenue U, his short, squat body topped by an over-size head, he looked like any one of thousands of rough working men, slowly being worn down by physical labor. That's the way Steven liked his appearance, but the truth of his work rested far from that scenario. He took tiny sips of a beer that he would not finish, as he awaited a contact already twenty minutes late. Curious, thought Steven, I have nothing to report. It is Izgoi who triggered the contact and they are late. It is very unlike Sergei's people.

Another ten minutes passed. Steven stood, left a five, and the half finished beer on the bar. He put on his jacket and stepped outside.

A chilly drizzle had started, and an oily sheen covered the surface of the road and pavement. It was past midnight and traffic had slowed considerably. Except for the bar, all the storefronts along the avenue were shuttered. Neon signs cast blinking lights, creating shadows like craters along the closed doorways and barred windows. Parked cars, bumpers almost touching, lined the street as Steven turned the corner. He walked a few yards to his car and took the keys from his pocket.

A shadow moved from the front of the auto, impossibly fast, faster than Steven's trained reflexes could respond. Although he kept in shape, it had been over two decades since he had used the fierce personal combat skills that might have saved him this night. But he had been too long ensconced in the soft cocoon of American life. The shadow launched a low kick. Steven didn't see it coming. It struck his mid section, doubling him like folded cardboard, followed instantaneously by an open hand strike to the temple that slammed his head against the parked car. Explosions of bright lights went off in Stevens' eyes and he went down with a soft gasp, his consciousness evaporating.

CHAPTER 17

Oklahoma City

I hugged LaToya outside the Soulful Rib before we parted, "Be careful, okay?" I told her, "Find out what you can, but be discreet, don't let that jive-ass…"

"Monkey-ass."

"Monkey-ass, sorry, I haven't kept up with my Ebonics. But seriously, be careful."

"I will, Gast. Two nights from now, right here okay? I could get used to these dinner dates."

She hugged Anthony next, and we left in the rented car.

"Where to now, boss?" Anthony asked.

"Let's find a motel to stay for the night and leave early tomorrow. We're going to pay a visit to Los Alamos."

"The lab near Albuquerque?"

"That's the place. How far?"

"A couple of hours flying time. Weather looks good for the next few days."

"Great, I'll hit them around lunch time. That always throws government workers for a loop."

CHAPTER 18

Brooklyn, New York

Steven opened his eyes slowly. His head throbbed and soreness filled his gut. He seemed to be paralyzed, unable to move his limbs, the movements of his head restricted to a few inches, and he barely managed to look down.

He sat on a high chair with sturdy wooden armrests on both sides. A captain's chair, the kind they have in the classier bars. His arms lay flat on the wood surfaces, covered with layers of duct tape winding around the wood. His legs were equally bound, and no matter how he strained, the tape didn't budge. Some sort of ligature held his midsection, tight enough to restrict his chest to quick shallow inhales. Unseen bonds that felt like cloth around his forehead restricted his neck and head. A musty odor of decay permeated the room as early morning light came in streams through the gaps between the planks covering the windows. Trash littered the room, barely visible graffiti covered the walls and the only upright objects in the room were a chair where a man sat, staring at him, his face shrouded in deep shadows. On the man's right side a series of instruments were laid out as if awaiting a surgeon's use: syringes, a portable dentist drill, pliers, wire, razors, and a variety of other unrecognizable objects.

Steven felt the pit of his stomach fall away as the man moved and a beam of sunlight fell on his forearm, illuminating a tattooed depiction of a fanged bear against a crimson background.

"Shatun," Steven whispered.

"You have heard of me," the man replied. "So you are not quite the innocent, are you?"

"Let me go," Steven said. "You have the wrong man. Whatever it is you want, I can't help you."

"Oh, I think you can," Zurinov replied. "You have information I need."

"I don't know anything. I've been here over twenty years. Any missions I might have had, ended many years ago. I'm just another harmless American citizen. Let me go."

Zurinov leaned forward and for a moment, the beam of light crossed his face, revealing the emptiness of his eyes. He spoke in a distant voice, as if what they discussed had little importance. "You are far from an ordinary American citizen. Who are the leaders of Izgoi? Where is Sergei?"

"I don't know. I can't help you."

"We both know you can. Where is Sergei?"

"Let me go and I will try to find out."

A smile, devoid of humor or humanity, crossed Ivanov's face as he answered, "Understand Stefan, that your life is over. You will die today, and that is an absolute certainty. The only choice you have is the amount of suffering you will undergo, because in the end, I will have the information. So choose, or I will make that choice for you."

He didn't reply, and Zurinov grabbed one of the syringes from the table and plunged the needle into Steven's right arm. It took only seconds for the pain intensifier to light up every nerve ending, as he began his descent into the bowels of hell.

CHAPTER 19

Los Alamos, New Mexico

Just a few cars were ahead of me, passing through the checkpoint at the entrance to Los Alamos National Laboratory. It was late morning and the rush hour had ended a few hours ago.

We had landed at Albuquerque at seven AM and rented individual cars. There was no way I could take Anthony, a civilian, along with me.

I reached the guard gate and held out my ID. "Federal agent, I need to visit your personnel office."

The guard looked at a clipboard, frowned and returned my ID. "You're not on the access list for today sir."

"I wouldn't be. I didn't call ahead because I'm only here to search your personnel records as part of an investigation."

The guard picked up the phone, said a few words and hung up. "See that building there?" He pointed. "Park right there and go inside, they'll handle it, sir."

I thanked him, parked where he told me to, and entered the building. Soon as I walked in, I faced a high and wide desk, similar to the kind found in hundreds of police stations throughout the country. I handed my ID to a young woman in uniform, wearing sergeant's stripes.

"ATF? Investigating something at Los Alamos? How's

that happen?"

"Last week a woman was murdered and I was a witness. The victim carried a Los Alamos ID. I want to confirm employment with your personnel records."

"Murdered? Why are you investigating and not the FBI?"

"We're running parallel inquiries. I'm the witness, remember?"

"All right Lieutenant Duval. Wait here please."

I sat on the bench while the quiet business of the Lab's police station went on. My nerves felt on edge and my side throbbed. I took a pill from my pocket and dry swallowed it. The pain started mellowing by the time she returned. She looked slightly puzzled and annoyed at the same time. She didn't need this to break up her quiet morning.

"ATF confirmed your identity. They also said you're supposed to be on convalescent leave and they don't know anything about an investigation involving Los Alamos."

"Sergeant, I'm an officer with the rank of lieutenant in a federal law enforcement agency. I can initiate an investigation on my own authority." It was an exaggeration, but I'd bet as part of the private police force providing security for the Lab, she didn't know a lot about the workings of federal agencies. "In any case, your Lab is not involved per se," I continued. "I'm merely checking employment and possible whereabouts in the hours before the victim's death."

She chewed on her lower lip, then turned and called someone. A young officer appeared. "William, please take Agent Duval to personnel," she said, handing me a pre-printed pass. I thanked her and left with William in a Lab police car.

Los Alamos reminded me of a giant theme park with broad avenues and wide roads flanked by meticulously landscaped borders, only all the rides had been taken out and replaced by serious looking buildings. Everything was painted a light shade of off-white, spaced with cryptic signs involving safety. William parked in a reserved space fronting a building marked "Human Resources."

Inside the building, I was introduced to an efficient looking prim woman. We entered her office/cubicle where she sat behind a desk containing only a computer monitor, keyboard and mouse and her nameplate on the front.

"All right Mister Duval, what was the name of the employee you were looking for?"

"Mary Orlowski."

"Is she currently employed at the lab?"

"Not anymore."

"What was her last known period of employment?"

"Not past last week."

She sighed and looked at me. "She died last week," I said, "She had a Los Alamos ID card on her when she passed away."

"Oh."

She concentrated on the monitor. The soft clicking of her fingers on the keys filled the cubicle. She paused, frowned, looked at the screen and muttered, "Strange."

"What's strange?" I asked.

"Her name triggers a search, but it comes up blank."

"That is strange," I said, but I wasn't surprised.

"No I mean what's strange, is that it should come up as negative without triggering a search. It's almost as if the record was taken out, but not completely."

"Try this." I gave her the number on Mary Orlowski's Los Alamos ID, "and try coupling the search with something called CF Project."

"What's that?"

"I don't know, but she was involved in it. It said so on her ID."

"Oh," she said again, and typed in the new information. No more than a few seconds passed until the computer emitted a series of beeps and chirps. She put her hands to her mouth and said, "Oh dear."

"What?"

"Its, it…It says Security Lockout. That never happened before, and…"

"And what?"

"Detain inquiring parties. Security notified."

CHAPTER 20

Sante Fe, New Mexico, State DMV office.

Shirley Case walked in, showed her ID at the front desk and asked for Thomas Kelly. A few moments later a tall man in his late fifties came through the door. He wore a dark suit with an American flag on the right lapel and a shamrock on the left. A shock of white hair topped a ruddy complexion and pleasant face. He broke into a smile when he saw her.

"Shirley! How's my favorite ex-big-city-detective-turned-hick-Sheriff?"

"You should talk, Tommy. You did just about the same thing didn't you?"

"Yeah, and I don't miss Boston PD or the Northside one bit. You?"

"Not on my worst day."

"You here on business Shirl?"

"Yeah Tommy, I got a strange one, figured you might be able to help."

"Shoot."

She told him about Mary Orlowski's disappearance from New Mexico DMV records and the issue of the non-sequential number that showed on her license, a license that supposedly belonged to a dead man. Thomas led her down two sets of stairs, and opened a door to the underground room. It stretched out of sight, illuminated by banks of neon lights that failed to keep away the stark severity of the place. It was a huge storage facility of documents that in the overwhelming majority of cases would never see the light of day. Shirley looked at rows of shelves, tiered to heights of ten, reaching the vaulted ceilings and flanked by ladders mounted on rollers. The concrete floor felt gritty under her sneakers. The air smelled like dried mold.

"Shit. My perps are going to retire and die of old age before I go through this crap."

"Relax Shirl, it's not as bad as it looks. I'll get somebody to help you. DMV paper records are stored in just two shelves. You'll probably find it before dinner."

Actually, she found it before lunch.

CHAPTER 21

———————◆———————

Los Alamos National Laboratory

I kind of felt sorry for this kid William. Here he was supposed to be a cop in a low risk, predictable environment, and now he faced a career-busting moment with no rules to be found anywhere.

"Look William," I told him as we stepped outside the building. "You know very well you don't arrest or detain someone without a solid reason or probable cause to believe a crime has been, or will be committed. Searching for a name in the database of a national laboratory is none of those things. In addition to all that, I'm a high-ranking federal agent. What does all that tell you William?"

The young man licked his lips, and I saw the slightest of tremor in the Glock Nine he held in his right hand. He looked like he wanted to be anywhere but here in this situation.

"You heard them on the radio. I'm to cuff you and bring you in."

After seeing that bunch from IRD in action, seeing how people seemed to disappear around them, the last thing I wanted was to be "detained" by them.

"I'll tell you what William, I'm going to get in your car and you drive us to your headquarter building, then I'll get out and go inside and I won't be your problem anymore. You have my word I won't run or anything."

"All right, get in," he replied.

Inside the car I pulled out my cell phone, speed dialed Anthony, then Shirley Case, explained things in a few seconds, disconnected, and hit the ATF number. I'd just gotten past the first secretary on the phone, and William had begun to turn into the parking space, when two Hummers with flashing emergency lights neatly blocked us in. Four men in suits got out. I recognized one of them from Mary Orlowski's murder scene in Arizona. I still held the cell phone in my hand and he slapped it away. The little phone clattered ten feet away and broke in two pieces.

I punched him, a solid straight-arm jab and I felt the satisfying crunch of cartilage under my knuckles, and barely had time to see the first spurt of blood from his nose when someone rabbit-punched me in the side.

The punch hit dead-on my not-quite-healed wound, and the pain overwhelmed me. I felt my knees buckling and my body sliding down the side of the car. I couldn't catch my breath as bright lights danced in my eyes. I felt someone hold me upright as hands dug out my wallet, ID-badge and gun. I tasted bile in my mouth and the pain paralyzed me, then the world spun out and turned black.

CHAPTER 22

Someone twisted a hot iron in my side, sending waves of pain radiating through my body like incendiary spasms. I coughed and smelled a dusty surface, felt bristles against my face as I moved my head, trying to tighten up even more into the fetus position. It took a few minutes before I could open my eyes and see the bristles of the carpet covering the floor I laid on. They felt scratchy on my face as I raised my head and sat up. My side throbbed and my stomach churned, and I had a sudden craving for a codeine tab mixed with a Percodan. Shit, I thought as I looked around and sat up.

The room was rectangular, about ten by twenty, and except for a plain table and two wooden chairs and the carpet they rested on, completely empty. I saw the outline of a door in the wall, but no knob. I stood, walked over to it and pushed. I might as well have been pushing against a boulder. No windows broke the stark surface of those walls. They appeared to be made of concrete, painted white. Bright light flooded every corner of the room from translucent plastic, covering neon fixtures built into the ceiling. Dead in the center of the ceiling, a bubble stood out, the kind used for surveillance in Las Vegas casinos.

I shouted, banged on the door-no reply. I started to get

really pissed off, building a head of steam. I moved the table until it stood under the bubble. I climbed on top and brought one of the chairs with me. Standing on the table, I held the chair over my head and the top of the chair back hit the bubble. I smacked it a few times and continued shouting. Each time the chair back struck the bubble, it made a hollow thumping noise and I could see it begin to dislodge. I'd bet I wasn't doing much good on the optic and recording devices inside. I was leaning back, winding up for another hit with the chair when the door opened and four men walked in.

I jumped down from the table, couldn't suppress a wince and muffled curse as my side flared up. I faced the men and recognized two of them. One had a thin bandage across his nose, a reward for stopping my knuckles. The other was the one who'd been in charge of the team that came to the scene of Mary Orlowski's murder in the Blackhawk. I couldn't remember his name.

"Agent Duval," he said. "I am Dallas Wilson, director of IRD. We are the ones detaining you."

"I can see that, you fucking Nazi, only I'd call it something else: How about assault on a federal officer? Kidnapping and unlawful imprisonment to start with?"

"Agent Duval you have interfered with a federal anti-terror investigation involving national security. You will remain here until we decide the appropriate course of action."

I didn't reply for a while and looked at the four men. "The appropriate course of action, Mister Wilson, is to follow the laws of the United States."

Wilson left the room without answering. The guy with the bandaged nose just stood watching me, holding a Taser in his right hand. I could see he would have dearly loved to use it on me. They took the table and two chairs out and left me in the now completely empty room.

The past is never far. It dodges our footsteps, haunting our thoughts and guiding our destiny. The only thing separating us from the past is time—an ephemeral presence that all the sciences of the ages has yet to explain. With the right circumstances, time itself becomes a presence.

Locked in this white room, without means of gauging the hours, I couldn't distinguish the passing of moments. I paced, counted, lay down in the deep carpeting, got up, exercised, but in the end, failed to construct any working measure of evaluating time.

Most of all, I thought of Amy. There was no way to avoid the ghosts that had haunted my psyche for the last twelve months. Perhaps it had taken this long, and exactly this sequence of events for me to stop dancing around the edges of reality.

Amy was dead.

I replayed the events leading up to this, worked the timelines and possibilities, and lucidity still evaded me. I returned to Amy's death, an inevitable trail my mind could not avoid. The last two and a half seconds of that raid in which I'd been shot, replayed themselves, raising questions for which answers might not exist.

We had practiced the moves so often it had become ingrained reflex. Two men led the way, one on either side of a steel battering ram so heavy it took both of them to work it. They held the handles on both sides in steady two-handed grips. As they approached the door, they used their momentum, adding to the considerable power of the battering ram. They blasted the door right off the lock, and stepped out of the way in one fluid move that spanned less than a second. Simultaneously, four flash-bangs exploded inside the house, fired through the side windows as I led the team inside.

I carried a custom AR-15 with shortened barrel and stock. Amy was behind me. Four agents followed behind her.

I didn't miss seeing him, but it was just a fraction of a second too late. He'd been concealed on the ground behind a pile of rags and debris. He rose to my right, and fired in the moment I looked away. I swung the barrel of the AR-15 and shot just a hair too late. He fired the .357 Magnum full-point Teflon round at the same time. The bullet caught me in the side, shredding the vest like cardboard, blasting out almost a pound of flesh and bone, driving me against the wall.

In the next one and a half seconds, a terrible clarity filled my mind. I knew I'd been hit, knew I was out of action, and time seemed to stutter like a movie played frame by frame.

He'd waited until I passed before firing, and now he was just level with Amy. She had shifted her attention to me, just one second off target, one miserable second and that's all the shooter needed. The shots came so close together it sounded like a rapid stutter. The rounds took Amy in the chest and mid-section, drove her off her feet into the dingy wall. I still remember the pattern, the peeling paint, and cracked masonry as Amy's body slid down the wall.

Soon as the rounds left the barrel the shooter dropped the weapon and the other guy emerged from behind the door. He held a silver barreled automatic, a Desert Eagle, and fired downward, straight into the shooter's head.

By that time the rest of the team had entered and he had dropped the gun, held his hands straight out, screaming "Police officer, police officer," and that was the last thing I remembered until I woke up in the hospital two weeks later.

The mind works in strange patterns. It's too bad we don't get an owner's manual with our brains. Things that aren't noticed at the moment, details passed, worm their way into the subconscious where they fester as they are slowly figured out. Then one day, seemingly out of the blue, a new question or an answer pops up.

The enforced period of solitude raised some questions in my mind. They bubbled up to the surface like bits of meat from the bottom of a stew pot.

The guy who had stepped out and killed the shooter, who was he? Why wasn't he charged? What had happened to him? I read the after-action reports on the raid so often, I had the thing memorized. Two suspects had been killed, and no arrests made. Everyone in the house had presumably been killed along with one agent; Amy, and one wounded: me. But there had been three in the house, I'm clear on that, and the guy who killed Amy's shooter had survived. Another thing came to me in that moment, and in retrospect, it should have been very clear: The killing of Amy's shooter had been an execution. Somebody wanted him silenced after he killed her.

A flap I hadn't seen before opened near the floor. It was about six inches high and a foot wide. A small bottle of water and a wrapped sandwich fell onto the carpet. I sat on the floor, drank the water and ate the sandwich, American cheese on white bread, dry, prison-style. I stood, walked to the middle of the room, and pissed on their carpet. It felt better than anything I had done since walking into Los Alamos.

CHAPTER 23

I didn't have the slightest hint they were coming for me. The door opened, and there they were, led by the guy I had decked, still sporting the bandage across his nose. The other three men were even bigger and built as if they spent their lives at Gold's Gym. There wasn't the hint of a smile between them. Nose-bandage held the Taser on me, while the other three took their spots on all sides, effectively boxing me in. The two goons behind pulled my arms back. They slapped on handcuffs, quick and professional-like, then bandage-nose stepped up, and punched me just below the waist.

It was a short punch, but solid and it hit just right, dead center in the solar plexus. I went down, and for a half-minute or so, I thought it was over, that my breath would never come again. I gagged and choked, curled up on the floor my eyes level with their shoes. The moments passed until finally I managed to draw the tiniest breath, then another.

They pulled me to my feet and I managed to stand. Each breath came with a razor stab of pain in my belly. Nose bandage came up to me until his face filled my vision and I could see the open pores of his skin and the rage in his eyes.

"Give me another chance fuck-face, just the slightest reason," he whispered.

I managed to hold his eyes, but couldn't reply. To tell the truth, I didn't want to answer, didn't want another part of a punch like that, handcuffed behind my back, mid-section strained and vulnerable.

"That's enough. Dallas is waiting," one of them said behind me.

Without a word he turned away, leading the small group, with me in the middle, out the door and into the hallway.

CHAPTER 24

They led me through a wide hallway, bleak as prison walls. We reached a door that slid back automatically with a hush of pneumatic pistons, and we stepped into yet another hallway. A short walk through a doorway, and we reached an open room surrounded by glass walls that reached waist level from the ceiling. Through the glass I could see several agents in shirtsleeves and ties working at desks, and two men sitting on a bench against the far wall.

The men sitting on the bench looked like they stepped off the cover of GQ, complete with expensive suits, silk ties and matching *pochettes*. There was a gray sheen to the glass, and I recognized it, had used it myself to interrogate suspects. The glass part of the walls separating the room I had entered, was made of one-way glass. We could see out, but they couldn't see in.

The sole furniture in the room was a single government-issue metal desk bolted to the floor as if someone would steal it. A portable phone remained the only object on the smooth surface. Facing the desk was a sole plastic chair, behind the desk another chair.

The man who had introduced himself to me at the scene of Mary Orlowski's murder, Dallas Wilson, sat on it. He looked up at me and waved at the chair. I sat facing him.

I have to admit that since I walked into that room, saw the people beyond, and Wilson at the desk, I almost felt as if I had entered a state of reprieve. Even though I didn't want to believe it, couldn't allow myself the conscious possibility that such a thing could really happen, the idea had been stirring in my head like the small whirlpools in a dark pond, made by some unseen creature just below the surface.

They could kill me. Who could trace it? Just another mysterious disappearance, like thousands that America generates every year. A quick bullet in the back of the head, the body dumped somewhere in the millions of acres of high desert country. The remains would desiccate, decaying to the bones that would rapidly turn to dust, scattered by the Santa Ana wind blowing from the mountains to the south. Yeah, it had been a distinct possibility, seemingly well within these people's capabilities. Only now it was too late for that, the moment had passed. I sat on the chair Wilson indicated, wincing at the sudden pain from my still-sore midsection.

"Everything all right, Agent Duval? You seem a little winded," Wilson said, the barest hint of a smile, cold as Artic pack ice, crossing his face. With thin lips and empty eyes, he reminded me of a reptile that had somehow inhabited a man's body.

"Nah, I'm fine," I replied, "after all, what's a few more violations of the Constitution among friends?"

The smile shut down on Wilson's face, as if it had reached its quota for the day. He leaned over and punched a button on the phone in front of him.

"Supervisor Fine, are you still on the line?"

"Yes I am," came the reply from speakerphone, and I recognized his voice: Assistant Regional Director Harry Fine, my direct supervisor.

"Supervisor Fine, I have in front of me one of your agents, Lieutenant Gaston Duval. Lieutenant, please identify yourself to your supervisor."

I said nothing.

He turned to one of his four men, "Please note Lieutenant Duval refuses to answer." The guy took a small notepad from his jacket pocket and quickly scribbled something.

"Gast? Are you there? Answer goddamnit," the voice squawked from the speakerphone.

"I'm here boss, I hear you."

"Okay Gast, got yourself in a bit of a mess here."

"No I didn't, boss. I made a legal enquiry into employment records held by a government laboratory pursuant to an investigation I instigated on my own volition as a federal agent confronted with suspicious activity."

"Not the way I hear it Gast. You failed to comply with the lawful order of a federal agency tasked with homeland security under Enhanced Patriot Act. You received a direct order to cease and desist and failed to obey it as you are required to do."

"So that makes me, a lawfully appointed officer, holding the rank of Lieutenant within the Alcohol, Tobacco & Firearm agency, subject to kidnapping, illegal imprisonment and assault? That sound right to you, boss?"

"That's all duly noted Gast, your attorneys have all ready submitted these details and accusations."

"Attorneys?"

"Yes Gast, your attorneys, McDougall, Gaffney and Weinstein. They're the only reason you're being released pending a hearing in thirty days."

"A hearing sounds good, Harry," I replied. "Then maybe we can dig out what these people are hiding."

Harry Fine didn't reply right away. When he did, I sensed he chose his words carefully, like talking someone through a complex and dangerous situation.

"Whatever needs to come out will come out in the hearing Gast. Until then you are on administrative suspension. You will continue to be paid, but you must turn in your weapon and badge to Mr. Wilson."

"He's already got them. I guess he's not giving them back."

"Your authority as a federal agent is hereby suspended

until the outcome of the hearing Lieutenant Duval."

A period of silence followed. Wilson and I locked eyeballs, and neither one spoke. Whoever opened his mouth first, lost. I'd be dammed if it would be me. A minute or two passed, slow and stretched as a root canal procedure. It was Harry Fine who broke the silence first via the speakerphone.

"For heaven's sake, Gast, give it up. Go on a real vacation like you were supposed to. Hide out in a resort, go get laid or something. If you just back off, this whole thing will go away."

I said nothing. He hung up. I stood, half expecting to be cuffed or hit again. Nothing happened. I took my eyes off Wilson, took a step toward the door, then a couple more and stepped out into the main office.

The two guys with the thousand dollar suits got up from their seats on the far bench. One of them waived me over. I made my way through the desks, filing cabinets and busy clerks until I reached them. The shorter one held his hand out. He looked like a wrinkled leprechaun and dressed like a photo shoot for the American Bar Association. His eyes blazed with intelligence and cunning. He must be hell on wheels in a courtroom.

"Agent Gaston Duval?" he asked. I nodded and he continued, "I'm Douglas Gaffney, partner in McDougall, Gaffney and Weinstein. This is my associate Bob Harris. We are your attorneys."

Now I remembered: Senator Douglass McDougall, affectionately known as "D-Mack" in the US Senate where he had served for almost three decades. His law firm was the most prestigious and influential in Washington DC. In a place like DC that had more lawyers than any state in the union, that was saying a lot. Since their fees must begin at six figures, and they didn't take just anyone as clients, especially some down and out federal agent, I had some inkling who had hired them. We shook hands and Bob Harris handed me a business card. He was a young guy who looked barely eligible for a driver's license.

Gaffney placed his hand on my back and gently prodded me toward the exit as he spoke, "I've got the particulars of this case and you have nothing to worry about. We fully expect your complete vindication at this hearing. Any negative connotations will be expunged from the record and I guarantee you that these events will not be a detriment to your career."

"Such as it is."

"Beg your pardon?" he said, and his leprechaun eyes locked on mine. "Look," he continued, "I suspect there's more to this case than meets the eye. However, my only concern is for you, my client. I would strongly recommend you forget whatever it is you're chasing that's disturbing these people so much. Take a month long holiday, come back for your hearing and everything will be fine."

"With so many people concerned about my leisure time, I guess I should take a vacation."

Gaffney shrugged and continued walking. We reached the exit, he opened the door and I stepped out.

We were still at Los Alamos, having just come out of the group of administrative buildings near the gate. The New Mexico sunlight scorched my eyes and the air seemed on fire. I stood still and slowly adjusted. Gaffney nodded to a white Hummer stretch-limo—the ugliest vehicle since the Yugo went out of business.

"I guess you know who hired us on your behalf."

"I have an idea."

He smiled and I pictured him next to some pot of gold, dressed in green. We shook hands and he headed toward the parking lot with his sidekick while I walked toward the waiting limo.

CHAPTER 25

Ten feet before I reached the limo, the front door opened and the driver stepped out, a big guy named Umberto I recognized from the Consoli estate. He nodded to me, opened the back door, and I got in.

It was cool inside the limo and the light was subdued, filtered by tinted glass. Anthony sat on the far seat sipping a Bud light. He handed me one.

"Thought you could use this after that little mix up."

"Wasn't a mix up. There's something going on, something people are getting killed over and some part of the government is involved. They're too sensitive about my enquiries and confident enough to illegally detain me and get me suspended for a month."

"By the way," I continued, "thanks for getting those high-power lawyers to get me out."

"Don't mention it. There's always somebody around who owes the old man a favor or two. So what are you going to do now?"

"Keep digging till I figure out what's going on."

"Well count me in."

I looked at Anthony, leaning back against the seat, relaxed, sipping his Bud light. I flashed back on how long we had been friends, fourth or fifth grade at least.

"Look Anthony, I don't know if it's a good idea for you to be involved like this. You got family and all."

"I ain't exactly helpless you know," he said, waving one hand around the limo. "Besides, I was getting bored with the corporate life."

"Alright, just stay on the edge of it, okay? Follow my lead."

"You got it Bro."

The limo pulled onto the road, heading toward the lab's exit. We passed through the gates and turned on the main road.

"Not for nothing Anthony, but this tub's a little conspicuous for a discreet investigation, don't you think?"

"Don't worry, I got it figured out."

We passed an old pickup parked on the side of the road with two guys sitting inside. A hundred or so yards back, I saw a dark sedan turn on the road behind us. Minutes later the pickup turned on the road, following the sedan.

After a few moments, the pickup accelerated and pulled out on the left lane as if to pass the sedan. Instead of passing, the truck veered hard to the right, hitting the left rear fender of the sedan. The big rear-wheel drive sedan went into an out of control spin, veered off the road and overturned before stopping. The pickup continued as if nothing had happened. It came to about ten yards of our rear bumper and held position there. Anthony and I had watched the action out of the back window. He turned to me with a wide grin.

"Yours?" I asked.

"Oh yeah. You remember Frankie and Gator from the neighborhood don't you?"

"The Percibelli brothers?"

"That's the ones."

"Anthony, we are not lugging these two psychos around. I mean here we are in what has to be the most conspicuous vehicle in New Mexico, followed by two guys with rap sheets longer than the state's constitution."

"Hey calm down, Gast. I got it under control. We got rid

of that tail didn't we?"

"Yeah, via a felony."

"Told you, I got it under control. Wait till you see what happens next."

"We bust out Charles Manson?"

"Hey trust me. Did I ever let you down before?"

"Plenty of times."

"Yeah, well this ain't one of them. Now relax and chill."

There are satellites with spy lenses so advanced they can pick out details like a scar on a person's face or the numbers of a license plate. We had used them a number of times during federal operations. Even though Anthony's men had gotten rid of our tail with their crash routine, there was no doubt in my mind we were being watched every moment. You couldn't miss a tank like this Hummer limo we were in.

The road wound through a congested neighborhood, packed with strip malls and housing subdivisions. Up ahead a big Exxon station sprang up with six gas islands covered by big overhangs. Four cars were parked at the islands, and a tow truck, also under the overhang, blocked the way. A convenience store fronted the islands. Attached to the rear of the convenience store was a wide building. A sign above the store advertised it as an auto repair & diagnostic center.

The limo pulled into the station. The pickup following us flew right past and disappeared in traffic. As the limo entered the station, the tow truck backed away, clearing a lane for the big vehicle. Umberto stopped the limo and parked it at the vacated gas pumps.

"Come on, this where we get off," Anthony said. I followed him in the convenience store. A couple of guys waited inside. They handed Anthony two cups of coffee and left the store without a word. I watched them get into the back of the limo. Anthony took the lid off his coffee and said, "More milk or sugar?"

"No, it's good," I said sipping the coffee.

"Glad you like it, now let's get moving," he said, walking

toward the back of the store.

Anthony led me through a hallway that opened into the repair shop. We stepped inside and I saw a Nissan Altima-nondescript, mid–priced, gray, one of millions of vehicles exactly like it. Anthony pointed to it as he spoke, "Yours. Papers are in the glove box. They'll have us on satellite but they can't see who's going in or out because of the overhang. The limo will pull out then I'll leave with this car." He pointed to a red Jaguar. "Cause I ain't driving something like you're getting," he grinned and continued. "Two other people are going to pull out with you, all going different directions. Keep in touch with me by using this cell phone only, okay?"

"You really did have it under control, didn't you?"

"Don't I always? Here, you'll need this stuff," he said, handing me a small leather bag. Inside was a cell phone and all the other stuff I had given him to hold before going into Los Alamos-Mary Orlowski's palm pilot and the envelope with the key in it, plus one other item: a black matte Berretta nine millimeter automatic with extra clip and a box of rounds.

"It's legal, under your name. That's the permit in the leather fold."

"Thanks Anthony."

"De nada bro, just keep me in the loop."

CHAPTER 26

———◆———

I dialed Shirley's cell phone number. She answered on the first ring.

"Hello."

"Hi, Shirl. It's Gast."

"Hey Gast. Got a new cell phone? This number is not identified."

"Yeah, I got it from someone who gets untraceable cells. They're going to try and keep me under surveillance. That should slow their asses down."

I told her how I was detained for a couple of days and how Anthony got me out. I didn't give her details about Anthony, just said it was an old buddy.

"Good thing you've got friends with connections. I can't believe this shit. Gast, there's something really weird going on, something that's getting squashed at some levels of government that are so high it's giving me nose bleeds."

"Well, we kind of knew that."

"Not like this, Gast. Something else happened that just blew my mind. I'm no longer the sheriff of Desert Spring County. I'm now unemployed."

"What the hell are you talking about Shirl? Sheriffs are elected and impeached, not hired and fired."

"In a normal world you'd be right. But like I said, there's

something weird going on. It reaches into very high places. Four days ago the governor of Arizona pulled state funding for Desert Spring County law enforcement. That's been taken over by a combination of Mariposa County Sheriff's department and State Police."

"Are you kidding me? They can't do that. Can they?"

"Yeah Gast, they can. When you pull the money, everything stops. The governor's office claimed a budget crisis, yanked the rug out, pacified county government with promises of equally effective law enforcement without the cost to the county. The cheap-ass retirees running the county grabbed the offer. My deputies were hired immediately by Mariposa County so there won't be any new faces to frighten the natives. I was told to put in an application for watch commander, automatic grade of lieutenant. They said the job was mine if I could stay out of trouble for three months. In other words, get off the Mary Orlowsky thing."

"So what are you going to do?"

"You know, Gast, this stinks. I'd like to blow the bastards up. I don't want their fucking job at the cost of letting murderers get away."

"Are you going to be okay, Shirl?"

"Yeah, I've got some money saved up, my bills are all paid. I got breathing room and I want to get on the case, shove this murder up their ass."

"Way to go Shirl. Next step is to check out Orlowsky's apartment, see what we can come up with. Can you get here fast?"

"I'll be on the next commuter flight. I'll call you with the details and you can pick me up. We'll kick ass and get to the bottom of this."

CHAPTER 27

Washington, DC

It was one of the messiest offices FBI Special Agent John Ford had ever been in—and he'd seen quite a few. A king-sized desk in the center of the room failed to contain all the various paperwork, without it getting stacked one on top of the other in a manner so disorganized, it appeared positively schizophrenic. Yet, Ford knew that the Senator had a reputation for immediately finding any thing he wanted in the cluttered office. His aides fought a constant battle to keep things in order, a battle they had apparently lost long ago.

The office where Ford sat belonged to Donald Weill, Senator from the Commonwealth of Virginia, a sixteen-year veteran of DC politics and chairman of the senate judiciary committee. The senator was running late for his appointment. His secretary had let Ford wait in the senator's office.

Special Agent Ford was there at the pleasure of his boss, the director of the FBI. The day before, the director had a discreet "working" lunch with his old friend, Senator Weill. The director had come away from that lunch visibly upset, and it wasn't because of the spicy food.

Special Agent Ford appeared average and medium in every respect. Average height, average features, medium built. His skin was café *aut lait* brown, inherited from his West-Indies immigrant parents. A pair of black-rimmed glasses lent him the air of a young scholar. He looked as dangerous as a hamster, except for one feature, a scar that ran bright-pink toward the back of his cheek, a memento of his teenage years. Ford had grown up hard, right off Avenue O, in the middle of the Bedford-Stuyvesant ghetto in Brooklyn, New York. Bed-Stuy was the toughest neighborhood of the toughest city on the East Coast. When Ford was growing up, the leading cause of death among black males in Bed-Stuy was homicide. The survival rate among that demographic group was as low as in any third world hellhole.

Ford heard a commotion in the outer office. He stood just as Donald Weill stepped inside. The senator paused. His eyes ran over Ford, appraising. He must have liked what he saw. A smile lit up his face as he stepped toward Ford, and held out his hand.

"Agent Ford? I'm Senator Weill."

His voice was a rolling baritone. In politics, the oratory power of voice was a tool to be honed and practiced. His handshake was also cultivated, firm, communicating sincerity and strength, a psychological tool by itself. The senator was in his sixties with a full head of white hair. Distinguished and patrician, he looked like the GQ model for the wise, elder politician.

"Special Agent John Ford."

"I had expected someone, well, I don't know…"

"Younger, tougher?"

"We have our preconceived notions, don't we?" the Senator said. Even though Ford knew the man was the consummate politician, he felt the sincerity of his tone. "I do apologize," Weill continued. "The director said you're his top investigator, you work strictly for him."

"Yes sir, I do."

The Senator put down his briefcase. He remained standing and reached in his jacket pocket.

"I'm going to commit a small crime in front of you Agent Ford. I hope you will find it in your heart to overlook it."

Ford smiled, but didn't reply. He had read all about the Senator's habits and affectations.

"I'm going to smoke in a federal building," Weill said. He tapped the bottom of a pack of Malboros, put one in his mouth, lit it, and blew the smoke away from Ford.

"I apologize for my rudeness, Agent Ford. I'm sixty-six years old, from Virginia, the tobacco state. I have few vices, but smoking is one of them, and I'm not giving it up. My newest colleague, that freshman senator from California, a certifiable celery-and-carrots health nut, took me to task on that. He's very proud that in his state you have to be 500 feet away from a building to smoke. You know what I told him, Agent Ford?"

"No sir."

"When his home town of San Francisco has its next earthquake, only the smokers will survive. They'll be outside while all the health nuts will be inside the buildings as they collapse."

The Senator laughed. Ford couldn't repress a chuckle. He understood why the Senator kept getting re-elected. You couldn't help liking the guy.

"But you're not here to hear my questionable humor, are you?" Weill said as the smile vanished from his face. "What you're here for, is to begin an investigation that may reach into some dizzying heights of power and money, some without a doubt, within this very government."

"That's what the Director told me, Sir."

"Did he tell you there would be danger to you, physically, as well as to your career?"

"There's always danger to our job, sir. That's understood."

The Senator nodded, smiled again and continued. "Good. Last year, the new administration decided that this country should finally get a handle on the energy situation. Global warming, our dependence on politically unstable regimes, continuing conflicts in the Middle East, amounted to a national catastrophe waiting to happen. We began a crash program to develop a new energy source. This program was headed by three of the top scientists in the required fields. I'm also on the appropriation committee, and I remember voting large amounts of funding for this project. The vote was behind closed doors because the project was kept secret. After all, you don't telegraph your punches to your enemies."

The Senator paused, walked over to the window, took a last drag on his cigarette and crushed it into the dirt of a flowerpot.

Outside, the wind had picked up. Dark clouds chased each other across the capital and fat raindrops spattered on the glass. The Senator turned back to the FBI agent.

"All my life, Agent Ford, I have tried to do good. Haven't always succeeded, that's for sure, but damnit, I've tried, tried as best as a human being with all his faults could do. I believe I've had a measure of success. Along the way, I've made many friends, people who know they could trust me. Six months ago I started hearing things, disturbing things, events that involved the suppression of successful results at Los Alamos to protect certain moneyed interests, disappearing scientists, and malfeasance by people in high places."

Weill reached into his briefcase and removed a manila folder. He handed it to Ford.

"Here, it's all in that file. It's never left my possession. The director, myself, and now you, we are the only people with this information. It must remain so."

"Yes sir. That's what the director said."

"In that file is a phone number, the name of my assistant, and a code word. If you need anything from me, call and give the code word. I'll be on the line within five minutes. Has the director given you sufficient access to resources?"

"Yes sir. He has."

"Good."

Both men stood. They shook hands and Ford headed toward the door. He paused with his hand on the knob as the Senator spoke again.

"Agent Ford?"

"Yes sir."

"Good hunting."

CHAPTER 28

The last commuter flight of the day had already left, so Shirley didn't get one until late the next morning. I waited for her at Santa Fe municipal airport. When she came out of the arrival gate, she looked even better than I remembered. She wore tight jeans and a plain white blouse, light makeup and her hair up, business style. She saw me and held out her hand. I took it and pulled her into a hug.

"How ya doin Shirl? You look good."

"You too Gast," she said, and she stepped back and flashed me a smile.

We went to the luggage carousel and retrieved her bag. It was small enough to have been a carry-on. When we walked out to my car, I understood why it had been checked in. She opened it, took out a Python .38, loaded a clip in it, and put it in her doublewide purse. She gave me the sweetest smile, slung the bag over her shoulder and said, "Now I'm ready."

It was noon by that time, and we were both hungry. I pulled into a diner, the old-fashioned railroad car-type. She ordered a grilled cheese and I had a burger with the works. She held her sandwich with two fingers and the thumb on each hand, nibbling, while I tore into my burger and fries.

"When did you eat last, a week ago?"

I shook my head and smiled at her. "Guess you got me my appetite back," I said.

We left the diner and I walked her to the passenger side of the car and opened her door. I paused there a minute, looking at her.

"Thanks Shirl."

"For what?"

"For caring about this, for helping."

She smiled that smile, a little dimple forming on the lower side of her cheek, just below the blue eyes. For a moment, I didn't think about Amy, and the day got a little brighter. She stood still, then reached over and gave me a quick kiss. I reached for her, but she turned and got in the car.

CHAPTER 29

What a stupid-ass detail, the man thought for probably the thousandth time. I mean, come on. Acting as manager of this pissant little group of a dozen or so condo units? And for what? Just so he could catch anyone inquiring about this Mary Orlowsky—who wasn't even supposed to exist. Well screw it. He was still getting paid his full salary with that IRD outfit, even if all he did was sit on his butt reading the paper all day. Problem was, it included the nights also. He had to live here and detain anyone who asked about Orlowsky's apartment. If nothing happened, he just called in once a week. Now it was Saturday, time to report. He picked up his cell and punched the speed dial number.

"Louis calling in, all clear," he said.

"Okay," a bored voice replied, and hung up. Louis shut his cell phone, unaware that a man had been waiting across the street, monitoring his cell calls, waiting for this particular one.

The IRD agent pulled the coffee maker out to make himself a pot. As he plugged it in, he glanced out the kitchen window and saw the man coming up the walk. There was something odd about the newcomer. He wore a New Mexico Power uniform and carried a small toolbox.

He was short and built like a fireplug with sharp angles and corners. The man's lower jaw protruded from a square face topped by a buzz-cut. He had angular shoulders, thick arms in short sleeves and legs in baggy pants. The only round thing on the man was an odd bump, a knot rising a few inches on his left shoulder. Even from inside the condo, Louis could see the scar on his forehead. The man reached the door and rang the bell. Louis opened it, said "Yeah?"

"You the owner?"

"Manager."

"Okay. I've got to come in, there's a voltage drop on this line. Got to make sure we don't have a short in here. Won't take but a few minutes."

Louis shrugged and said, "Sure." Then it happened so fast, the IRD agent would have little recollection of the actual event. Before he could react, the man swung the toolbox, catching him in the belly. Louis folded like cardboard and the man caught him with an overhand chop, and the lights went out.

Louis revived very slowly. He struggled to open one eye, then the other. There was an ache in his head and he gasped as another sharp pain stabbed through his stomach. He tried to rub his eyes, but his right hand wouldn't move more than a couple of inches. He was in the condo's walk-in closet. A hole had been cut into the wall, exposing a structural beam. A chain had been looped around the beam and his wrist was bound to it with handcuffs. A leg shackle bound his right calf, also chained to the beam.

The "repairman" from New Mexico power sat on the floor in front of Louis, his legs crossed yoga-style. He held a knife in his hand, long and thin with a slight curve, the kind of knife used to fillet large fish.

"Do not speak," the man said. "If you speak, I will cut your throat. Nod if you understand me."

The man's voice was soft, almost a whisper, but it carried the unmistakable promise of certain death. Louis nodded.

"Good. I will be taking your place for a few days. I will bring you food, water, and a bucket to relieve yourself. If your cell phone rings, I will have you answer it. One week from now, if we are still here, you will call in as usual. If you are smart, and do all this properly, you will live. If you fuck up, I will kill you. Do you understand?"

For a moment Louis couldn't find his voice, so he nodded.

"Good," the man replied.

"But…but what if they come to check on me? What should I do?"

"You will do nothing. You should pray that this does not happen, because then, you will die."

The man stood and gave Louis a thin smile that didn't quite make it to his eyes. Then he turned and left him in the closet. Unconsciously, he rubbed the knotted protrusion on his right shoulder. Then he sat in the kitchen where he had a good view of the street and waited.

He was very good at waiting.

CHAPTER 30

"Oh for cryin'out loud, Gast. What do you think this is? A date where you have to be careful I don't get my cutesy hair-do messed up?"

"Come on, Shirley," I replied. "You been in law enforcement long enough to know you don't go in without backup."

We sat in my car, parked on the street about fifty yards away from the entrance to Mary Orlowsky's condo. A wall ran twenty feet before the entrance path, hiding our car from whoever might be inside the manager's unit. It was late afternoon. Shade from the tall buildings across the street, blanketed the car. In spite of that, the temperature still ran in the nineties and I had the engine going and the air conditioner on.

Shirley rolled her eyes, leaned her head against the headrest, and turned to look at me.

God, she looked gorgeous.

"Gast, listen to me," she said slowly, as if I was one of her less-bright deputies. "First, this is not an arrest or take down, okay? I'm just going to talk to the manager and get information and access to Orlowsky's unit. Second, people will speak more freely to a woman alone. Third, I still have an Arizona private investigator's license, which makes this legal for me. Fourth, you're on suspension with the ATF, which makes this illegal for you. Now that's just for starts. You want me to come up with four more reasons?"

I said nothing. She put her hand on my shoulder. It felt warm and soft.

"Come on, Gast. I tell you what, give me twenty minutes. If I don't come out, you jump right in, deal?"

"Ten."

"Fifteen."

"Okay."

We both got out of the car at the same time. She stood on the passenger side and just looked at me.

"Hey, I'm just stretching, staying right here until..." I looked at my watch. "Five twenty two."

I smiled at her. She smiled back.

"See that you do, buster," she said, then turned and walked toward the condo's entrance.

I stayed where I was and watched her until she stepped onto the walkway, out of sight. I went over to the wall where I could see her ring the bell on the manager's unit. The door opened immediately. He must have seen her coming. They guy was short and thick as a stump. Even at this distance, I could see the scar on his forehead. I settled down to wait.

I'm not good at waiting.

CHAPTER 31

Fifteen minutes passed and Shirley still didn't come out of the condo. I took the Berretta Nine that Anthony had given me, pushed off the thumb safety, and placed my coat over it. I got out of the car and walked casually toward the complex, as if I was just strolling, carrying my jacket. I reached the door and rang the bell.

The guy who answered was short and squat. A poorly healed pink scar ran across his pale forehead as if tracing the bony ridge above his eyebrows. He looked like some NFL linebacker that somehow had been compressed to five feet six without losing muscles. A twitch ran across his mouth and the scar danced with the movement. I guessed that's what passed for a smile.

"Yes?" he said. His voice was mild, out of character with his appearance. The tone carried traces of what sounded like some East European inflection.

"I'm looking for a friend who came in here a little while ago to ask about an apartment."

"Ah yes. Come in," he replied and stepped out of the way. I took two steps in, pivoted toward the guy, trying to keep the gun under my coat pointed in his general direction.

The man closed the door and moved with the speed of a

bad thought. Somehow he got behind me, encircled me with arms that felt like iron bands tightening around my mid-section, pinning my arms. I squeezed the trigger and a shot went wide into the carpet. I reared back, trying to head-butt the guy, but it didn't work.

I felt my breath come in ragged pulls, dark spots moved in front of my eyes and pain flared in my side. I didn't want to risk another shot with the gun pinned so close to my body.

Another guy rushed in from the open door of the adjacent room. I got a fast impression of dark coveralls, salt and pepper hair, hard eyes. Something white covered my face, pressing into my mouth and nose.

I smelled a harsh chemical mixture of chloroform and held my breath. The guy in back contained me as efficiently as if I was tied to a tree with steel wire. The rag was pressed mercilessly into my face by the newcomer. I struggled for a few minutes until the urge to breathe became a primordial overriding instinct. I gulped in a lungful of foul, chemically-laced air. I felt my limbs slacken, nothing seemed to work, and the lights went out.

CHAPTER 32

He was an old man, his face wrinkled and brown as only a lifetime broiling under a desert sun could produce. Thin and slightly stooped, his clothing wrinkled, not the cleanest, but not filthy either, as if there was no one to take care of this old man, yet he made a valiant effort at hygiene and neatness, best as he could. He stood in the body of the truck, facing the open side window, operating a machine that whined as he applied the business end of a butcher knife to the spinning stone. The sign painted in weathered letters read:

Henri's Sharpening Service. Lawnmowers-scissors-knives renewed at fair prices!

The street was pretty much empty. Few individuals braved the hundred-degree heat of a Sante Fe afternoon, yet the old man continued working, his eyes fixed on the blade he was sharpening.

It had taken Zurinov over an hour to put on the make up and clothes needed to transform from assassin into old desert rat. Now he held the knife under the spinning stone, but the utensil would never be properly sharpened. Zurinov's concentration rested on the two monitor screens below the sharpening machine.

The truck was parked some five hundred yards from

Mary Orlowsky's former residence. Surveillance cameras mounted on the AC unit on the roof of the truck brought images on the coming and goings to the screen. Another camera he had placed on a telephone pole last night showed him the other side of the condo complex. Between the two monitors, he had a 360-degree view. He had seen the IRD man posted in the condo. He had been told that would happen.

Now, two days later, the New Mexico Power "repairman" had arrived and never left. Zurinov was not surprised. The gait of the man, his body language, the way he took in his surroundings, all told him the newcomer was far from a utility worker. Zurinov did not recognize him. Still, he thought, it would be intriguing to discover what the man was after. A trap set by government agents, now reset by unknown individuals. Curious.

Then, a half hour ago, a couple had arrived, and parked their auto down the block, but not out of view of Zurinov's state-of-the-art cameras. The man and woman obviously didn't want to be seen by the occupants of the apartment since there were plenty of parking spaces in front. The woman had walked up to the condo, knocked on the door and been admitted by the repairman.

Now the man got out of his car and walked up to the condo's door. The way he held his jacket in his right hand, under a scorching sun, told Zurinov he probably had a weapon concealed. He watched the man stepping up the to the apartment door. There was something in his walk that Zurinov's experience interpreted as another military-trained fighter, American by his features. The slight hesitating limp on the right side spoke of an injury, either permanent, or not fully healed.

"Hey, you got a permit for that thing?"

Zurinov's combat senses had been trained to a razor's edge, and tempered by the killing fields of Afghanistan and Chenchnya. He remained aware of his surroundings at all times. Survival depended on knowing the battlefield as intimately as one's body. He had not been surprised by the policeman's approach. Zurinov's right hand rested lightly on the butt of the Makarov machine pistol concealed just below the sharpening machine.

He looked up, smiled at the policeman who looked like a high school weightlifter.

"Yes sir, officer. I have permit. I paid for it," Zurinov replied, letting the Slavic accent come through. After all, it was in character. He reached with his left hand, picked up the framed certificate and held it up for the officer to see. The cop looked at it for a moment and nodded at Zurinov.

"Okay sir. Have a nice day."

The policeman walked back to the patrol car parked on the curb a few feet behind Zurinov's vehicle. He got in the passenger side and opened a bag, handing a sandwich and plastic cup to his partner in the driver's seat.

Wonderful!

Now these two young idiots were going to have lunch while something obviously was going on in his surveillance target. Zurinov briefly considered killing the two policemen, then barging into the condo and killing everyone inside. No. It would cause too much trouble and he could not be sure he had all the pieces in place. He would wait. There were other ways to handle this.

CHAPTER 33

I opened my eyes to darkness, felt constrictions through my hands and feet and on my mouth, and a coarse surface pressing on my eyelids as they opened. Movement transmitted itself through my body from the cylindrical tube that held me. I could tell it was cylindrical because no matter how I tried to move my arms and legs, they encountered the same coarse surface.

I was cocooned inside this unbreakable tube. To make things worse, they had tied me up with what I guessed to be duct tape: the all purpose fastener. Although I couldn't figure out yet what the cylinder was made off, I knew I was in some sort of vehicle. I felt it moving, sensed its vibrations and the rumbling noise of the engine.

Sharp lances of pain flared in my side with each heartbeat. My head was pounding and the stench of the chloroform lingered in my sinuses. I gagged and tried to keep the retching under control. If I vomited, I could suffocate, not the most pleasant way to die.

I felt the cylinder being lifted, then rolled. Dim light flooded my eyes as the rolled-up carpet was opened and I sat up. A hand reached from behind and removed the tape from my mouth with surprising gentleness. I swiveled my head and saw Shirley sitting on the floor, her hands and feet also bound with duct tape.

We sat on the floor of a large van. There were no windows. Light came from the front compartment where I could just make out the back of the driver's head and a passenger. The van had that new smell in spite of the remains of carpet that we had been rolled up in.

"You okay, Gast?" Shirley asked me.

"Yeah. Where the hell are we?"

"We're guests of this gentleman," she said, nodding to a spot behind me.

I turned my head around and saw a man sitting on a box, near the rear doors of the van. He looked familiar, and for a moment I couldn't place him, then I remembered: he was the second man, the one who had held the chloroform-soaked rag on my face until I took a breath. I looked at him, trying for my best ass-kicker stare.

Even squatting in the gloomy interior of the van, I could tell he was tall. His face was pale with the complexion of people whose ancestors spent thousands of years in a part of the earth where sunshine was rare. He carried a wintry look about him, as if tragedies were a normal part of his life. The hair was a military style brush cut, salt and pepper, beginning to recede from the forehead. His eyes were a light gray, overhung by droopy lids that emphasized the appearance of some vast sadness. Yet, there was strength in those eyes and in the body as well. Muscles rippled beneath a dark tee shirt and jeans. He was obviously in shape for someone I pegged as about mid-fifties.

There was a tattoo on his right forearm that looked familiar. I stared at it for a while then remembered where I had seen one like it. I looked up at him and our eyes met again. The slightest hint of a smile lifted the corner of his mouth.

"You are ex-military, yes?" He said softly.

"Rangers."

"Ah yes, excellent soldiers. Then you will recognize this," he said, turning his arm slightly, displaying the tattoo.

"Yeah. Spetznaz, Russian special forces."

"Former. Many years ago."

We continued to stare at each other, but the hard edge had gone somewhere else. There was a subtle rapprochement, a mutual respect of veterans from elite units.

"What's this? Homecoming week?" I heard Shirley say. Before I could reply, the man spoke again.

"My name is Sergei, and I do apologize, miss, for the way we took you. It was deplorable, but as you will soon discover, necessary."

We rode for another half hour or so in silence. From the speed and straight path of the van, I surmised we were on some desert road. Finally the vehicle slowed, turned, ran about a hundred yards at low speed and stopped.

Sergei opened the van's rear doors and motioned to us.

"Place your feet outside. Yuri will cut the tape. Please don't try anything dangerous."

Yuri was the short, squat guy with the scar on his forehead. He held a thin, wicked looking knife. Without a word, he reached over and sliced the tape holding my feet. He turned to Shirley and did the same.

We jumped out of the van, and my knees gave way. I felt Sergei's arm holding me. I straightened up and looked around.

We were a hundred yards off a curving two-lane macadam road. Hills rose in the distance and further out the San Mateo Mountains reflected orange from the setting sun. The air smelled like baked rocks and little dust devils swirled in the late afternoon breeze. The temperature had dropped to about ninety, and would continue to drop through the desert night. A house stood off the driveway leading from the road. It was a two-story frame house, unusual for these parts where almost every structure was some form of concrete or stucco.

Our hands were still bound in front of us as Sergei motioned us toward the house. Yuri led the way, while the other man who had sat in the front with him, remained outside, cradling one of Mister Kalishnikov's finer products: An AK47 assault rifle, best thing the Russians had made since Stolichnaya. Yuri carried one also. He looked like he had been born with the thing in his hands. We climbed the three steps to the porch. Sergei opened the front door and waved us in.

We stepped inside a wide room with high ceilings. There was a U shaped alcove in one corner, flanked by tall windows looking out to the front of the house, the driveway, and the road. Yuri pulled a chair toward the window and sat down facing out. The AK rested lightly on his lap as he stared out. He looked like a modern day troll who had escaped from under a bridge.

The furniture in the room seemed functional, but mismatched, as if the owners had bought everything at separate garage sales. Two easy chairs flanked a low-slung coffee table on the far wall. Facing them were two more chairs, a couch and end tables.

"Please, sit," Sergei said. We sat, and he pulled one of the chairs closer, facing us.

"You are not our prisoners," he said.

"That's like saying a bear never shits in the woods," Shirley replied.

At that moment an old man walked in the room. He had unruly white hair, like Albert Einstein on a windy day. His eyebrows were bushy and a scraggly mustache hung from his upper lip. He wore a wrinkled white shirt, brown pants and slippers. There was a dignity about him, like a scholar of divinity who couldn't be bothered by earthly matters such as appearances. At first glance, he didn't hold anyone's attention. That is, until you looked at his eyes—blue, as bright as a Caribbean sky, and brimming with intelligence. A smile curled his lips, wrinkling the loose skin of his jowl. He looked from me to Shirley then turned to Sergei.

"Why are our guests bound with this tape? Cut them loose at once."

"In time, Poppa, in time," Sergei replied before turning back to us.

"Mister Duval, Miss Case, I'd like you to meet my father,

Doctor Yakov Katamay."

Something sounded familiar about the name, but I just couldn't place it. The old man's eyes flitted back and forth from Shirley to me. He took a few steps and turned to his son.

"Sergei?"

"In a moment Poppa, I must talk to them first."

"Very well, five minutes," he replied then turned to me. "You like Ghoulash?"

I had a sudden disconnect. It took me a moment to understand the question, as if he had asked me my great-grandmother's date of birth or something.

"What?"

"Is my English not good? I'm speaking of Hungarian Ghoulash. I make the best in the world. Learned it at university in Budapest in 54, would you like a bowl?"

Before I could reply I heard Shirley pipe up next to me.

"I'll take one doc, a big one, with bread and butter, and a Diet Pepsi."

"Ah, a woman after my own heart, and so beautiful, you are a lucky man," he replied, turning to me.

"Not yet he isn't," Shirley said.

"Forget the Pepsi, my child. I will not have that horrible chemical mixture in my kitchen. I will bring you Evian, the best water in the world, even if it comes from those insufferable French."

"I'll take a bowl too," I said.

"Of water?"

"Uh, no, you know what I mean."

Katamay chuckled and nodded. He turned, took a few steps toward the kitchen, and stopped.

"Sergei, when I return, I expect to see our guests completely freed. We are *Izgoi*, not gangsters."

Second time I had heard that term. I remembered it had been on Mary Orlowsky's Palm Pilot, with a phone number.

"Of course Poppa," Sergei replied.

CHAPTER 34

While Sergei sat in front of us, I noticed some things I had missed when I first saw him. A network of scars ran along the right side of his face and his nose had a slight bent, as if it had been broken and poorly set. His body spoke of obvious strength and oozed specialized military training. Put a Green Beret, or a Delta Force uniform on him, and he would have been right at home. Yet, there was softness to the eyes and the set of his mouth. I sensed that this was a man who had killed out of necessity, and loathed it. His eyes were darker than his father's, but in his face I recognized the resemblance to Yakov Katamay. I also remembered where I had heard the name.

"Your father," I asked. "Is he the Doctor Katamay who was in that Nobel Prize flap a few years back?"

"Yes. We are Jews, and some journalists believed that the prize was denied to my father because most of the winners that year were also Jews. There might have been some truth to that, or maybe not. Either way my father did not care. The prize meant nothing to him. All he wants is to continue studying his nuclear physics, his atoms and electrons."

"Obviously you didn't follow his footsteps."

"It was the great disappointment of his life. He envisioned the Katamays, father and son, discovering the secrets of the universe. Unfortunately for my father, science bored me. I wanted to be a soldier, so I joined the Red Army at the earliest age possible. Sixteen, pretended to be seventeen. Went airborne, Spetznaz, the whole nine-yards as they say."

We sat quietly, watching each other. From the kitchen came the light clanking of pots and cutlery. It was a comforting domestic sound in contrast to this overall strange situation. In the hallway we could hear the ticking of what was probably a grandfather clock. Across the room, Yuri sat like one of those gargoyles atop ancient European cathedrals. Instead of a pitchfork, he held that assault rifle, staring out the windows as if he expected an enemy regiment to storm the house. It was Shirley who broke the silence first.

"That was a pretty rough take down, the chloroform and all. Why did you do it?"

"Again I apologize," Sergei replied. "I simply could not think of a way to pull you out of a certain trap you were about to walk into. You would not have listened to us."

"You could have tried," I said.

"Yes. I could have tried, just as I tried a few weeks ago to talk another person out of danger. That person would not listen, as you would probably not have listened."

"Oh yeah, who was that?"

"Her name was Mary Orlowsky."

We all sat silent a moment. The pots clanked, the clock ticked somewhere in the hallway, and a desert breeze whispered around the eaves of the house.

Sergei leaned forward in his seat. The veins of his forearms bulged, emphasizing the dagger-tattoo of the Spetznaz. When he spoke, his voice had a soft, yet strong, tone of conviction.

"You are truly not our prisoners. I am going to cut your bonds. I ask only one thing. I will tell you a story, and you will listen carefully. After I am done, you are free to go if you choose. That is all we ask. Do you agree?"

Shirley and I both said, yes.

"Yuri," Sergei called out.

The man rose and walked across the room until he stood in front of me. He held the AK-47 in his left hand and reached behind him with his right. Now he held a long, thin-bladed knife.

"Hands," he said, eloquent chap that he was.

I held out my hands and he cut the tape in one motion. That pig-sticker of his could put Ginsu knives to shame. He walked over to Shirley. She held out her hands and he did the same. Without a word, he turned his back and returned to his post in front of the windows.

"Now I will give you proof of our sincerity, providing that you both give me your word you will not cause us any trouble."

"Okay, you got mine. Shirley?"

"Yeah, mine too."

Sergei picked up a leather shopping bag laying at his feet. He reached inside twice, and came up with a gun each time: mine and Shirley's. He placed the pistols directly in front of us on the coffee table.

"Whatever you choose to do when we are done, you may take your weapons. After you have listened to what I am about to tell you, we will be the last persons you will want to use them on."

"Okay," I said, "tell us a story."

CHAPTER 35

Zurinov drove the sharpening truck into the wide garage his support team had rented for him. He left the truck and opened the door of the Lexus SUV parked there for his use. He sat in the driver's seat a moment and surveyed the interior before starting the engine and engaging the gearshift. Once outside the garage he stopped the vehicle again.

He was on a side street of an industrial area, well chosen for its remoteness. The road ran parallel to a series of warehouses before disappearing into the desert. The sun was ready to vanish over the horizon and the remaining light threw long shadows from the buildings of the industrial park.

The seat of the SUV had been changed. Instead of the stock bucket seats, a single split-bench seat had been installed. Zurinov pushed a hidden button and the top of the right side of the seat sprung open. In the recessed well beneath the seat cushion, lay the tools he would need: A grenade launcher no longer then three feet, next to it, six rounds that would fit with surgical precision into the barrel. A paratrooper's machine pistol with folding stock, an M-14S military rifle with mounted scope and custom elongated barrel, still one of the most potent sniper rifle in existence. Along with this mini-arsenal, stored in the lower tier of the seat, were a half dozen hand grenades and all the ammunition he would need.

Zurinov closed the seat and turned on the monitor set in the dashboard. He keyed certain commands on the touch-screen and the device picked up the signal from the intelligence geo-satellite. A map of the area sprung into view. In a far corner a red circle blinked as it slowly moved. The satellite had kept contact with the vehicle he had designated earlier with the laser.

Even though the satellite had infrared, night vision capability, Zurinov knew the odds of losing the vehicle in the dark were very high. He touched another command on the screen and the map changed. A glowing orange line showed him the best route to reach the tracked vehicle.

Zurinov engaged the gearshift and accelerated toward his target.

CHAPTER 36

"Once upon a time," Sergei began, "the government of the United States decided that a radical new source of energy had to be found. The environmental problems caused by petroleum fuels, the political issues from unstable oil producing countries throughout the world, and the approaching global crude oil shortage, created a dangerous situation for America and the Western world— But where to go? New energy sources such as solar, wind, ethanol and other exotic sources were decades away from the kind of wide, productive use needed. It was time for something else, something radical. Congress created the Charles McHenry congressional sub-committee. It was a top-secret issue of the intelligence oversight committee. Senator Charles McHenry was drawn to my father's work in the field of cold fusion. He believed correctly, as my father did, that cold fusion was possible if we created the equivalent of a Manhattan Project."

"Hold it right there, Sergei," Shirley said. "I'm a cop from Boston. I don't know cold fusion from a cold beer. Talk plain English, slowly."

"Perhaps I will let Poppa explain those concepts. He got very good at it from having to cajole funding from politicians."

The aromas of exotic spices wafted through from the kitchen and tickled my nostrils. I suddenly realized I hadn't eaten since that morning, and I was starved. Noises of clattering pots and cutlery drifted in, comfortingly familiar noises in these strange circumstances.

Doctor Katamay walked in carrying a large wood tray. He made a face and pushed aside our guns, then set the tray down on the table, the guns on either side. Four large bowls sat on the tray, surrounded with spoons, paper napkins, sliced, crusty Italian bread and two sticks of butter. He took a bowl, two slices of bread, a spoon and napkin, carried it to the other side of the room, and handed it to Yuri.

"I already took it to your guard in front," Katamay said as he returned. "Is that really necessary, Sergei?"

"You take care of the physics, and I take care of security, alright Poppa?"

The old man shrugged, mumbled something about insolent children, and handed everyone a bowl and spoon. He took a couple of slices of bread, buttered them, and handed them to Shirley.

"Here you are beautiful child. You two oafs can take care of yourselves."

Sergei looked at me. We smiled and dug in. It was easily one of the best meals I ever had. Katamay brought seconds, and even then, it was all I could do to stop myself from licking the bowl like a kid.

Katamay took the empty bowls one at a time, stacked them on the tray then turned to us with a deadly serious expression.

"Now I'm going to tell you a secret. You must promise to keep it only for your own use."

"Sure," I said, while Shirley nodded and leaned forward.

"Ghoulash must be made the day before and not served for 24 hours. That way, the spices and juices marinate properly. Got it?"

I looked at Shirley, and we both burst out laughing. Katamay and Sergei joined in. Finally Katamay leaned back in his chair and nodded at Sergei.

"Go on, finish the story."

"In order for this new government initiative on energy to be successful," Sergei resumed, "there had to be four elements in place. The first was a location containing the most advanced nuclear research facility in the world. They had that, at Los Alamos National Laboratory, right here in New Mexico. The second component was the keenest mind of its day in the field of nuclear physics. Poppa fit the bill. He is the unquestioned expert, specializing in atomic fusion. The third element was expertise in the field of energy plasma. Instead of wires, coils and solid generators, the new energy would be converted and transferred through a variety of ion plasmas. The expert in that rarified field was Doctor Mary Orlowsky, formerly of Cal Tech. The fourth piece of the puzzle was Professor Nathan Ragowski who was head of Nano-technology research at Brookhaven National Lab for nine years."

"Nano technology is the science of microscopic things isn't it?" I asked.

"Actually, it's much more than that," Doctor Katamay cut in, "you see that light switch?" he asked, pointing to the wall, "It weighs about a pound or two, made of metal, wire and insulating plastic, about two by four inches and another two inches deep. Nano-technology would replace it with a series of sentient atoms, thinking nuclear particles and molecules so small they would be invisible without an electron microscope. They would weigh literally next to nothing, never wear out or malfunction. They would be to that wall switch what a modern jet-turbine driven ship would be to a medieval sailing barque. Such advanced controls would provide a quantum leap in energy generation and applications."

Now it was Shirley's turn to ask a question.

"We were present at Mary Orlowsky's death. Agent Duval here was a witness, and at the time, her murder fell under my jurisdiction. The investigation was squashed at high levels. It appears there's an entire branch of federal law enforcement, this Investigative Research Division, whose only function seems to be suppressing the facts of her murder. Why? Wouldn't they want her murder solved and the research protected? And what do you people have to do with all this, anyway?"

"While we're playing ten questions," I added, "what the hell is the Izgoi? That's the second time I've heard that term in connection to all this."

There was a moment of silence. The only sound was the steady tick-tock of the clock in the hallway. I heard Yuri's seat shift at the other end of the room, and from the corner of my eye, I saw him stand. Then I heard the metallic click of the Kalashinkov in his hand, chambering a round.

CHAPTER 37

———◆———

Zurinov pulled the SUV to the side of the road. For the last four miles he had been running with just the parking lights in the squid-ink night of the empty desert road. He shut off those lights and waited a few minutes for his eyes to adjust.

Now he donned the night vision goggles, and the darkness sprang into green and white highlights. A coyote stalked across the road, just fifty yards from him. Closer still, the small pinpoints of a pair of rodent's eyes twinkled under the darker shape of a cactus. The road lay ahead, curved here and there where the engineers had found it easier to go around the boulder formations that dotted the landscape. There was a dry smell to the air that penetrated the interior of the SUV and blended with the vehicle's scents of leather and plastic. The night had a feel to it, an atmosphere that Zurinov recognized as approaching death. He found himself excited by the killing violence he would bring in just a few moments. For Zurinov, it wasn't just about the money. It never had been.

He looked down at the screen mounted in the dashboard, where the satellite readout was displayed. The blinking O representing the target, and the steady X showing his position had almost merged. The distance readout indicated less than three miles. Further in the distance, a glow indicated the actual target position. It hadn't moved for almost an hour now.

Zurinov pulled the SUV completely off the road, shut down the engine and got out of the vehicle. He took the grenade launcher and three grenades. Next he strapped on the machine pistol, a nine-millimeter, and his favorite close-in weapon, a US Marine K-Bar knife. He walked across the road, moved some fifty yards into the desert and headed toward the target. He walked rapidly with the high-stepping, experienced gait of the practiced night fighter. The soft crepe-soled shoes landed silently, each step guided by the clear image from the night vision goggles.

CHAPTER 38

For a second, I thought Yuri had received some kind of silent signal to kill us all. I reached out and retrieved my Berreta from the table. But Yuri wasn't interested in us. As he pointed the weapon out the window, there came a volley of automatic gunfire. We all instinctively ducked, and Sergei knocked the lamp from the table. Now the only light came from the kitchen.

There came the crackling of shattering glass as Yuri broke the windowpane. He kneeled, shouldered the AK and fired a series of three round bursts. Steady, controlled firing-the mark of a professional.

I reached the table and grabbed my Berretta nine. I saw Shirley to my left, taking the Python, and clicking off the safety. Sergei rose in a crouch, put both hands out flat toward Katemay, Shirley and me.

"Down, stay down," he whispered. "We will control this."

Yuri fired another three round burst, then turned violently, as if stung. For a fraction of a second I saw the look across his face, the immediate realization that this was the absolute end of his life, and nothing could take it back. I believe he saw that grenade come in, a blink of an eye before the possibility of any escape.

* * *

I've been near rocket propelled grenade explosions before. Twelve miles from Kandahar, I crouched in a shallow depression, trying to claw my way into the rock, as a grenade exploded a few feet away. I've had artillery rounds impact a dozen yards away, their thunder shaking the thick walls of the concrete bunker. But I've never been in an enclosed space when a grenade went off.

Even though we crouched with the heavy oak table in front of us, the explosion was stunning as an apocalypse. The concussion slammed the table against my body, hurling me to the wall. I saw Shirley knocked back against the chair, and Katamay rolled to the other side by the air pressure. The windows and the frame that held them, the plaster of the walls, simply disintegrated, blowing out in a storm of dust and pulverized debris that filled the room. Yuri's body took the full force of the explosion. Lacerating shrapnel, jagged and launched to killing speed by the detonation, penetrated his body, shredding organs from neck to groin.

Sergei had been directly behind him, which is probably the only thing that saved him. The stink of cordite mingled with the coppery smell of blood. The room filled with a mist of exploded dust and smoke.

I turned to Shirley and helped her up.

"Shirley, you okay?"

Her face was covered in dust. Bits of plaster and shredded wallpaper hung from her hair. She shook her head, focused her eyes, and her mouth moved, but not a sound came, both of us temporarily deafened by the explosion. She nodded her head yes, pointed to Sergei and went to help Katamay.

I picked up the AK-47 that had been blown out of Yuri's hands. I kneeled and fired several bursts out the gaping hole where the windows had been. The weapon operated flawlessly, as if nothing had happened. They always did, that's why every soldier since Vietnam loved them.

The darkness outside the house seemed alive with menace. I continued firing until the clip emptied out, then took another one from a belt on Yuri's corpse and reloaded.

Behind me Shirley had helped Katamay. The old man was coaxing Sergei up while Shirley tried to get his arm over her shoulder. His eyes kept rolling in his head. Each time the white showed, Katamay would slap his cheek, speaking urgently in Russian. His face was bloodied from a number of insignificant shrapnel cuts. His right shoulder was blood soaked where a bullet had passed through, and a number of shrapnel wounds peppered his torso. His biggest problem however, was the concussion from the explosion.

A buzzing shriek rang painfully in my ears, but some of my hearing was starting to come back. I turned to Katamay, and Sergei seemed to find his bearings as he nodded toward Yuri's body on the floor. I shook my head no.

"He's dead. We can't do anything for him, and if we don't get the hell out of town pronto, we're next. Is there another way out?"

Sergei's mouth opened over bloody lips, but no sound came out.

"Come on doc," Shirley hollered at the old man. "Is there another way out?"

I turned back toward the open wall and fired another burst. Whoever had attacked, I just needed to slow them down a bit. I turned back to Shirley. She had Sergei on one side and Katamay helped on the other. The big man's knees buckled as he tried to walk.

"Let's go," Shirley yelled. "The doc says there's a basement garage with entry through the kitchen. He says there's a vehicle in there that can get us out of here."

I pushed Katamay aside and took Sergei by the waist. The old man scooted in front of us into the kitchen. We followed him as he opened a heavy door leading to a concrete stairwell. The door was solid oak lined with steel. That should buy us a few minutes if our attackers charged the house.

We went down the stairs. Shirley slipped and fell several

steps before stopping on her rear. I barely managed to keep Sergei upright and we both sprawled onto the concrete floor at the base of the steps.

The basement room was more like a square concrete cavern than a garage. It was completely empty save for a large vehicle squatting there, at the edge of the ramp leading upward to a closed, wide garage door.

The vehicle was a Hummer, but different than any I had seen before. It was an early type, going back to when they had first been adapted for civilian use from the military Hummvees, and gasoline sold for less than a buck and a half a gallon. It looked as if the builders had changed their mind, wanted to revert it back to military use, but had gone too far to do that. It was painted a dark green, not quite Olive Drab, but not exactly designer colors either. The wheel well openings had been enlarged to accommodate extra wide tires that protruded almost a foot on both sides. There was a massive look to the vehicle that reminded me of an armored personnel carrier. I hoped the thing could go faster than thirty miles an hour, but what choice did we have?

I got in the driver's seat and Katamay took the front passenger side. Shirley hustled Sergei in the rear, propping him up, and tied his seatbelt on. Muffled sounds of gunfire came from upstairs. We didn't have too long.

I looked at the dash but couldn't find the ignition switch.

"Where the hell's the key?"

"Just step on the gas," Katamay said.

"You gotta turn it on first. Where's the ignition switch?"

"Just-step-on-the-gas," the old man said through clenched teeth.

An explosion burst into the basement from the stairwell. Pieces of the door blew down into the garage and hit the Hummer. Clouds of heavy black smoke rolled down and the acrid smell reached inside the closed vehicle.

"For Christ's sake, do what he says," Shirley screamed. "Step on the fucking gas."

I jammed the gas pedal to the floor and nothing could have prepared me for what happened next.

CHAPTER 39

Hubert Montrose III stared out the window from the conference room on the 13th floor of the Louis IV Hotel-the exclusive domain of the *Committe Des Cinq*. Lines of dark clouds rolled across the sky to the far horizon, pushed by a low-pressure front coming in from the nearby Atlantic. Far below, traffic choked the *Boulevard De La Victoire.* Everyone in Bordeaux was trying to get home early and beat the storm.

Montrose reached out and touched the window. Sometimes, it all seemed like an illusion, as if everything could just disappear at the whim of capricious gods. For the first time since this whole affair had started, he felt twinges of concern.

Dallas Wilson, who had seemed so implacably efficient at the start, now faltered. Instead of an early progress report laced with success, he had left a terse message of delay. Well, he couldn't dodge it forever. The time had arrived for his pre-arranged private report.

Montrose nodded at the silent technician at his console. The man replied with a soft, "yes sir," typed in some commands at a keyboard and left the room. Montrose took a seat at the conference table.

The column of light appeared from the hidden recess in

the ceiling, and the holographic image of Dallas Wilson materialized. Montrose knew it originated thousands of miles away in the American West, and was broadcast through encrypted satellite signal and reconstituted here. Still, you had to be impressed with the technology, he thought.

"Good morning sir," the image of Dallas Wilson said, clear as if the man stood right there in the room.

"It's late afternoon here in southwest France, Mister Wilson. You have failed to render an early solution to our problem. Instead you sent a message of delay for this report. All this leads me to believe your efforts have not worked, and the enormous amounts of money we have spent, a substantial amount on you personally, I might add, have failed to bring fruit. Please tell me I am wrong, Mister Wilson."

"It is true that we have not closed the case as anticipated, sir. However, we do expect termination very shortly. We have Doctor Katamay and his protectors on the run thanks to that Zurinov. Naturally, he would not have been nearly as successful without our assistance."

"So exactly where are we on this?"

Wilson hesitated, and licked his lips.

"Well Mister Wilson?"

"Zurinov found them through surveillance of a stakeout we had set up at Orlowsky's old residence. He then tracked them to a safe house in the desert where he attempted to terminate them. He was unsuccessful."

"For heaven's sake Wilson! It took literally billions, billions do you understand, to get you in control of this new American security agency, this IRD. Once you had this location, why didn't you flood the area with agents? Capture and terminate them, destroy these loose end."

"That's hardly fair, sir. Zurinov may be a legend in covert assassinations, but he works on his own. He doesn't share information. It's a one-way street with him. We can't track them down as he did. We just don't have the resources he has within the Russian expatriate community, especially with those dammed Izgoi."

"What the hell is Izgoi, Wilson?"

"Without going into too many details, sir, Izgoi is a loose association of former deep cover agents from the old Soviet Union. When the iron curtain fell and the USSR disbanded, these people found themselves without controls, hell, without even a country. They're secretive as hell, impossible to penetrate. We know that ex-Spetznaz soldiers are among them, including Doctor Katamay's son. They are the ones hiding and protecting him."

"I will talk to the people running Zurinov."

"There's something else sir."

"What?"

"When they got away from Zurinov, they escaped in the prototype. It's still in their hands."

CHAPTER 40

When I was about twelve, my parents took me to Las Vegas. That was in the days when the city of sin was trying to attract families. Excalibur had just opened, New York, New York was going full blast, and the MGM Grand had the Wizard of Oz animated on two acres of its front lobby. In the backyard, was a seventeen-acre amusement park with nanny services and supervision for the children. The idea was that mom and dad could put the kids in care of the amusement park. The kids would have a ball while the parents blew their college fund in the casino. They had a new ride there called the Screaming Sky Launch. This monstrosity catapulted a car with six riders up a ramp. The acceleration was incredible. It scared the shit out of me.

When I stepped on the gas pedal of this strange Hummer, I felt like I had returned to that ride. No pause, no hesitation, no noise. The vehicle exploded forward as if the space shuttle rocket was tied to its ass. I was pinned across the seat as the vehicle shot out straight into the garage door.

The door had to be solid oak with steel swivels, hinges and rollers, and it didn't even slow it down. The roll cage protecting the front of the vehicle pulverized the door. The Hummer became airborne for what seemed an eternity, but couldn't have been more than half a second. It landed with a bone-shattering jolt. My pelvis hit the steering wheel, and my head smashed into the thankfully-padded ceiling. In the back, Sergei and Shirley were tossed like bugs captured in a can held by a hyper three-year old. Katamay was the only one to remain in his seat, strapped in by an elaborate seat-belt/shoulder harness.

The Hummer continued, barely slowing even though my foot was long gone from the gas. It smashed into the wood fence surrounding the property, and that didn't even put a dent in its speed. Plowing through dozens of thick cactus, bouncing over stones, and running through sandy patches, the vehicle finally crossed the road and came to a stop about two hundred yards down. There was complete silence, but then again, apart from objects smashing into the steel bars of the grille, the vehicle itself emitted no sounds.

We sat there, speechless and happy to be in one piece. Finally Katamay said, "When I told you to step on the gas, I did not mean all the way down."

"Where the hell d'you learn to drive, Gast?" Shirley said from the back. "Talk about women drivers."

A metallic ping sounded from the rear, followed by a loud crack rolling from the direction of the house, the sound of the shot catching up to the supersonic bullet. Before I could react, a second shot came and blew out the left rear cowl window. Instinctively, I stepped on the gas again, gingerly this time. The Hummer shot forward, plowed into a stand of cactus and kept going in total darkness. I fumbled around the dash until I found a light switch and toggled it on. Powerful halogen beams lit the night, pointing out the road to our flank. I turned into it, away from the house.

"Shut the light, Gast," Shirley yelled from the back. "He'll see us."

"He sees us now. He's got NVG's."

Now I noticed a single digital readout in the dash, miles per hour. The front wheels hit the road surface, straightened, and less than three breathtaking seconds later, the readout displayed 95MPH.

The Hummer gobbled up the road in silence. I heard the wind whispering around the boxy surface, the tires singing on the asphalt, but that was it. No engine noises or gears whining. I had to back off the gas when the digits reached 120. The stripes in the middle of the road whizzed by as if it was a single, solid line. Cactus and road debris flashed on the side of the road and vanished instantly. There was a sensation of great speed, but well controlled. I stepped lightly on the brakes and the Hummer immediately dropped to 70. I spiked it up to 100 and held it there.

"Stay on this road," Katamay said from the passenger side. "It will hook up with Route 4 and you can take that to the 550."

"We need to get Sergei to a doctor, Gast," Shirley said from the back.

"We cannot take him to a regular doctor," Katamay said. "They are required by law to report a gunshot wound. That would be a death sentence for us. We will take him to another safe house. There will be medical attention there."

"I hope it's safer than your last one."

"I don't know. My son takes care of that."

"So where is it?" I asked.

"I will show you," Katamay replied. He reached into a dashboard compartment in front of him and pulled out a standard GPS. He plugged it into a 12Volt outlet beneath the dash. The screen came up and the device indicated it had located our position. Katamay keyed in a waypoint from the machine's memory. A pleasant female voice came from the machine and said, "Continue 84 miles to Highway 4 and turn left." At the same time, the screen showed a three dimensional view of the road. I pushed the gas down a quarter inch or so, and the Hummer speed shot up to 120.

"Just follow the directions," Katamay said.

"What about gas?"

"It will be fine."

"Are you kidding me? This thing must use as much gas as a jetliner."

"It will be fine."

"How do you know? There's no gas gauge on this thing. What's it run on anyway, rocket fuel?"

"Water."

"Say what?"

"Water, it runs on plain water."

CHAPTER 41

A desert sunrise is something everyone should see at least once in a lifetime. The orange tint of the horizon through the windshield of the Hummer told me I would experience another one before we got to our destination.

I'd been driving most of the night. I felt the weariness through every pore of my skin, below that, to the bones and vital organs. I must have had a multitude of contusions, and black and blues, the results of the various violent events of the previous day. My nervous system screamed for a Percodan, afterwards, a beer, and a cool place to sleep.

Katamay dozed on the passenger's seat. His head rolled on the high back, displaying features and wrinkles that emphasized his age. Sergei hadn't slept at all. Shirley kept him awake to stave off the potential fatal results of the massive concussion he had received. She on the other hand, had nodded off about two hours ago. Her head rested on Sergei's shoulder, her blond hair draped over her forehead and down her shoulder. Dirt, plaster and dark smears covered her face. She was a mess, and she still looked beautiful. I caught Sergei's eyes in the rear view mirror and he spoke softly.

"Thank you," he whispered.

"Hey, you would have done the same for us."

"Yes I would have."

"So who were those people back there, the ones who attacked the house?"

"Not people, just one. His name is Zurinov. He only works alone. They call him Shatun."

"That's a cute nickname, what's it stand for?"

"In my place of birth, the great forests of Russia, there are bears. They are terrible in their strength. They must be to survive, for there are no conservation efforts or friendly park rangers as in America. Only the fiercest survive. These bears hibernate. They shut themselves into their dens for the long Russian winter. They emerge in spring. During their long sleep, a very few, maybe one or two each year, are affected in a particular way."

Sergei's voice was a soft, easy whisper. It blended well with the susurration of the wind passing over the frame of the Hummer at 90 MPH. That and the low whistle of the tires on the road were the only sound of our travel. We had entered an empty part of the desert, just past canyon country, where roadrunners and reptiles were more frequent than people. The GPS told me we were less than a half hour from our destination. I listened to Sergei as he continued.

"Something goes wrong in the brain of a very few bears during hibernation. Science has never explained it. The old *Babushkas* tell the legend that it is the devil and his minions who have possessed the bear, taken his spirit. You see, the bear awakens with a murderous rage. He will kill any living thing he sees. It is the most feared creature of the forest, and will not stop until something stronger kills it. A bear like that is called the *Shatun*. The only other thing in nature that can do that is men with guns...big guns. That is Zurinov, that is why he is called Shatun, a devil with a killing heart. In times such as these, it has made him very rich."

"So why does this, Shatun, this Zurinov, want to kill you."

"We have, how you say in America, a history, Zurinov

and I. He has been hired to kill my father. That is business. Killing me will be for pleasure."

"Nice circles you run with, Sergei."

We hit a small bump. At our speed, it became a serious jolt. Shirley's eyes sprang open. Katamay continued to sleep. I guess it's true about seniors and their naps.

Shirley sat up; she blinked. Her head swiveled until she finally figured out where she was. She leaned back and closed her eyes again for a moment.

"Shit, shit, shit," she said. "I was hoping this was all a bad dream."

"Welcome to reality, Shirl," I replied.

"You know Gast, I mean, nothing personal here, but since I met you, my life, such as it was, has been going down the tube rather fast."

"Thanks. I have that affect."

She yawned, and blinked in the rays of the newly risen sun. She turned to Sergei, took his head between her hands, and moved it back and forth, examining his eyes and the caked blood on his facial wounds.

"You don't look too good," she said. "But you'll live. There's a doctor where we're going, right?"

"Better."

"A hospital?"

"No: A Russian nurse."

"Oh."

CHAPTER 42

Oklahoma City.

LaToya knew something wasn't right. Last night someone had followed her. She was certain that she had seen the same face at least four times in different places. He looked like Mister Average. In fact, LaToya only vaguely remembered the man's features. She certainly couldn't have identified him from a line-up. Although LaToya had never been in the field, she had been trained at Quantico like any other ATF agent. She understood surveillance. She felt the thrill of fear in her gut as she realized that her inquiries had now made her a target.

LaToya left the federal building on time, right at the end of her shift. She just walked out the front door and turned into the parking lot. She reached her car, a Hyundai sedan. She passed it, looked in the rear seat to be sure no one was hiding there. Empty—of course—they were professionals, nothing as crude as an occupied carjacking.

She unlocked the door with her remote, opened it, got in and drove away. Three times over the next few miles, she spotted a brown sedan. Coincidence? Then another, a white Japanese job this time. *Christ girl*, she thought, you're getting paranoid. There must be gazillions of white Japanese sedans like that. She reached her apartment house, but didn't stop. Around the block one more time: Nothing.

Her hands shook on the steering wheel. Where was Gast? Why wasn't he answering her phone calls? The answers she had dug up pointed to an incredible conspiracy, something that would make Iran-Contra and other scandals look like petty cash. Gast could help her figure it out, even that Tinia Protocol thing. He was great with stuff like that. She pulled into her parking spot on the side of the apartment house and got out of the car.

She'd barely taken two steps when it happened. The same white Japanese car she had spotted earlier roared into the parking lot and stopped directly in front of her. Two men erupted out, one from each side of the car. She froze for a second, and it was all the time they needed. They grabbed her on either side, pinning her arms. She screamed. One of the men backhanded her. There was blood in her mouth and something hard pressing into her side. She knew it was the barrel of a gun. They brought her to the car, her feet dragging on the ground, as they hustled her inside, into the middle of the front bench seat. The driver started the car and they drove away, LaToya squeezed in the middle like the captive she'd become.

The driver made a fast U-turn in the parking lot and drove out into the wide avenue.

A brown sedan waited for them at the curb. It was a big American-made machine. It accelerated and the right front fender smashed into the white car bearing LaToya and her assailants, wedging the smaller car's nose against a parked van.

LaToya saw a man get out of the rear of the car. Tall, wearing a stained white "wife beater" tank top and porkpie hat, with arms knotted with ropy muscles and wild, scary eyes. He frightened LaToya more than the two who had abducted her. She saw another man get out from the other side. He made the first guy look small. He carried something in his hand.

The man in the porkpie hat reached the driver's door and yanked it open.

His eyes got even wilder and spittle flew from his mouth as he screamed at the driver.

"What're you fuckin' stunata? Look what you did to my car!"

The driver tried to stand but only got half way. The man hit him, a straight-arm professional punch. The driver's head snapped back and he fell, sitting heavily on the car seat. He reached in his jacket, the butt of a gun in his hand. Before he could pull it out, the other man slugged him across the arm. This time he had a short, lead sap. LaToya heard the bone crack. Another blow, this time flush across the face, and the man slid to the ground.

At the same time, his companion pulled a silver automatic from a shoulder holster under his jacket. He hadn't quite gotten it out when the window on his side exploded inward. The other man from the brown sedan had come around to that side and he had a baseball bat.

The bat continued its arc through the car window and caught the other man in the head. The gun flew out of his hand. A spray of blood and teeth splashed the interior.

LaToya screamed.

The man in the porkpie hat reached for her. His eyes were even wilder than before. He smelled like sweat and garlic. He pulled one arm around her side and his other hand on her arm. She felt the strength of his grip, his fingers like granite. He pulled her out of the car. She screamed again.

"Will ya shut the fuck up, lady? Please?"

LaToya shut up.

They pulled her in the back of the sedan. She was wedged tight between the two men, afraid to even breathe. The driver didn't turn around, just pulled the big sedan right out and disappeared around the corner. Even though to LaToya it had seemed like forever, the whole thing had taken less than three minutes.

CHAPTER 43

I slowed the Hummer and stopped in front of the turnoff indicated by the GPS. It was nothing more than a trail winding up a hill of boulders, red sand and loose shale; the proverbial badlands. Only the best four-wheel drive vehicles could hope to negotiate that. I suspected the Hummer topped that particular list.

Katamay pulled out a hidden control panel beneath the dash. He toggled a switch and small digital letters appeared above the speedometer readout: All-Terrain Mode

"There," Katamay said. "Now the gas won't be so sensitive and you won't kill us all."

He was right. It was much easier to work the gas and brakes. The Hummer took to the hill like a sidewinder on a sand dune. In spite of fatigue, aches and pain, I seriously enjoyed driving this thing.

The trail, such as it was, leveled off to a plateau. I stopped the Hummer and got out to stretch. The sun rose, its rays a living gold against the horizon. Peaks of distant mountains glowed pastel and indigo standing against a sky so blue the hand of God could have painted it. I took a deep breath. The air felt so pure, like the first day of creation.

There's something about a sunrise, a renewal, banishment of fears that the night had brought. I felt refreshed, ready to take on whatever strangeness the last few days had awakened.

I pulled out the cell phone and looked at the speed dial registry. There were two numbers there: Anthony's and LaToya. I keyed Anthony's first. He answered immediately.

"Gast, where the hell you at? It's been two days."

"Some shit hit the fan, old buddy," I said, and told him everything that had happened. He was silent for a moment.

"You really shouldn't do this stuff alone," he finally said.

"I didn't, I got Shirley with me."

"That the cute sheriff you told me about?"

"Yeah, she's also ex-Boston PD."

"Okay, but all in all, you should have some muscle with you."

"Don't be a chauvinist, Anthony."

"I'm a guinea from Brooklyn, comes with the territory."

"You talk pretty tough until your wife hears you. Maria'd kick your ass all the way to Flatbush Avenue for that remark."

"You're right about that. So where the hell are you now, bro?"

"Near as I can tell, somewhere at the base of the San Mateo Mountains."

I gave him the GPS coordinates I had memorized when I stopped the Hummer.

"Now don't go sending anybody here, or coming yourself. Let me figure this thing out here. I'll call you in 24 hours. Got it?"

"Got it."

"And listen, Anthony?"

"Yeah?"

"Call LaToya. I was supposed to check with her a couple of days ago."

"Like checking in with me?"

"Yeah, but as you might guess, I've had my hands full, didn't have a chance to call momma. Did you get anywhere with that key thing?" I asked him.

Before we split up, I had given him the key that I got from Mary Orlowsky at the scene of her murder. I had asked him to see if he could trace it, but I really didn't expect much. After all, it was just a key. No markings, no ID, nothing.

"I got it," Anthony answered.

"What?"

"I said: I got it. It came from a storage business on Pablo Road in Santa Fe. They rent storage pods and lockers. This was a key to one of their smaller units. We cleaned it out. It's all here at the estate now."

"How the hell you find it so fast?"

"Bowditch Investigations and Security, they provide all the security for our casinos—we're their number one clients. I gave them the key, told them to find it quick or I'd get a new outfit. I guess they put everybody they had on it. They figured it out in one day. What'd you find in the locker?"

"Records, notes, scientific crap that I don't understand. LaToya's going over it now."

"LaToya? Anthony, did you say LaToya is there now?"

"Yeah, she called me a couple of days ago. She'd been trying to get you, but you were AWOL. She was afraid, thought somebody's been following her, so I sent Franco and a couple of the boys to watch out for her."

Franco and a couple of the boys: that would be enough security for the President of the United States.

"Anyway," Anthony continued. "Make a long story short, a couple'a mooks tried to kidnap her. I hope those guys were federal employees cause they're going to need the health benefits."

I didn't reply as I imagined Anthony's people rescuing LaToya. I would have given up a box seat to the World Series to see that, then again, maybe not. I'd seen enough blood the last twelve hours.

"So," Anthony said. "We've been feeding her good Italian food and primo Chianti. She likes it here."

Yeah, she would.

"She also said she's got some information that'll knock your socks off. Soon as you get here, we can pull all this shit together and figure it out."

"Okay, give me a day."

"One day, bro, that's it. Then, I'm coming after your sorry ass."

CHAPTER 44

It was early afternoon when I stepped outside in the heat, but the altitude had taken the blast-furnace quality out. Puffy clouds hung in a sky blue as ever, and a cratered full moon hung there, ghostly pale and still visible in spite of the bright sun.

The "safe house" Sergei had led us to, was actually a camp: Two double-wide trailers side by side, three storage-sheds, and two open structures that looked like outsized car-ports. Crates hung about, stacked in various locations, a couple of Harley-Davidsons leaning on their kickstands and a weathered, 4WD pickup sporting a rebel flag bumper decal. The other bumper carried a faded sticker proclaiming that if your heart wasn't in the West, you'd best get your ass out. Hanging from long aluminum poles imbedded in the hardscrabble, great sheets of desert camouflage stretched over every item, large or small, from trailers to packing crates. The place looked like a survivalist camp run by paranoid bikers fearing aerial attack. After yesterday's events, I wasn't too surprised.

No one was up and around, not even the two people we met when we'd arrived at dawn. They had spoken briefly to Katamay and a woman had come in and treated Sergei's wounds. This morning they had all vanished.

I spotted the Hummer, covered under one of the carports. I couldn't get over the performance of that machine. I wanted a close look at it. On the outside, it looked like any other Hummer except for the extra wide tires and front impact cage. That alone wasn't too strange, I'd seen plenty of big 4WD vehicles customized like that.

I turned the latch on the driver's door. It was unlocked and opened easily. I looked under the dash. A single, thick wire harness, wrapped in electrical tape, ran from the dash and disappeared under the hood. That was it, no more than seven or eight wires instead of the monstrous arrays of electronic stuff that filled the dash of every vehicle I had ever driven. The accelerator and brake pedals were hooked up to a spring loaded device that held what looked like sensors. No mechanical or hydraulic connections. There was a sterile smell to the vehicle that took me a moment to identify: Ozone, the smell of electricity, like the aftermath of a lightning strike.

I pulled the hood release lever, stepped away from the interior and opened the engine compartment. It looked like nothing I would ever expect.

Right in the middle of the compartment, where one would anticipate the engine to be, laid a box the size of a large suitcase. It was made of some kind of dark metal, burnished to a dull hue. I reached out and ran my hand over it. It felt silky, neither hot nor cold. I had touched material like that in certain exotic weapons and combat aircrafts; titanium alloy.

The case-I didn't know what else to call it—hung suspended by six steel struts bolted to the vehicle. The struts disappeared inside apertures within the case that must have contained some sort of support structure. A wire harness ran from a box on the firewall and disappeared inside the titanium walls of the case. From another opening within the case, four thick cables reached outward. Each cable was engulfed in thick insulation, the kind used to protect against high voltage. Four cables: one for each wheel.

I followed a cable to the right front wheel. It terminated at a big industrial electric motor. I couldn't make out the markings on the case of the motor, but I'd bet it was a hundred horsepower at least, probably more. The motor itself was bolted to a platform that was part of the independent wheel suspension, allowing it to move up and down with the motion of the wheel. A thick output shaft protruded from the motor and disappeared into a thick constant velocity joint that drove the wheel. I looked under each wheel. They were all identical to the same strange electric power set-up.

I looked around for battery wells, knowing I wouldn't find any. You needed more than batteries to provide the kind of performance I had experienced last night. You needed a whole generating station, yet the only thing it had was that case under the hood.

Could they have figured out how to transmit significant amounts of electric power through the ether? I vaguely remembered reading about an eccentric genius, a man named Nicholai Tesla. He claimed to have discovered that secret back in the thirties, even built a station for it in Shoreham, Long Island, funded by J.P. Morgan. The whole thing fell apart when Morgan got impatient and cut the purse strings. Could these guys have discovered that secret? Is that what this was all about?

I stood and walked a few steps back for another perspective at this vehicle, when I heard Shirley's voice behind me.

"So did you figure out how it runs?"

She had showered and applied some light make up that she must gotten from God knows where. She looked good and stood close enough that I smelled her scent, a provocative mixture of hyacinths and other exotic stuff. It's one of the mysteries of life that women will always smell good no matter what the circumstances are, and men will never figure out how they do it.

"I've been dying to check this thing out since I woke up," I shrugged.

"How disappointing, Gast. Here I thought you'd be concerned about me," she said with a half grin. Her teeth were white and a small dimple appeared on the right side of her cheek when she did that half-grin thing. I stood still and looked at her.

"Well, I didn't want to tell you."

"That's a mistake," she replied softly.

"You know," I said, "when this is over, I'd like to take you out, I mean do it right, flowers, romantic restaurant, wine, candles."

"Sunsets."

"Full moon."

"Long walks."

"Liniment."

"Ben-Gay."

We laughed at the same time, and I put my hand on her shoulder.

"Don't you have someone special?" I asked softly.

"Not since my ex left me, I'm a cop, remember? No one can stand to be married to a cop."

"What a fool."

"How about you, Gast? Got anyone?"

"I did. She died, got killed in a raid a year ago."

She put her hand to her mouth. "Oh, Gast. I'm sorry. Was that the one, I mean, that raid?"

I nodded, I'd never forget Amy, never. Still it had been a year. Maybe it was time. I had a sudden flash of her, and her eyes seemed to approve.

"Yeah," I said. "I think she would have wanted me to go on. I mean, she was that kind of person, you know?"

Shirley stepped a little closer. Her scent and presence filled my universe. I reached out, my arms went around her and it felt as natural as rain. She molded her body to mine, and I kissed her. I kissed her hard and she returned it as if there would be no tomorrows. She was fierce and she surprised me. I liked it.

CHAPTER 45

Special Agent John Ford believed all crime scenes, at first, had that same feel. It was later, when you got the emotional angst of the carnage that had taken place, that each place developed its own unique sense. Ford thought there was some psychic element, a beyond-the-senses thing that imprinted itself on the investigator's mind. Or, it could have just been his subconscious at work. Either way, this scene would talk to him.

His driver, a new, young agent, parked the car behind the half dozen Valencia County Sheriff vehicles, New Mexico State Troopers cruisers, and the two, unneeded as it turned out, Paramedics and Emergency Rescue vans. As it turned out all they needed was the coroner.

The road remained completely blocked and a pass-through lane had been marked on the hard packed desert floor with red traffic cones. The driver shut the engine off, and they both got out of the car. A state trooper, thin with the military bearing of a West Pointer, yelled at them from behind the cones.

"Hey, keep moving gentlemen, nothing to see here."

Ford walked behind the cones and held up his ID.

"FBI. Who's controlling the scene?"

The trooper looked at their credentials and waived toward

the house.

"State police, detectives are inside. Not sure who's in charge."

"Thanks, we'll look around a bit before going in."

"Sure."

It was a little past noon and officers from the various law enforcement branches stood in small groups. Some drank out of water bottles and ate wrapped sandwiches. Ford saw a few looking at them and speaking softly. Word would get out fast that a couple of FBI "boots" were out and about, probably OJT: On-The-Job-Training. Even though he was much older, Ford appeared to be in his early twenties, his driver barely twenty-four with no experience. Together, they looked like a couple of college geeks in nice suits, and it was fine with Ford. Their appearances tended to give bad guys a false sense of security, while other cops and witnesses seemed to open up a bit more.

Ford walked to a spot about fifty yards across the road. The area was marked off with tape and guarded by a trooper. Several little flags on six-inch wire mounts stood planted in the ground marking the location of evidence to be processed. As Ford examined each spot he saw they contained the same items: footprints, tire marks, and one cartridge. He kneeled, looked close at the cartridge but didn't touch it. After a moment, he stood and walked toward the house followed by his driver.

Several troopers and deputies moved aside as he reached the front. A body lay under a sheet, outlined by spray paint on the hardscrabble dirt.

Ford pulled the sheet back, looked at the body for a long moment then covered it up again. He motioned to the driver to stay still while he slowly walked two concentric circles, expanding with each turn. At one point he stopped, pulled a pair of latex gloves from his pocket and snapped them on with quick practiced moves.

He squatted, picked up a piece of twisted brown plastic, examined it then put it back where he had found it. He turned and walked toward the house with his driver following close behind.

The great room looked like a bomb had gone off in it, which indeed it had. Another body lay twisted on the floor, surrounded by blood splattering and outlined in white chalk. Flies buzzed and the stench of corruption hung in the air. The ground felt gritty under their feet. Crime scene technicians had erected lights that reached every corner of the room, banishing any shadows created by the late morning sunlight pouring through the windows. A man kneeled in the center of the room, examining a spent cartridge. He looked up, saw Ford and his driver, and stood. He wore a dark jacket with bolo tie and a Stetson, what they called back east a cowboy hat, low over his head. He had that thin weather-beaten, Western look.

"So here's the FBI," he said. "Where's the rest of your crew?"

"We're not here to take jurisdiction. We'll just look around a bit."

"Training, are you?"

"Something like that."

"Knock yourself out," the detective said. "Be sure to share your wisdom with us," and went back to scrutinizing the cartridge.

They stayed a little over an hour. Ford looked at everything but touched nothing. They walked around the house where he spent some time examining the blasted out wall and remains of the shattered garage door. Finally, he led the driver back to the car and they left without a word.

After driving in silence a while, the driver turned to Ford and spoke.

"Not very friendly, are they, Agent Ford?"

Ford sighed, looking straight ahead, and pushed his glasses back up on his nose.

"No they're not, lots of rivalry between law enforcement agencies out here. You've got the Sheriff's Office, Santa Fe PD, New Mexico State Police, FBI, ATF, Secret Service, and God know what else. Of course the FBI has the most resources and authority, really pisses them off. Plus, a veteran detective in his fifties is not going to appreciate what seems to him like a couple of kids jumping on his turf."

"I guess not. But can I ask you something?"

"Yes, but I may not answer. You know the rules."

"Yes sir, I do," he replied. "This case is an eyes-only, need to know basis. I'm here to assist and learn. I'm not privy to the details, so don't answer if I'm out of bounds."

"I won't."

"All right then. So how did you know about this crime scene? I mean it only happened last night."

"We were tipped off by a note delivered to a senator's office by a messenger service. Now pull over here. I'll drive a while. I want you to take some notes for me. I'll put them together in my report."

The driver pulled the car off the road and they switched places. Ford drove and waited for his aide to get out a small notebook and pen before he started speaking.

"Due to the high incidence of meth labs and drug related violence in this part of the country, local authorities will conclude this was probably a drug dispute. That is not the case. This was a battle between professionals with an advanced degree of military training. There are indications of links within the federal system."

The aide stopped writing and looked over at Ford.

"How…"

Ford took his eyes off the road and looked at his aide.

"What's your name again…William is it?"

"Yes, sir."

"You're bright William, and you graduated top of your class at Quantico. I saw your record. You also got some field experience in New York, all well and good. It will make you realize how little you really know, how much work lies ahead of you."

"Uhmm, yes sir."

"The attack was by one man. He infiltrated to within 50 yards of the lookout and took him out with one shot. I found the cartridge back there, one 7.62MM NATO round, probably an M-14S, dammed good sniper weapon. The sentry's body bore tattoos found only in elite military units of the old Soviet Union forces, so sneaking up on that guy and taking him out with one shot required a certain degree of skill not found among your average outlaws and meth dealers."

William scribbled in his notebook. When he was done, he looked at Ford again.

"Where do you get the links to the federal system?"

"Two clues: First he leaves the spent cartridge behind. He's already shown himself to be effective, not careless. He would know enough to take the cartridge with him. The fact that he left it there shows that he believes he's protected. When he reaches the house he fires two rounds from an M-79A2 grenade launcher."

"How can you know that?" William asked.

"The original M-79 is a Vietnam-era weapon. The M-79A2 is an improved version of that weapon. It incorporates a two-inch booster in each round, a small rocket motor that ignites one quarter second after the round is fired. It increases the range and accuracy of the shot. When the booster ignites, it blows off a brown plastic cover separating it from the charge. I found one of those expanded covers at the scene. Only about eight hundred were manufactured by Colt Arms, before a new infantry weapon incorporating a grenade launcher was adopted by the armed forces. To get an M-79A2 requires access to federal armories and storage facilities. You don't buy them on the surplus market, therefore: Federal collusion at some level."

They came to a major intersection and Ford turned onto US84, heading north.

"Where are we going?"

"FBI office in White Horse."

William nodded, said nothing, waiting for Ford to resume.

"Now our lone attacker is apparently spotted by someone inside the house who shoots at him—probably the second body, the one inside. Our man fires the grenade and kills him. From the number of spent shells inside, they return quite a volume of fire, giving them time to escape. From the abandoned food bowls, we have at least five people in there, including the dead man. From the blood trail, at least one of them is wounded. One thing for sure, they expected to be attacked."

William stopped writing, looked at Ford and waited. The agent put his forearms on the steering wheel, laced his fingers ahead of him, and cracked his knuckles. He yawned and said, "God this heat makes me tired. Tell me why I know they expected an attack?"

"They were armed, they had posted a lookout."

"And what else?"

"Uhmm, I'm not sure."

"The garage."

"The garage?"

"Yes," Ford continued. "The door had a false front, what's called a *Trompe-d'oeil*. That's French for fool-the-eye. You couldn't tell that was a garage door hence the attacker wasn't prepared for whatever monster truck blasted through. That's why they got away."

"Oh."

"Here's what I want you to do, William. Call the director's office. Use the special number I gave you. You'll either get him or his top assistant. Authenticate with a code I will give you. Tell them you want any available satellite surveillance of the area. If that truck is on film somewhere, I want to know where it went."

"They'll have that? I mean satellite surveillance?"

"Big brother is alive and well since the Enhanced Patriot Act passed, and it's not always a bad thing. There may be photographic records of activities in this area. Next, tell them about the M-79A2 let's get a parallel investigation going in that area. Last, get some agents to track down whoever made this garage door. You don't see that every day and they dammed sure didn't build it themselves. Maybe that will lead us to whoever had this made."

As their car headed toward the FBI office, the aide booted the laptop and established the link with the office of the director of the FBI.

CHAPTER 46

Brookhaven National Laboratory, Upton, Long Island, New York.

The line at the security gate stretched to a dozen cars ahead of Doctor Jawaharla Bhindra. It moved pretty fast as security scanned the ID of each driver and passenger. When Bhindra reached the gate, he held his ID out the window. The guard used the portable scanner, got the okay from the machine and waived him through.

Bhindra drove on the main road of the lab that used to be Camp Upton, back in the forties and fifties until the Atomic Energy Commission took it over from the US Army. The streets and avenues of the lab were built wide to allow platoons of marching soldiers and military vehicles to pass easily. Buildings rose on either side. Some were old army barracks, upgraded for administrative use. Most were newer concrete structures housing various research units. The one Bhindra worked in was the newest addition.

Initially, the lab was slated for nuclear research in 1958. The first reactor had been built there and wasn't dismantled until 1997. Back in the sixties, the Atomic Energy Commission had turned into the Department of Energy. Bhindra headed the latest nuclear reactor research facility. It had been built a scant four years ago. A section of the building housed the newest, state of the art reactor. This made Brookhaven National Lab the birthplace of the first reactor as well as the current site of the latest nuclear generator. What only a very select few people knew, was that it was also used for nuclear weapon research.

The gate was the first and easiest level of security. Bhindra drove to the end of the main avenue, turned right and came to a second gate. Eighteen-foot fences ran in concentric circles topped by razor concertina wire. Armed foot patrols with attack dogs walked in the path created by the fences. At fifty-foot intervals, motion sensors and cameras topped the wires. An entire platoon of specially trained soldiers was assigned to this particular place that held the nation's latest nuclear research commissioned by the Department of Defense.

Bhindra parked his car outside the gate and walked in. Once again, his ID was scanned, but this time he placed his hand on a flat screen fingerprint ID. The machine buzzed its approval and Bhindra walked in. He would go through two more security levels, including retina-prints before being allowed into the research facility he headed.

As Bhindra walked into the outer area of his office, his secretary greeted him.

"Good morning James," she said. Bhindra insisted everyone called him by the closest English version of his first name, Jawaharla. "You have visitors."

"Visitors? How did they get in here?"

"Some big muck-a-mucks. They have full DOD authority and confirmed credentials. Said it's for a routine security review. Same people that were here a few months back."

Bhindra felt the bottom of his stomach fall away. He had dreaded this moment since those horrible people had walked into his office in March—had it been really been only six months? Not a moment went by that he didn't have their visit hanging over his head like the malevolent demons of his boyhood. He felt the blood pound in his temple, and clasped his hand in his pocket to stop the trembling. In spite of the cool air of the room, he sweated as if someone had planted him in a sauna.

"James, are you all right?"

"Uh, yes. I will be fine, just something I ate last night."

"Can I get you some water? Should I tell these people to come back? They're not very nice you know."

"No, no. That's quite all right. I will see them now."

"They're waiting in your office."

He had to make a conscious effort not to slow down, as if anything could make this exceedingly bad karma go away.

Bhindra opened the door to his office, walked in, closed the door behind him and stood still.

"Well hello doctor J," Dallas Wilson said. Lack of respect was the least unpleasant thing this man had brought into Bhindra's life. "Come, come," Dallas continued. "After all, this is your office. Sit behind your desk like you're in charge. You never know who could be watching."

Dallas sat in one of two seats opposite Bhindra's desk. The IRD director had his hands draped over the seat's armrests and his legs crossed. He appeared very much at ease, comfortable. The other man with Dallas did not. That man stood, leaning against the bookcase on the opposite wall. There was an air of barely restrained violence about him. His eyes flickered up and down Bhindra's slight frame. He looked at the scientist as if he had found him wanting, somehow lacking a characteristic important to this man.

"This is my associate. He is an IRD deputy director," Dallas said. "He has the same authority I do. I wanted you to be sure that everything would be carried out as we promised, should you fail to hold your end of this bargain."

The man said nothing. He held Bhindra with eyes so cold they should have been in a jar somewhere in deep-freeze..

"Bargain?" Bhindra asked as he walked toward his desk. "You make it sound as though I have a choice in this matter."

He sensed the thin, government-issue carpet under his feet, felt every step as he walked behind the desk and sat. Even that simple act seemed to have been orchestrated by

Dallas, somehow.

"Oh but you do have choices. Perhaps, it's time to review them so we're clear on what is at stake for you. Would you bring Doctor J up to date?" Dallas said turning to his deputy.

The man took the few steps separating him from the front of Bhindra's desk. He reached inside his jacket and pulled out three photos. He held the first one in front of the scientist.

"This was taken at the one-fifteen recess at the Ridge Elementary-Middle School."

The photo showed a little girl about six. She was on a swing. The camera had caught the delight on the child's face, the gap-toothed smile and her hair blowing back.

Now he held another photo in front of him. "This one was taken at eleven AM inside the school," he said.

The photo showed a boy perhaps nine or ten. The child's mouth was slightly open as he looked at a spot behind the camera.

"And this one is at the Middle Island King Kullen supermarket, about two o'clock, before the kids would have gotten home from school." The picture showed a slight, and pretty, dark featured woman. She wore a pantsuit, western clothing contrasted by the black dot on her forehead. The camera caught her in the act of putting grocery bags in the trunk of her car.

Bhindra felt as if he stood at the edge of a pit while something slithered in the darkness below as he stared at the photos of his wife and children. Bile rose in his throat and he coughed. He opened his mouth but no words came out. It took another try to just whisper the words: "Please…How could you do this…"

Wilson's deputy placed both hands on Bhindra's desk and leaned forward until his face was less than two feet from the scientist. Bhindra swallowed. It was painful, he felt stifled.

"You'd better understand something," the man said softly, the tone of his voice infinitely more threatening than a shout. "You and your family don't mean shit to me. You're just a little brown monkey. I'd just as soon kill you right here."

"Now now," Wilson said from his seat. "Let's not frighten the good doctor unnecessarily."

The man smiled and stepped back.

"Before we get started James," Dallas said, "I thought we should review what would happen if you fail to follow our instructions. You and your family may have been in this country for a dozen years, but you are still on a research visa. At the slightest hint of a problem your wife and children will be whisked away to McArthur Airport, just twenty minutes from here. There will be a private chartered jet waiting. It will be a long flight to the Kashmir tribal lands. You've heard of the place haven't you? Your native India is a few hundred miles away, across the mountains. Is there any doubt in your mind that we can do this, doc?"

Bhindra couldn't move. His vocal cord seemed paralyzed and he couldn't' stop his hands from shaking. He barely managed to croak out a pitiful "no."

"There's a warlord there," Wilson continued. "His name is Ali Kharan. He is a CIA client, and a very distasteful one at that—a sadist of the worst kind. However, we must be pragmatic. This individual is instrumental in the war on terror for that part of the world. A source of income for Kharan is the brothels he runs. That part of the world is host to some of the worst men, literally the scum of the earth. These brothels cater to their often brutal, desires. One such brothel is populated by children none older than twelve. Your family will be given to Kharan for his brothels. Mercifully, they probably will not survive beyond a year or two. None of them do."

Bhindra sat very still. His hands were drawn up in tight fists, resting on the surface of the desk. The knuckles whitened as the fingernails dug into the soft flesh of his palms. No one spoke. The only sound in the room was the soft whisper of the climate control system. All that Bhindra heard was the sound of the blood in his veins and his heartbeat. All he felt was anguish, unbearable, worse than any medieval torture.

Wilson smiled, as cold and distant a smile as the reaches of outer space.

"But let's not dwell on the negatives, eh doc? Let's assume you will follow our instructions. In that case, your job will be secure with automatic citizenship. In case anything happens to you, there is a five million dollars policy on your life with your family as beneficiaries."

Bhindra just looked at Wilson. He wished he could be back in his native land. Even the teeming hovels of Bombay seemed better than the situation he was trapped in.

"Doc?"

"Yes…I will do as you ask."

"I'm glad to hear that doc. We have activated the Tinian Protocol. The Cold Fusion Generator will arrive at Brookhaven in about twenty-four hours. You will have twelve hours to install and prep the device. You have it in readiness as we demanded?"

"Yes."

"Good," Wilson said as he stood. "There is no need for us to take any more of your time. I'm sure you have plenty to do."

The two men walked out and the door closed softly behind them. Bhindra looked down at his hands as he opened them. A single drop of blood lay on his palm, like the tiny red eye of a small predator.

CHAPTER 47

We sat in the shade of an overhang, Sergei facing Shirley and me. He had bandages across two parts of his face and on both arms. Outside of that, the shrapnel and concussion didn't seem to have had any serious effects on him.

A dry desert breeze blew in from the mountains, evaporating any sweat generated in the ninety-degree heat. Sergei spoke softly, his voice clear and slow.

"The vehicle you drove here, that Hummer, is a prototype powered by a CF generator. There are only two such generators in existence. It works by cold fusion. Do either of you know what that is?"

Shirley and I shook our heads no.

"Cold fusion is the Holy Grail of nuclear physics, as elusive and legendary as that religious icon. Up until a few years ago it was thought impossible...until my father solved it. Cold fusion is the fusing of hydrogen atoms together after they are separated from the oxygen atoms. They use the components of ordinary water, $H2O$, without a mass release of heat and energy, a nuclear explosion as in fission."

"So what happens when you have this cold fusion?" Shirley asked.

"A massive outflow of electrons, which is commonly called…"

"Electricity."

"Correct. It is generated and controlled by the work of Mary Orlowsky, the foremost authority on plasma generation and Nathan Ragowski, a leading expert in nano-technology. Combined with my father's work, the CF generators produce unlimited amounts of electric energy, with no emissions or any other environmental affects, using only distilled water, and very little of it at that."

We both sat still for a moment. It was hard to comprehend the magnitude of this accomplishment.

"But it must be very expensive to make these things?" I asked.

"For now, but the technology, once applied is not that complicated. It doesn't require anything that is not commercially available right now. Give it a year or so, and CF generators can be mass produced for about the same cost as an automobile engine."

Sergei stood, looked around as if he suddenly realized where he was. "Think of it," he continued. "For a couple of thousand dollars and with a few gallons of water, your car will run practically forever. Put one in your house and you have endless electricity for heat, air conditioning, appliances. You can adapt them to boats, airplanes, eventually space travel."

"My God," Shirley said. "Why isn't this discovery being shouted from every channel, but…" she stopped, as the answer came to her.

Sergei looked at her, guessing her thoughts.

"Yes, the world will change, overnight, when this is made public. Think of it—oil wells, refineries, electric generation plants, nuclear or petroleum, obsolete overnight—trillions will be lost as entire industries become suddenly worthless. There will be a power shift such as never seen in the history of the world."

I began to understand what was happening. The entrenched power-that-be would fight tooth and nail to keep this from happening. That's what this was all about. Lives meant nothing to them and it really pissed me off.

Sergei's eyes locked on mine. There were secrets in there, untold things that I sensed like a rustling of leaves from a breeze, presaging the approaching storm. He looked away as he spoke again, but his words were for me more than anyone else.

"There is something else you should know, Gaston Duval."

I said nothing.

"Your late fiancée…"

I looked at him and he turned his head, his eyes on mine once again. My world had narrowed to this tunnel, Sergei and his coming words. I sensed Shirley's hand squeezing my arm. I felt grounded by her presence.

"Amy, she was a very brave woman."

"Yes," I whispered.

"And…" Sergei continued. His breath came in a sigh, as if his lungs needed to be empty for this revelation. "She was Izgoi."

CHAPTER 48

I felt a rage, arcing like downed power cables across a storm-swept road. Sergei told me that Amy had been Izgoi and grew up without knowing it. Her parents had lived somewhere west of Odessa, inside Russia's Charm School, steeped in American life and culture.

The Charm School was an American city in every respect. Any farm boy from the Midwest could have been dropped in there, and found himself right at home with McDonalds, Burger King, Genovese drugs, cars, roads, even TV, radio and Hip Hop. It was Middle America all right, except it was in Russia, a training ground. Amy had grown up there until she was six years old, then her parents had been transported to Ohio. A job waited there. Their ID's were indistinguishable from the real thing, backed by records planted years ago. The family fitted right in, and to Amy, it seemed like an ordinary move, the kind of move countless American families make all the time.

She had gone to college and found law enforcement all on her own. We met as ATF officers and until the last year of her life she didn't know she was Izgoi. Then they killed her. Some monstrous, shadowy evil, slithering within the US government like malevolent killer bacteria hugging the bowels of a dying patient, murdered her. Mary Orlowsky, this other scientist I had never met, Nathan Ragowski, and God knew how many others, killed without a second thought.

I had always felt secure in the orderly world I was born into. Throughout my years growing up in Brooklyn, the military, ATF, even the Consolis and their wise guys, there were rules, codes everyone followed. You get up in the morning you don't know what the day will bring. But you do expect certain things-the lawn and sidewalk in front of your house will be there, the street will be there, the sky will be above you, the ground below, rain, shine, snow or storm-certain things will be there. Now I felt as if everything had been yanked away. A chasm lay before me, dark and unknown with no horizon or sky.

I took the Berretta, pulled the clip, checked the rounds, and replaced the weapon in the rear holster where I carried it. I looked off toward the distant mountain peaks, but didn't really see them. I wanted to murder those responsible, I needed revenge. But most of all, I wanted the world back as it should be, and I wanted to protect Shirley. There was an attraction there. Whatever happened between us, I wanted it to be a result of what we wanted, not cut short by an assassin's bullet.

"Are you alright, my friend?"

It was Sergei. He took a seat on one of the packing crates facing the one I sat in. We were at the fringes of the camp, just before the desert swallowed the edges of the cleared land.

"Yeah, Sergei. I guess, I don't know."

We both sat in silence with our thoughts for a while. It was mid-afternoon and the heat descended from the sky and rose from the ground. The air was clear and smelled like sulfur.

"So what comes next?" I asked Sergei.

He looked down and scratched the bandage on his forehead. His voice was low, hesitant, and it seemed out of character for a man like him.

"I'm not sure, Gaston Duval. I'm trying to keep everyone

alive and I haven't succeeded very well."

"I'm not letting this go, Sergei. You know that don't you?"

"Yes, I am glad. It will take men like you to expose this. We cannot do it alone."

"My friend Anthony will be here before nightfall. He owns a large airplane. He will fly in at the base of the mountain, land on that flat road below. I asked you earlier if you would come with us. You didn't answer."

"I discussed it with my father. There are other places we could go. Perhaps we would be safe, perhaps not. But if we went with you, we would not be as safe."

"You don't know Anthony and his associates."

"You do not know Shatun and *his* associates."

"Maybe, but if you stay with us, we could put our heads together. With our combined knowledge, we could blow this whole stinking thing like a rotten cantaloupe."

"That is why we will go with you," Sergei replied.

CHAPTER 49

It's another late afternoon in the desert where the air, drier than cement dust, still held the kiln-like heat of the day. The sun was less than an hour away from passing below the horizon and a few puffy clouds reflected golden light from a sun that would soon turn crimson.

We'd come down the base of the mountain, right where the foothills ended and the flat, clay and sand desert began. A road, straight as a longitude line on a surveyor's map lay before us. It wasn't much of a road, just a clear, hardscrabble path. But it was firm, clear and long, an ideal landing spot for an aircraft.

I had called Anthony earlier and given him the coordinates where we awaited him. Sergei sat on a rocky outcropping, scanning the desert, the AK-47 cradled loosely in his arms. Shirley dozed a few feet and Katamay sat across from me.

The old scientist rested on a portable canvas stool. He wore a floppy hat with a brim as big as the Mexican hats they sell in tourist shops in Tijuana. He had a little plastic cooler with some ice and bottled water. He passed me a cold 16oz Evian. I opened it and took a swig; desert heaven!

"I still think it's a mistake, leaving that Hummer," I said.

"I mean, I could have driven that sucker to Arizona in a day."

"And what good would that do?"

"Well, if they get it, they could either destroy it, or copy it and keep it secret."

"Yes, they could destroy it, but the vehicle means nothing without the science. They are trying to kill that by killing us."

"They could just duplicate it and keep it secret."

Katamay looked at me under the brim of that ridiculous hat. He wore sunglasses, the big wraparound kind that seniors with light sensitivity wear. He smiled, chuckled and took a sip of water before he answered.

"They can't reverse engineer the CF generator. They need to know the science. If your friend, Anthony, has managed to get Mary Orlowsky's notes and records, then only we can create something like this."

"I guess," I replied. "Maybe you're right. So tell me about these people who are after us. Is it really only one man, this Zurinov guy? Sergei said he's got in for him, Why?"

Katamay looked off into the distant hillside and sighed.

"It is so hard to explain to Americans."

"Why? We're pretty smart."

"Oh yes, very intelligent, and you have created a paradise in your land. Americans have made a nation that is so unique. It is a country of freedom and prosperity such as never before seen in the history of the world. That's why certain people hate you. They are jealous and want to destroy that which they cannot have."

"I think you just explained the gist of terrorism."

"I don't think it's quite that easy. Your real problem as Americans is that you don't realize what a wondrous world you created here. You tend to forget that. You forget that unpunished and unrestrained violence is routine in many places throughout the world. It is in such a place, Chechnya, that Sergei and Zurinov became enemies."

"In Afghanistan, we fought Islamists trained in Chechnya."

"Yes Mister Duval, it is a training ground, a place where failure equals death."

"So what happened between them, Sergei and Zurinov?"

The sun had dropped to within inches of the horizon. Long, thin clouds stretched over the horizon, colored red and orange by the sun beneath them. The temperature had dropped a few welcome degrees in the last half hour. Katamay took off the sunglasses, his eyes locked on mine.

"Sergei and Zurinov were in the same combat teams when they were ambushed. But attacking a hardened Spetznaz detachment is not the same as ambushing a company of Russian conscripts. There were heavy casualties on both sides. Sergei was wounded. The Chechens managed to take a prisoner and confirmed Zurinov's identity. He was captured before he could escape. Of course by then he was notorious."

"Notorious, how?"

"For his actions, savage even by the standards of that part of the world. It was Zurinov's unholy appetites that brought him down. You see he doesn't like women, or men for that matter."

"Doesn't leave much in between."

"Unfortunately it does. It leaves boys, small ones. Zurinov is a pedophile and a sadist. He likes to hurt them as he rapes them."

I stood there, in the desert sunset. No rational person could doubt that such beauty had to have a divine creator. On the other hand, how could that same God allow such evil to exist in the same world? It's an age-old question. I can't even begin to fathom the answers, but I do understand one thing: Knowing what I know, it would be very easy to pull the trigger if Zurinov ever came into my crosshairs.

Katamay removed the dark glasses, rubbed his eyes and continued.

"Zurinov raped and murdered a number of children. His depravity was such that it sickened the hardest souls of that tortured part of the world. They put him in a hut for housing pigs, and tortured him for three consecutive days.

Then things got worse for Zurinov."

"Worse?"

"Yes, he was turned over to a clan that'd had three children murdered and tortured at his hands."

"Poetic justice, isn't it?"

"I don't think I would classify this kind of evil as poetry."

"Yes, you're right," I replied, "but it's something we hear often when such crimes are committed. Turn the culprits over to the victim's family."

Katamay sighed, a weary expelling of breath as if he had reached a point where nothing could ever surprise him again. "No, my friend, the revenge is not worth the loss of one's soul. In this case, it turned out to be a mistake. They underestimated Zurinov's resourcefulness, even after the most hideous torture. He escaped, but not before..."

"Before what?"

"Before they castrated him."

That one stopped me cold. Katamay is right. Wrapped in the safety and civilization of the United States, we Americans have a difficult time understanding the everyday savagery of those places.

"How...I mean, how could he escape after something like that?"

"Castration is not necessarily fatal. His captors wanted him alive to torture him a few days more. They cauterized the wound with a white-hot iron."

"While he was conscious?"

"Of course. It was rumored that his guards became careless. They believed he was no longer a threat because of the intense torture he had suffered. They were wrong. Later that night, when the solitary guard came too close, Zurinov ripped out the man's throat—with his teeth—and escaped."

"Now he wants revenge on Sergei for not rescuing him?"

"To this day Zurinov believes it was Sergei who leaked his identity and left him to die at the hands of the rebels. This is the source of the blood feud between Zurinov and Sergei."

"So he's here for revenge?"

"Oh no, much more than that. He's being paid a very large sum to kill me, as well as Sergei. It is what baseball fans would call a home run."

At the end of the road Sergei had set up four lanterns to mark the runway for Anthony. In the growing darkness, the lights threw long shadows on the desert floor. The sun had vanished below the horizon leaving a diminishing orange glow on the distant mountain peaks. Soon even that dim illumination would disappear. The warm air carried the drone of Anthony's plane as it lined up with the road and descended. I felt a waft of desert air on my face. Scents of distant vegetation mixed with volcanic ashes rode the breeze.

"Your friend," Katamay said, nodding toward Anthony's airplane, now taxiing toward Sergei's lights. "He is rich, no?"

I frowned for a moment. I didn't think of Anthony that way. To me he was the guy from the neighborhood, my life-long friend.

"Yeah, I guess he is," I replied.

"Do you trust him?"

"With my life."

"That is good. You may have to."

CHAPTER 50

———◆———

I walked with Katamay to where Anthony's airplane was taxiing. Shirley met me there and we hugged briefly.

"You okay Shirl?"

"Yeah, Gast. It's kind of scary out there, you know? I keep thinking this guy is going to pop out from under some rock. I'm glad your friend came before it got too dark."

I looked over at Sergei. He kept scanning the surrounding hills, the AK held loose in his hands, as familiar to the Spetznaz veteran as another limb. He walked closer and our eyes met. I felt a sensation, a presence out there in the shadows of the hills. The little hairs on the back of my neck felt electrified. There was an edge to the air and the growing darkness thickened.

"He is out there," Sergei whispered. "I feel him."

He didn't have to explain. I knew what he was talking about. Only soldiers who have hunted dangerous men in forbidding places can understand it. I said nothing, just nodded at him.

Anthony closed the distance to where we waited, and brought the airplane to a stop. The big machine's idling engines had the sound of a primeval beast growling for prey. The aircraft was the latest product of American-Lear Industries. Big enough to hold ten passengers with twin engines that looked like rockets with propellers attached. Anthony had once told me the engines were manufactured by Rolls Royce. They combined cutting-edge turbo-prop and ramjet technology. Whatever made it go, that was one hell of a fast machine.

There were two doors on the side of the plane. One located toward the rear, a cargo door, and one near the front for passengers and crew. The front door opened, steps unfolded automatically until they reached the ground, and Anthony stepped out. We did a brief sports-hug, and I introduced him all around. We got on the plane with our weapons.

"What'd you guys do, rob an armory?" Anthony asked as he strapped himself back in the pilot's seat.

"You should talk," I said, "with your little army back at the house."

"What? We got the right to bear arms. It's in the constitution."

Anthony worked the throttles, turning the plane around. We were airborne in less than a minute. Like I said, it's a hell of a machine.

Anthony set the automatic pilot as the aircraft reached its cruising altitude. At this speed, we would arrive at the Consoli estate in Arizona in no time.

I brought Anthony up to speed on the event of the last twenty-four hours including our escape in the Hummer powered by this cold fusion generator. He listened quietly and looked at me as if I had grown a second head.

"What?" I asked.

"You think this is all over this new energy source, what you call this cold fusion thing?"

"Of course, Anthony. Some very powerful people want to keep this secret."

"Watch the news lately?"

"Yeah, I've been staying at Club Med. How the hell could I watch the news? We've been stuck in the boonies with some dangerous assholes trying to kill us. Entertainment hasn't been high on the list of things to do."

"You really don't know what's going on?"

"No, I really don't."

"This cold fusion generator is all over the news. They made it public. The Department of Energy is sponsoring a demonstration at that new National Laboratory in Felton, Delaware. CNN, CNBC, Fox News, that's all they're talking about. Whatever's going on with you, it can't be to keep that cold fusion process secret."

CHAPTER 51

Zurinov stopped the Landrover behind an outcropping of volcanic rocks, less than a quarter mile from where he estimated the camp was located. He got out of the machine without making a sound. All the vehicle's hinges and latches had been sprayed with sound-deadening foam. The exhaust system was equipped with oversized mufflers that kept it quiet even under the duress of four-wheel drive operation. Zurinov had arrived with no more noise than the proverbial, silent, grim reaper.

He wore a dark, desert-camouflage combat suit lined with the latest Kevlar mesh. Resistant to shrapnel and most firearm projectiles, the suit was light and fitted specifically to his body. He carried two fragmentation grenades taped to his sides, a Glock nine millimeter in an ankle holster, and a Marine K-bar knife on the other ankle. On his head, secured by a chinstrap, a dark cap would prevent any light reflections from his bare skull as well as hold the night vision goggles affixed to the brim.

He leaned into the Landrover and removed a Negev-11 automatic rifle. The weapon was the latest to come out of the Israeli arms development labs. Fabricated from light composite materials, accurate to 1000 yards, capable of an appalling rate of fire and reliable as a German railroad, the

Negev-11 was considered the best infantry weapon in the world.

Zurinov thumbed the safety, pushed the slide back allowing the first round to enter the chamber. The whole operation made no more noise than a cotton-ball falling on carpet.

The sun would set in a few moments. Zurinov was just another shadow among those of boulders, cactus and distant hills. His passage was insubstantial as if he didn't exist. He was a ghost, a practitioner of the Ninja arts of stealth.

He reached the edge of the camp and stopped. His practiced eyes swept over the structures and found no signs of occupation. He padded into the camp, concealed by the back of the buildings, weapon at ready. In moments he quick-searched the trailers and car-ports—empty. He stopped at the edge where a foot trail wound into the outcropping of hills. He picked up a cigarette butt and flaked open the burnt ends in his fingers. It was extinguished but still held a trace of warmth. The tobacco ashes had the consistency of recently burned embers. Further out he saw the boot prints, barely visible in the hard desert surface. He set out on the trail at a jog, weapon always at the ready.

Night falls a little slower in the desert. Light, coming from the horizon created by the mountain ranges, travels over the flat surfaces unimpeded by rolling lands and forests. Zurinov made it to the base of the boulder-scattered hill before full darkness set in. He squatted down and used the powerful riflescope to scan the desert floor and road below. At the same moment, he heard the drone of twin aircraft engines.

Zurinov swung the rifle scope toward the end of the road and saw the plane landing. He scanned the area again and picked up Katamay walking toward the aircraft, now taxiing toward them. Walking with Katamay was the tall man who had been trapped in the house with the woman. They were the ones Sergei had taken. Apparently they were now all in league.

Sergei! Whenever he thought of that name, Zurinov's gut surged. Unconsciously he rubbed at his crotch, feeling the tortured mass of scar tissue that was all that remained of his genitals.

In the growing darkness, Katamay stayed clearly in his gun-sight-an easy shot-but where was Sergei?

Katamay was the target he was being paid a million US dollars to kill. But Sergei, he was the traitor, the betrayer. Zurinov would never rest until he'd eliminated him. He wanted to do it close, to look in his eyes, to feel the man's death at the end of his arm.

Zurinov watched Katamay and the other man get on the plane. Then the woman and finally Sergei appeared. Now it was too late to kill them both together as he had planned. A headshot for Katamay and gut-shot for Sergei. Give the younger man enough time to live so Zurinov could take his retribution. He wanted Sergei's departure from this world to be as painful as possible.

The plane's door closed. The engines revved up. The aircraft turned around and began a take-off run.

Zurinov noted the tail number and dialed his cell phone.

CHAPTER 52

---◆---

I left Anthony at the controls and walked back to the rear section of the airplane. The passenger compartment consisted of three rows of twin recliner seats on one side leaving room for an aisle. At the end was a small couch with enough seating room for three people. A tiny kitchen filled the remaining room. There was a minibar, a fridge and small microwave. Katamay and Sergei sat on the couch in the rear. Shirley occupied one of the two seats in the first row. I sat next to her. She smiled and I kissed her for a long moment. When we broke it off, her eyes were soft and shining.

"We'll have that romantic moment yet," I whispered.

"For sure, but it's not going to be here and now."

"I guess not," I sighed.

"So tell me about your friend," she said, nodding toward the pilot's cabin. "You introduced him as Anthony Consoli. Any relation to the Consoli Mob from New York?"

She laughed and stopped when I didn't.

"Vito Consoli is his dad and my godfather, I mean, in the Catholic sense, not the Mafia kind."

"Gast, will you get serious?"

"Okay, he's my pizza delivery guy, alright?"

"You're not kidding, are you?"

"No Shirl, I'm not."

Her mouth opened and her eyes widened. She looked cute as hell. She couldn't have been more surprised if I pulled my hair back and showed her a third eye growing out of my forehead.

"Gast, are we talking about the same man here? Don Vito Consoli, the only mob guy to reach *Cappo Di Tutti Cappi*, then retire and disappear from view?"

"That's my man," I said, then gave her a brief history of growing up in Brooklyn and my lifelong friendship with Anthony. She still looked puzzled and shook her head.

"I'm blown away by this, Gast. I mean, you're ATF, a lieutenant no less. How…I mean…"

"It's no big deal, Shirley. I disclosed it from day one on my application. There's no conflict. I've never done anything illegal, and neither has Anthony. We're both decorated veterans, former army officers, Rangers. Anthony's business is legitimate. He was never involved in any of the family's underworld affairs. Vito Consoli and Franco made sure of that."

"Franco? You mean Franco "The Hammer" Squillante? Consigliere under Vito Consoli? Shit, Gast. These people were crime legends even in Boston PD, let alone New York."

"Shirley, these guys have been retired for ages. They're both old men now. Vito is eighty-five and Franco's somewhere in his late seventies, early eighties. You'll meet them both in less than an hour."

"Swell. Will Charles Manson be there?"

"Shirley…"

"Come on, Gast. What do you expect? I've stuck with you on this murder. I want to see justice done, and I admire you for risking everything. That's what people like us are supposed to do, the right thing. Now I find out our biggest allies are some kind of renegade ex-Russian spies and the New York mob. What other surprises you got for me? I don't…"

At this point, I just grabbed her face between my hands

Patrick Astre

and kissed her. She struggled a little and tried to say something. I flicked my tongue in her mouth and it met hers. I felt her body relax, her tongue slipped against mine, and she closed her eyes. After a while she moved her head against my chest and nuzzled my neck, then moved her mouth to my ear.

"You're something else, you know that?" She whispered as her soft lips nibbled on my ear lobe.

CHAPTER 53

Brookhaven National Laboratory, Upton, Long Island, New York.

Dr. Jawaharlah Bhindra worked alone on this night for he could never explain to any assistants the work he was now doing. He had been preparing this for the last three months. By working late on the same three nights, he had gotten the staff used to his hours. Now that the time had come for the real thing, he couldn't afford any interruptions. The lives of his family hung in the balance. For Dr. Bhindrah, nothing was more precious, not even his own life.

The Cold Fusion generator had been delivered from Los Alamos just a few hours ago. He had removed the cover from the burnished titanium case. The generator sat on the steel laboratory table with its innards exposed. He saw magnetic coils flanking tungsten plasma conductors, pulsing arrays of gaseous flexible pipes holding billions of "nano-bots and other nano-technology machinery." There was a self-contained miniature cryogenic unit, conduits that defied explanations and miles of connecting solid-state circuitry. The workings of the device were embedded in the emerging science of quantum mechanics, and Bhindra couldn't begin to fathom its operation. But then, he didn't have to, not for what was expected of him—that, he knew how to do.

Dr. Bhindra removed the stainless steel bolts holding the end of the case and replaced it with the end-piece he had manufactured a week before. The new end was almost two feet wider, allowing space to accommodate the device he would plant in the innards of the cold fusion generator.

The device itself was eighteen inches long, blunt on both ends and thick as a medium fire extinguisher. Dr. Bhindra thought he felt it buzzing with an alien life of its own, but of course it was his imagination. The shielding was manufactured to such exquisite tolerances that nothing escaped and the dosimeter gauge, sensitive as it was to any radiation, stood perfectly still.

With the device now secured inside the generator, Dr. Bhindra began the meticulous task of wiring it in. He concentrated on his work, trying to keep his mind blank, not to dwell on the consequences of his actions. To keep such thoughts at bay, he pictured his family. It was the only way he could keep from going mad.

As he worked through the night, he thought about what lay secured in a lockbox in the bottom drawer of his office, in the visitor's section outside the security perimeter: A thirty-eight caliber target pistol, the only firearm he had ever owned.

CHAPTER 54

Anthony had built runway lights at the landing strip flanking the estate. He turned them on by radio control as he began the descent.

There's an ethereal beauty about a night landing in Arizona. The climate is conducive to clear skies, more often than not. On this night the atmosphere held not a drop of moisture. The moon and myriad stars created a bright dome of picture-card beauty above us. Below and to our left the city of Scottsdale glowed with thousands of jeweled lights. More pinpoints twinkled to the far horizon, indicating homes and buildings, like upside down reflections of the stars. The runway lights grew larger as the aircraft descended and finally touched down.

Two men, guards, waited for us as we left the plane. They carried machine guns. Anthony asked them why they were here to meet him.

"We're on lock down, Boss," one of them said. "This LaToya woman we picked up in Oklahoma, she's got some information on government big-shots. The old man thinks they might try something against us."

Anthony stopped and looked at him a moment.

"You for real?"

"Yeah, Boss."

Shirley frowned as she listened to the exchange.

"Things are kinda upside down, aren't they?" I said to her as we walked through the gate.

The airstrip is adjacent to the estate, but it's not fenced in like the rest of the property. One of the gurads closed the gate and activated a security button. The gate once again became part of the electronic security perimeter. I knew that included motion, sound and light detectors and other alarm and surveillance devices. Inside the house were a score of heavily armed men.

As we walked into the main house, LaToya was the first to greet us. She wore a colorful shift and her hair was wrapped in a Jamaican bandanna. She looked good, but I could swear she had put on a few pounds—no big surprise after a stay with the Consolis—of course I couldn't say that unless I wanted something broken. She gave me her usual bear-crush hug.

"You got some good friends there, Gast. They saved my poor, government-owned black ass. They been taking good care of me."

"I can see that, LaToya."

"What'chu mean by that?"

"Nothing."

"Oh yeah? Who's this little gal you brought along?"

"Oh, this is Shirley, that Sheriff I told you about?"

"Ex," Shirley said. LaToya looked her up and down and smiled. "You don't look like no sheriff I ever saw. Girl, you as pretty as a desert orchid."

For a moment I could swear that Shirley blushed. Maybe it was just the light. Anyway, LaToya saw the way I held Shirley's shoulder, her grip on my arm.

"So you two are an item now?"

"Well, we're on the way," Shirley replied.

"I tell you what, girl, don't you let him get away. He's a good man. After what he's been through, he deserves something nice in his life."

"LaToya…"

"Hush up, Gast. I ain't saying nuthin but the truth."

It was now past midnight. Maria came out of her and Anthony's bedroom and gave me a sleepy-eyed hug. I introduced her to Shirley. More hugs.

"I heard all about you," Maria said.

"Yeah, what's he been putting spec sheets out on me?"

"You should see what's on them." Anthony let out a whoop and hi-fived with LaToya. Maria smacked him on the arm. "Shut up, idiots. You'll wake the kids," she said.

The housekeeper brought out sandwiches, a pitcher of Sangria, beer and coffee. Everyone helped themselves. When they were done, Anthony showed them to their rooms. I had a permanent one on the second floor.

I showered, put on a bathrobe and stepped out to the balcony. Anthony had told me Bowditch Security was now keeping an extra five-men detail on the estate. Three manned the gate, the remaining two conducted continuous foot patrols within the security perimeter. I know Bowditch security. They hire veterans and cops looking to make more money legitimately. They hire the best and the toughest, and pay very well.

I heard a soft knock at the door, went back inside the room and opened it. Shirley stood there holding two glasses of wine. She wore a filmy semi-transparent gown, her hair was down and she had that exotic lilac scent.

"You going to invite me in for questioning, officer?" she said softly.

I must have had some nights as equally good as that one, but for the life of me, I couldn't remember when.

CHAPTER 55

Zurinov ended the terse conversation and disconnected his cell phone. He watched the lights of the aircraft carrying Katamay, Sergei and the others as it gained altitude. His eyes didn't stop watching until the wing strobes grew tiny and disappeared completely. Only then, did he flip on the NVG's and began the walk back to the Landrover he had left parked in the hills.

The light from the moon and stars rendered the countryside as bright as noon under the light-enhancing goggles. He saw a jackrabbit bolt out in front of him, avoided a big diamond back rattler on the hunt, and continued on the trail.

A less well-trained man might have felt the weight of the weapons he carried, but to Zunrinov, they were no more difficult to bear than the appendages of his own body.

Once again he passed by the camp. The stillness of the place testified to its complete emptiness. He continued on the trail until he reached the Landrover hidden behind an outcropping of boulders. He opened the back door, put the weapons on the floor, got in the back and promptly fell asleep.

The early dawn light awakened him before six AM. He drank some water, ate a chocolate protein power bar, and waited as the sun rose and the heat of another desert day came up.

It was seven thirty in the morning when Zurinov's cell phone trilled. He answered it immediately.

"Yes."

"Shatun?"

He recognized the voice of Dallas Wilson and replied.

"Yes."

"We have traced the aircraft. It is at the estate of a well-known and powerful man, a former gangster."

"Ah, I am familiar with such people. Get me there today."

"The place is heavily defended. You cannot do this alone."

"You do not know what I can do. You are here to assist me. I work alone. Get me there today."

"I will, but I have thought about this. It will be easier this way, and you can still do this alone."

"Tell me."

Wilson told him. When he was done, Zurinov smiled.

"Good," he said. "I agree. I will be waiting for you."

As was his habit when there was waiting to be done on a mission, Zurinov sat on the ground in the lotus position. Insects buzzed about him as the air slowly built to a scorch. Light reflected from the desert floor in heat waves and a hot breeze blew dust across his eyes. He ignored it all until he heard the distant sound of helicopter rotors coming closer. A distant moue played across his mouth. Tonight he would be in Arizona, near Scottsdale, where Sergei believed he had found safety. Instead, Zurinov would bring him death.

CHAPTER 56

When I woke up, Shirley had gone, either gotten up early or returned back to her room. Maybe she wanted everything to look proper. I got up, shaved and showered and put on fresh clothes. Coming to the Consoli estate always made me feel like a kid again. My room was always ready and stocked with everything from toiletries to my favorite beer in the little fridge. It felt great.

I went downstairs and found Shirley and Maria talking in the kitchen.

"Hey," I said.

They looked at each other and giggled in that conspiratorial way women have when they're talking about you.

"What?"

"Nothing," Maria said. "Well, gotta run and get the kids up for breakfast."

"School?"

"No, swim meet."

"Wise ass."

"No, doofus. I'm serious. There's no school today, teachers conference, but they have a swim meet in Scottsdale."

"But they're only six and nine."

"So? It's a junior meet. That jock stuff is good for them."

Maria left and I sat next to Shirley. There was a pot of coffee on the table and I poured myself a cup.

"Sugar?" Shirley said.

"Put your finger in it."

She smacked my arm. "Maria's right. You are a wise ass."

I took a sip of the black coffee. It was delicious. Vito Consoli, like every Sicilian I ever knew, loved his coffee. From Espresso to regular morning java, it had to be perfect. He ordered it direct from some exotic plantation in Puerto Rico. I looked at Shirley and smiled. She smiled back.

"So how do you like them?" I asked her.

"They're nice," she answered. "I met the old man, Vito. He was down here earlier, went out for his morning walk. I can't believe it's the same people we read about."

"Like I told you, that's the way I've always known them, grew up with them. I've never dealt with their other side. Anyway, it's long gone now. Only the connections remain and it comes in handy once in a while."

"I suppose. I also spoke with Katamay this morning."

"What'd you do, decide to get up at four AM and become the ambassador? Talk to everyone?"

"Better than sleeping late like you and letting the world go by."

"So what'd Katamay have to say?"

Shirley stood and walked to the refrigerator to get milk for her coffee. She wore designer jeans and a plain, short sleeve blouse. I guessed she'd borrowed them from Maria. They were about the same size. She also wore the Colt Python at her waist in its leather holster.

"Nice accessory," I said nodding to the weapon.

She shrugged. "The way things have been going, it should come in handy."

"You think?"

"Anyway, Katamay seems to believe there's something big brewing, that this whole thing with the cold fusion generator going public is meant to create a disturbance. Maybe get the excitement going and show it to be a dismal failure instead of suppressing it."

"Could be. Where's he at now?"

"In the den with LaToya and Sergei, going over the stuff LaToya found."

We took our coffees and walked to the den. Anthony had joined them. We sat on the big, sectioned couch, watching a morning news special about the cold fusion discovery. Paula Zhan from CNN was hosting along with a "talking head" energy expert.

"…at Brookhaven National Lab where the machine is currently undergoing final calibration and testing." At this point Paula Zahn turned toward the side and addressed a question to the expert whose head appeared in a corner section of the screen.

"Professor, I guess we have to wonder why Brookhaven Lab in Long Island? Why not finish everything where they created it, at Los Alamos?"

The guy was an old codger with bushy eyebrows, bald on top with long hair on the sides. He looked as nervous as a mouse in a serpentarium.

"Uhm, well Paula, I would have to guess the answer to that question would be a couple of unique scientific tools that are only available at Brookhaven Lab."

"What kind of tools Doctor? Why can't they just be transported to Los Alamos? I mean, this is the scientific discovery of the ages isn't it?"

"Indeed it is Paula. When I say tools, I don't mean things like power drills or something. We're talking about PAMPA and NURAG."

"PAMPA and NURAG? You're going to have to explain those to our viewers, Doctor. In layman's terms, please."

"Yes of course. PAMPA stands for Phased-Array Multi-Particles Accelerator, and NURAG, Nuclear Resonance Alignment Generator. How these devices work is…"

Katamay clicked the button on the remote and shut off the TV.

"Pardon my language, ladies," he said to Shirley and LaToya. "This is complete bull shit. These people are up to something, and it's going to be very bad."

CHAPTER 57

Special Agent John Ford always wished an owner's manual had come with his brain. Sometimes, things, ideas and solutions just came to him. If only he could figure out the process there wouldn't be any mysteries he couldn't solve. But right now, his inspirations and intuition seemed to be on vacation. He had a variety of information that he should have been able to put together into a cohesive plot. He should have been able to unravel all this like a kitten with a ball of twine. Instead, all he had was this mind-map leading to a seemingly endless variety of solutions. To hold endless solutions, is to have no solutions at all. One of his professors at college had once told him that.

First, and most disturbing, was the information on that new agency, IRD. The way it was created and funded was unique. Most of its efforts seemed to be concentrated around Los Alamos and much of its activities were, at least in Ford's mind, questionable. But Ford wasn't the only one with that thought. That was why Senator Weill and his friend, the director of the FBI had assigned him this can of worm.

He had bits and pieces relating to IRD and it was time to bounce them off someone else. He smiled as his aide came into the room.

"You wanted to see me, chief?"

"Yes, William. I want to play twenty questions."

"Sir?"

"Brainstorm, work our logic muscles. Let's see if we can put some of these pieces together, just like an exercise at the Academy."

"Okay."

"First, what is the Tinian Protocol?"

"Uhm, I don't know. I looked up the name and Tinia is the old African God of thunder. It's mentioned several times in IRD communications we picked up."

"Which we cannot admit to receiving because we listened illegally, thanks to the resources of someone very high up in the bureau, someone who must remain nameless."

"Alright, sir. Interesting though, Tinian is mentioned as something having to do with the cold fusion generator."

"Which is another question. Why is IRD so focused on this CF thing? I mean they have complete charge of it."

"Complete with allegations of people disappearing, and that curious affair with that ATF officer."

"Yeah, that is strange. This Lieutenant Duval is squeaky clean, decorated, a military hero and ATF hero. He was on the fast track to Captain, maybe even skipped to Inspector rank until he ran up against those IRD folks."

"You think he's involved somehow?"

"I think he may have discovered something and got squashed for his troubles. He's an interesting man. I had a copy of his personnel file faxed to me. There's something else very interesting as well."

"His, ah, relations, with the Consoli crime family?"

"Ah, you read the file, William?"

"Well yes sir. You told me to go over all the material we had and see what I came up with. But I don't see what that has to do with anything. I mean he disclosed it, he grew up in the same neighborhood, went to war with Anthony Consoli."

"True. Now look at this last report," Ford said. He handed the young man another computer printout.

William read it, and looked up puzzled.

"This airplane belongs to Arizona Enterprises. What's it got do with anything?"

"Arizona Enterprises is the corporate organization that owns the plane. The Consolis own Arizona Enterprises. That same plane was shown on surveillance last night as landing on a deserted road near the suspected encampment where our participants escaped to. They were followed there by someone, probably the same person or persons who attacked them at the house. We are also not the only ones interested in them. Once again, someone else requested and received this report before us and the NSA will not tell us who it is."

"Isn't there a way to force them?"

"Probably, eventually. But not quickly. This is the National Security Agency, after all."

"Humm. So what's our next move sir?"

"I think we should pay a visit to the Consolis at their place in Arizona. Get some of those HRT honchos to come with us. A show of force always impresses people like the Consolis."

CHAPTER 58

The day kind of flew by for me, lazy and sweet after the tumultuous events of the last forty-eight hours. There was a domestic simplicity to its passing that I had sorely missed. We went to the swim meet with Anthony and Maria. Gina, the nine year old, argued non-stop with her brother, six year old Michael. There must have been about a thousand kids and hundreds of parents in various stages of confusion and/or aggravation. The kids loved it. They kept jumping in the water while the coaches worked desperately to line them up for a semblance of swim races.

Later we all went to McDonald's and took up half the dining room. We sat at the biggest table in a wonderful confusion of shouting, squealing kids, mounds of hamburgers and spilled French fries and sodas, everyone eating everyone else's stuff. Vito Consoli sat at the head of the table like the Sicilian clan leader he actually was, but misplaced in that quintessential American setting. The old man didn't eat anything. He never ate anything that wasn't two hundred percent Italian. Macdonald's might as well have been the planet Mars when it came to that.

The bodyguards sat at the adjacent table like a group of dangerous gargoyles. The kids stayed away from them, quietly warned by concerned parents, the exception being of course, Anthony's kids who constantly crawled all over them.

Shirley and LaToya loved the whole thing. LaToya came from a large family and was used to it and missed it. Shirley, a single woman, cop, and sheriff to boot, seldom experienced the kind of chaos that passes for a large family outing, but seemed to like it as well.

We got back late in the afternoon. The housekeeper had been told we would be eating out, but still had a large antipasto spread on the dining room table along with lasagna, Chianti and espresso for Vito Consoli.

As the evening fell, Shirley and I took some iced Coronas and sat by the pool. We were alone. Shirley held my hand.

"So what next?" she asked.

"Well I guess if everything remains quiet, we put together a case with everything we have and find the right authorities to bring it to."

"I know that. It wasn't what I meant."

"Oh."

"I mean what about us?"

"Well I'm on suspension and you're unemployed, so…"

"I don't mean that either. You know exactly what I'm talking about, okay?"

"Yes."

"Well think about it, alright? We'll talk tomorrow."

"Okay."

CHAPTER 59

———◆———

Zurinov sat quietly in the Blackhawk through the entire ride to Arizona. He never said a word to the two IRD pilots who picked him up. They didn't say anything to him. Everyone knew their jobs and needed no discussions. Zurinov liked that.

It was late afternoon when the big machine dropped altitude. The pilot flared the engine and landed in a small clearing surrounded by low hills. Zurinov jumped out and took the pack that had been left for him on the Blackhawk. The helicopter immediately rose a few feet, rotated on its axis, dropped its nose and accelerated back to where it had come from.

Zurinov walked over to the edge of the clearing. There was a lean-to sheltering a sturdy ATV, the kind used in special operations. He reached inside his pack, took out a GPS and fastened it on the mount on the front of the ATV. He turned it on and when the machine located itself, he tapped a preset waypoint labeled "Consoli."

He got on the machine, started it, and headed toward the Consoli estate following the directions from the GPS.

Zurinov had about ten miles to go before reaching the outer perimeter of the estate. If the helicopter had approached any closer, it might have been spotted by one of the guards, thus the approach by ATV.

The terrain was rough, strewn with rocks, boulders, sand and tough, stringy desert vegetation. The ATV with its fat tires, four-wheel drive and independent suspension was ideal for that kind of travel. The engine was so heavily muffled that it emitted only the barest whisper. As darkness fell, he put on the NVG and navigated by amplified ambient light. Two hours later, he arrived at his destination: a ridge-line forming the base of an outcropping of rocks. He shut off the ATV and climbed the hill. When he neared the top, he fell to his belly and crawled the last twenty yards.

Slowly he lifted his head so he could view the estate below him. Spotlights blazed from posts every twenty feet on the fence surrounding the property. The pool area, tennis courts and houses were all washed in the light of powerful halogen lamps. Even the landing strip and the hangar where the plane was secured remained lit up. Zurinov guessed they would leave it like that all night, as if lights could protect them from an onslaught of his martial skills.

He studied the small diagram of the estate that they had given him. Wilson, the IRD man had told him it was accurate. Zurinov believed him. The success of his mission was in their interest.

He saw the guard-post at the entrance, at least three hundred yards away. Might as well have been on the moon for all the good it would do them.

He turned his attention to the three houses, all clustered together with the pool and cabanas in the center. The small house off to the left was where the most dangerous guards stayed. He would neutralize them first. On the other side of the main house was a bungalow where the gardener and his family lived. That could be ignored. The main event would take place within the big house. That's where Katamay stayed—and Sergei.

A window opened on the second floor. A man stepped out onto the small balcony. At that distance, Zurinov could not tell who it was with the naked eye. He raised the binoculars and looked. The person on the balcony was the tall man that had joined this little group in Santa Fe. He was the one his sources at IRD had warned him about, the inquisitive lawman from the American ATF agency. The man looked directly out and for a second, Zurinov's heart stopped. It seemed as if the stranger looked directly at him, saw him in his hiding spot. He almost ducked instinctively, but of course that was nonsense. It would be impossible for anyone to see him in the dark folds of the hill from under those bright spotlights. The man turned as if responding to someone in the room. He stepped away from the balcony and closed the French doors behind him.

Zurinov removed the electronic device from the bag and laid it out beside him. It was quite simple really, just two LED's and one switch. He liked that. Simple things worked better. He looked down at his watch and read the glowing little digits. Ten PM.

Three hours to go.

CHAPTER 60

"Will you stop pacing," Shirley told me. "You're worse than a guy in a cast with fleas. You're making me nervous."

"Sorry. I can't help it. It's like we're missing something. Why did they suddenly leave us alone? If that cold fusion thing is the cause of all these problems, why are they releasing it all over the news? Something's not right."

"Well you're not going to fix it tonight, Sherlock."

I looked at her. She sat on the edge of the bed, still wearing her jeans and blouse. LaToya was right—pretty as a desert orchid. I went to her and she stood as I came close. She put a hand on my chest and it felt soft and warm.

"Make a deal with you," she whispered. "I'm going to take a nice, long bath and you forget all this for tonight. Go get us some champagne, I saw a couple of bottles in the big refrigerator downstairs."

"Why Sheriff Case! Are you suggesting I abscond with Mr. Consoli's bubbly?"

"Yeah, big guy, do just that."

She put two fingers to my lips, then turned and stepped into the bathroom. I went downstairs and found the champagne, rummaged some more and found an ice-bucket and two glasses.

When I came back to the room, Shirley was still in her

bath. I went to the French doors, opened them and stepped out on the balcony. I was barefoot and the stones felt good on my toes, still warm with residual heat from the day. The air smelled clean. Dry and warm, it carried mixed scents of flowers from the estate's gardens, and volcanic dust from the nearby hills. The ridges marking the edges of the property blended with the more distant hills and mountains into a solid dark mass. The dazzling lights of the estate rendered it that way. I stared out into the night, wishing they had placed a little less light. The place was on display for anyone stalking in the dark folds of the hills.

"You staying out there all night, or are you going to offer me champagne?" Shirley's voice drifted in from the room. I turned away, stepped inside and closed the French doors behind me. I saw the digital clock on the dresser.

It was ten PM.

CHAPTER 61

The First Alarm Company had its base office on Redondo Boulevard in Scottsdale, about two-dozen miles from the Consoli estate. The firm specialized in sophisticated security systems for upscale mansions. It had installed and maintained the high-tech system for the Consolis. Although their systems were stand-alone, the office was manned around the clock for any tech support or repairs its wealthy clientele may require.

At ten PM that night only one man was on duty at First Alarm. He was a supervisor and if needed, could call upon a technical crew that was on standby.

The door to the office opened. A man walked in. He was big with hard features and a brush cut. He wore a gray suit, dark tie and black shoes. He looked like a movie version of a tough FBI agent. He walked right up to the supervisor's desk and flipped open a leather ID case.

"IRD agent, command grade."

The supervisor looked at the ID. It seemed genuine enough, government-grade alright.

"Okay. So what can I do for you?"

"We're conducting an anti-terror operation. I will be answering your phone for the next hour. Here's a Federal Judicial Order under authority of the Enhanced Patriot

Act."

The agent handed him some legal-sized papers that looked like a court order. The supervisor read it and frowned.

"But what if I get a technical call or a service problem from one of our customers?"

"Then I'll turn it over to you. I'm interested in one call only. Starting now, I'm answering all your calls. If you got a problem with that, I'll have two agents down here to lock your ass up for obstructing anti-terror operations. Believe me, son, you don't want no part of that."

"Uh, yeah, okay. I'll just sit out there," the supervisor replied, and showed the agent how to work the phone system.

"Now one more thing," the man said. "Give me the security codes for communication with the Consoli estate."

The supervisor swallowed hard, blinked, said, "Okay," and gave him the codes.

CHAPTER 62

It was half past eleven when the van pulled up to the front gates of the Consoli estate. It was a Ford Econoline, brand new, white with First Alarm painted on the sides and the company logo right below that. The driver got out of the van and walked up to the gate. He wore blue coveralls with "Danny" stenciled on the breast pocket. A uniformed Bowditch Security man holding an automatic pistol at the ready, met him there.

"Hey, I'm Danny from First Alarm. You guys got a glitch in your security system. I'm here to look at it."

"It's fine. We don't have any problems with it."

"Yeah, you do, might be nothing or a false reading. We run diagnostics by internet contact four times a day on all our systems. Yours just came up with a trouble code. Can I bring my van in?"

"No, come inside, just you."

"Okay, let me get my tool box."

"Not yet, just you for now."

Danny shrugged, and the man opened the gate. He accompanied Danny to the guardhouse and waived him to a seat. Another guard stared at Danny as if daring him to try anything.

The first guard looked up a number and dialed it. It was

answered on the second ring.

"First Alarm systems. Night supervisor speaking."

"This is Bowditch Security at the front gate, Consoli estate. One of your guys is here, says there's something wrong with our system. What's your security codes?"

The IRD man read him the complex code verifying that he was indeed First Alarm. The Bowditch guard matched it with the one on his pad. It was correct.

"System seems fine on my end," the guard said. "What's supposed to be the problem?"

"Intermittent code 19," the IRD man replied. "Could be a minor problem, false signal. Can't ignore it, that's why we get paid the big bucks. My technician's going to run a few tests. If he can't find anything he'll hook up a diagnostic recording device and we'll come back tomorrow to check it out."

Satisfied, the guard said, "Okay." He told Danny he could get his toolbox, but leave the truck outside. One of the guards would accompany him every step of the way.

"Knock yourself out," Danny said.

Danny spent ten minutes in the terracotta shed next to the guardhouse. The cramped structure housed the controls and computers for the electronic security systems. He hooked up gauges to a service port and took a number of readings. When he was done he turned to the guard who had watched every move he made.

"Can't find anything wrong, not unusual for a code 19. I'm going to hook up a recording device that will monitor in constant diagnostic mode. The system won't be affected."

"Go ahead."

Danny plugged a black box the size of a cigarette carton into the diagnostic port.

"I'm going to activate it now," he told the guard. "Just leave it alone and I'll come back in twelve hours and get the readings, okay?"

"Sure."

"Danny" pushed a tiny switch, activating the device. He knew that somewhere in the dark hills, the little device they had given Zurinov would receive the "ready now" signal.

CHAPTER 63

Zurinov waited, he was used to the long stalking waits required to successfully hunt human prey. He had waited in better places as well as much worse than this section of Arizona. From the luxuries of the big Western cities to the forsaken territories of Tajikistan, Afghanistan and Chechnya, he had waited.

Sixteen years had passed. His patience would soon pay off. The final three hours were not more painful or elongated than all the time that had passed before it. His eyes never wavered from scanning the Consoli estate. Even though they had placed themselves on alert, they had fallen into a routine, one that Zurinov would easily pierce.

Sergei, he thought. Your hour has arrived. I am here.

Zurinov crawled over the lip of the ridge. The darkness was absolute, made even more so by the reflected lights of the estate. It prevented the eye from developing any night vision. But that was alright. Zurinov wouldn't need it. He continued crawling to within fifty yards of the outer fence, just out of range of the pool of light. If he went any further, he would trip the detection devices.

Zurinov held out the little control box the IRD man had given him. Two LED lights and one button—simple. The LED on the left blinked red every three seconds. He pushed the single button and waited. The red light stopped blinking and the second LED lit up a steady green. That meant the device the phony alarm technician had planted worked. The systems were disabled without the guards knowing it. The cameras and monitoring system went into closed loop mode, replaying the last hour. Since nothing had happened, the guards monitoring it would not know the difference.

Now Zurinov dashed flat out, full speed to the fence. It was not a reckless move. He had timed it carefully. The two men on foot patrols were out of sight, at the other end of the oval forming the property. By the time they returned, Zurinov would be ready to deal with them. His first task was taking out the gunmen in the smaller building adjacent to the main house. Over the last three hours, Zurinov had observed them and understood their patterns. One would always be awake and alert, prowling the property, armed and ready. After one hour, he would go inside and wake up one of the other men who would take his place.

He had observed the big American go inside. Next, the Mexican had come out. The man was a chain smoker. At this moment he leaned against the wall by the corner of the house, a Mac-10 machine pistol dangling from his belt, the cigarette in his hand. Yes, Zurinov thought, the Americans were right about the dangers of tobacco. The Mexican was about to die because of that smoking break.

Zurinov hurled himself straight up on the fence. He climbed the links like a crab on the pilings of a dock, smooth, quiet and fast. When he reached the top he paused to remove a dark canister from his waist. He aimed it at the top of the fence and pressed a lever on the canister. A rubberized plastic sheet shot out of the container, propelled by a CO_2 cartridge. The material settled itself over the razor wire topping the fence, providing a protected pathway the width of a man's body. Zurinov scrambled over it and let himself fall to the ground. He was inside the Consoli estate.

He landed softly with barely a sound, legs flexed, ready for any unexpected encounter. He paused for a moment, scanning the area. Nothing—exactly as he expected.

Zurinov covered the distance to the house in seconds. His practiced steps, muffled by specially made crepe shoes, were as silent as they were swift. He flattened himself against the wall, moved to the edge, crouching as he passed each window. He stopped at the edge of the wall. Around that corner, the Mexican had stopped and lit a cigarette. Zurinov smelled the tobacco smoke and musty odor of his clothing. He heard him mutter something in Spanish, and it was like a "go" signal for the Russian assassin.

He whirled around the corner in a combat crouch, knife held low, blade out. The Mexican didn't have a chance and Zurinov was not the sporting kind. The Russian moved his knife so quickly the guard couldn't even raise his arms in time. The honed blade burst through the larynx, jugular and windpipe, and whipped out just as fast. The Mexican barely had time for a muffled gurgle when Zurinov grabbed his head in a two-armed jiu-jitsu grip, broke his neck instantly and gently lowered the body to the ground.

He stepped over the corpse and continued along the wall until he reached the air conditioning unit. He took a multi-purpose tool from his pocket, unscrewed the four retaining screws and pulled the inspection cover off. The main duct that supplied cold air throughout the house was held by a spring-loaded clamp. Zurinov unfastened it, removed another canister from his belt, twisted the pin on top, placed it inside the duct and refastened the clamp. He listened for a moment until he heard the canister hissing softly inside the duct.

About a decade earlier, Chechen separatist rebels had taken control of the Moscow Opera House and over a hundred hostages. After a period of unsuccessful negotiations, Russian Special Forces had attempted a rescue. During the night they pumped the Opera House with knockout gas. It would have worked except the gas wasn't right and more than twenty hostages lost their lives. Since then, the Russians had perfected the gas and that's what Zurinov used. The remaining guards inside wouldn't wake up for about eight hours.

With the primary threat out of the way, Zurinov moved on to the main house. He had memorized the layout and knew exactly how to get in and where to go: The children's room, Anthony's children, Vito Consoli's grandchildren.

CHAPTER 64

The knock woke me instantly. There was a rapid-fire urgency to the sound. The voice calling me through the door sounded desperate, as if its owner was about to break down into incoherent noises.

"Gast…Gast…Please, Gast, open up, open the door…"

I barely recognized Maria's voice. I had never heard her like that. I jumped out of bed, threw on my jeans in about two seconds. Shirley sat up in bed as the desperation in Maria's voice shattered any remains of sleep we had. I rushed to the door and threw it open.

Anthony's wife stood there, dressed in just her nightgown. Her lip trembled and there were dark streaks under her eyes where tears had cut a path down her cheeks. Her eyes held the desperation of the truly horrified. Her voice trembled and her body shook.

"Gast, please, its Gina and Michael. He's going to kill them."

"Who, Maria? What's going on?"

"Just come down, Gast, now. Please?"

"Yeah, I will, right now. Where's Anthony?"

"He's got him too. Please, come down, he'll kill them all."

She was close to the edge of hysteria. I sensed that another moment might bring some kind of breakdown.

I reached for my gun on the night table. She screamed then stifled her mouth.

"No guns, Gast. Please, he said no guns or they're dead. Just come down. You too, please," she implored Shirley. "He knows exactly how many people are here and where they are. Just come. There's no time left."

She ran down the hallway then the stairs. We followed her, stopping at the landing at the end of the steps.

He had positioned himself exactly right. When we got off the stairs he had us all covered. He sat quite at ease, his legs crossed. He wore a dark tee shirt, having removed a black jacket that lay next to him. The muscles of his arms rippled, making the red bear's head tattooed on his forearm appearing to move on its own. His face wasn't remarkable. He could have been an accountant, or computer technician. It was the eyes that gave him away. There was a glacial feeling to his gaze that said he was a bringer of death, a demonic quality as if he was far beyond any redemption. I had never seen him, yet I recognized him.

Shatun.

Directly in front of him, tied together with masking tape, Anthony's children sat in a wide high-backed captain's chair. Propped up by their ligatures, their eyes were closed and their heads kept from lolling by a strand of cloth tied around their foreheads to the back of the chair. The man's gun was casually trained on the children.

Anthony was on his knees on the other side of the room. His eyes were feral in his helplessness. He was handcuffed to the leg of the big dining table. I heard Maria behind me barely stifle a sob, heard Shirley whisper something to her.

"I am Zurinov," the man said, quietly. "I will explain the situation as I have explained it to the parents of those children. Presently, they are unharmed. In a few hours they will awaken from the effect of the gas I made them breathe as they slept. Providing, that is, that you do exactly what I demand immediately."

I said nothing. My mind raced through all the moves I might make, and came back without possibilities.

"I am one of the best shots in the world with this weapon," Zurinov continued with a deceptively small wave of the muzzle that covered both the children. "I can put two bullets in each of their heads before you can draw a breath. You understand that, do you not Mister Duval?"

I said nothing. Behind me I heard Maria gasp. Anthony glared steadily at the man. My friend's eyes burned with anger, frustration and overwhelming fear for the lives of his children.

"Steady Anthony," I told him quietly. I returned my eyes to Zurinov. "What do you want?"

"They told me your name and who you are along with your friend, the police woman. From you, I want nothing."

He reached into a small bag next to him, pulled out some things and tossed them on the floor in front of us. It was a pair of plastic ties, the kind used by law enforcement to restraint prisoner's hands. He must have brought only one set of handcuffs. Two might have rattled. He had correctly used it on the most dangerous person—the children's father, Anthony.

"You," he waved to Shirley. "Put them on him. You know how it is done. Do this in front of me. If you hide my view I will shoot a child, then you."

Shirley stepped to my side. She never took her eyes off Zurinov as she bound my wrists together with the sturdy plastic ties. She appeared calm, but I felt the imperceptible shake of her hands.

"Tighter."

Shirley pulled and the plastic tightened through the loop. The thin strand turned my wrists white. I felt the tingling as the circulation was cut off.

"Kneel."

I knelt as Zurinov told Maria to bind Shirley's wrists like mine. She obeyed with shaking hands, her eyes wandering to her children, pleading for help that would obviously never come. I had realized one thing, certain as the very rotation of the earth and the passing of time.

Zurinov would not let any of us escape alive.

CHAPTER 65

There came a scuffling step from the stairs. Each footfall was deliberately heavy, as if the newcomer wanted to let everyone know he was on his way. His legs appeared then the rest of him. He held his hand out, palm up, to show he had no weapons. He stopped and spoke softly.

"It is me Zurinov. I am the one you came after. I'm here, unarmed."

Zurinov didn't reply but kept his weapon trained on the newcomer as he emerged into full view.

It was Sergei. He walked gently with no sudden moves if crossing a room filled with the most fragile of things and he feared knocking them over. We were all on our knees and Sergei stopped next to us.

"It has been a long time, Zurinov."

Zurinov licked his lips and took a breath. He seemed barely in control of himself, as if a gargantuan rage swept through his body.

"Sixteen years," he finally whispered.

"Let these people go, Zurinov. They have nothing to do with this."

"It is too late for that now. Where is your father?"

"I have restrained and hidden him where you will not find him."

"Then I will destroy this house."

"Then you will never be sure, and neither will your paymasters."

The two men stared at each other. It was as if some demonic energy had been released and left hovering between them, waiting to unleash itself as Sergei spoke again. "You have been wrong all these years, Zurinov. It is time to let it go or finish it. Take me. I will go with you willingly. Leave my father and these people."

Zurinov stood. He transferred the gun to his left hand. The muzzle remained trained on the children.

"Perhaps," Zurinov said. "Come to me."

Sergei stepped toward Zurinov. Strong, confident steps, he didn't hesitate, and closed the distance between them.

I have never seen a man move that fast. Not in combat, not in sports or martial arts training. Sergei stood no chance. The knife seemed to come out of the very air as Zurinov took him at mid-step.

A Marine K-Bar knife is an awesome close-combat weapon when properly maintained and used by someone who knows how. It is the military equivalent of the Bowie knife, and Zurinov was an expert. He buried the eight-inch blade just below Sergei's sternum. It made a sound that will haunt me for the rest of my days, a soggy, gurgling whisper.

Sergei froze in mid step, his eyes opened and his pupils rolled back in their socket. He made a gasping kind of noise and slowly collapsed on Zurinov's arm. The Russian assassin pulled upward on the blade. The steel moved a few inches more, widening the wound, cutting through arteries and organs. Zurinov pulled the blade out and gently pushed Sergei. A jet of blood came out of the wound and splashed both men's legs and shoes. Some droppings landed on Zurinov's shirt and he looked at it. His eyes blazed, the pupils narrowed and his breathing came in ragged. He looked like a deranged man in the throes of a blood orgasm. Sergei fell to his knees and collapsed in a crumpled fetus position. The charnel-house stench of blood filled the room.

I heard a keening wail, a sound that carried all the agony of the world and turned to see Katamay rushing down the stairs. Sergei hadn't restrained him after all, or maybe the old man had escaped. He carried a gun and several things happened at the same time.

Katamay fired at his son's killer. The old man's shot went far to the right. We all ducked and Zurinov raised his gun toward Katamay.

It must have been the last burst of his life force, one last directed convulsion before his death. From the floor, Sergei grabbed Zurinov's ankle and pulled. The assassin lost his balance, fell forward and the shot went wide. Katamay stumbled and fell the last few steps to the floor.

I rushed Zurinov. I knew it was the only moment I would ever have. Leaping with your hands tied in front of you disturbs your balance. The body is out of sync and the movement is spoiled. I missed Zurinov. He kicked the coffee table toward me. I stumbled on it and fell. He rose with the gun held in his hand and pointed it at me.

I've experienced this phenomenon before. I think it's a shared experience among those who faced death at one time or another. Time just seems to slow down. You see things in great clarity. Events that take fractions of a second pass by with maddening slowness, as if the entire scene is played through air with the consistency of thick syrup. In Afghanistan, I swore I could actually see the bullets arcing through the air toward our position. This night, I saw Zurinov's gun moving toward me. The black end of the barrel was a dark eye from which death would erupt, first for me, then everyone else in that room.

CHAPTER 66

Vito Consoli came to America from Sicily in the nineteen-forties. Throughout his rise in the American Cosa Nostra, right to the title of Don, he'd used his Sicilian wiles. Cunning, treachery and death were a quintessential part of his world. No matter the height of your position, the strength of your friends or weakness of your enemies, you always had to have an ace. Sometimes you hold an ace and never use it, but you've got to have it. After all, you never know.

On this night, Don Vito Consoli would use his ace. At eighty-five he felt pitifully slow even though he would have made a sixty year old proud. He'd heard the noises downstairs through his own private monitoring system, saw his grandchildren tied and that *gavone* of a Russian holding them all with his gun.

Vito Consoli moved through the passage as quickly as he could. Even though in his old age he had become quite thin, it was still tight. The secret passages had been built for stealth and surprise, not comfort.

He made his way down the stone steps. At only sixteen inches of width, they were narrow and he had to move sideways. The tiny glow-lights along the floor were almost useless to his old eyes, forcing him to move at a maddeningly slow pace.

He came to the end of the cramped stairs and walked toward the narrow, dark corridor where two glow lamps indicated the secret door. Don Vito Consoli grasped the steel handle, counted down silently to three and pushed open the door.

CHAPTER 67

Maybe I was dead already and these were just hallucinations. The kind of tricks your mind plays on you to anesthetize the pain of dying.

A section of the wall behind Zurinov opened. It was a part of the wall where no doors should have existed. It just opened without a sound and a hand holding a shiny little twenty-two caliber pistol emerged from the opening. The pistol fired and the bullet hit Zurinov on the side of the head. He went down like someone had hit him with a two by four. The big gun fell from his hand and clattered on the tiled floor. Now he was level with me, both of us on the floor, five feet apart. His eyes were opened, moving, as a trickle of blood came from the hole in his cheek. He tried to stand.

Vito Consoli stepped out from the hidden door that had opened in the wall. The old Sicilian's eyes burned with anger as he mouthed some ancient Italian curse. He leaned down, placed the muzzle of the little automatic against Zurinov's head and pulled the trigger—three times. Afterward, he threw the gun to the floor, cursed again, and spat on Zurinov's body.

The twenty-two is a cheap weapon firing a low velocity small round. Commonly called a Saturday night special, it's often the weapon of choice for professional hit men and the *Coup-De-Grace*. The bullet's got just enough power to penetrate the skull but usually not enough to exit. It just rattles around the soft tissue a while, destroying the insides without fail.

Zurinov lay face down on the floor as blood poured from his nose, mouth and ears. He was as dead as could possibly be. The satiny flow from the orifices of his head filled the gaps separating the tiles until it reached Sergei's body where it mingled with his blood in a single coagulating puddle.

CHAPTER 68

I watched Katamay as he closed his son's eyes and held his head. Sergei's face looked peaceful. Death had chased away the facade of agony from his last moment.

I squatted next to Katamay, my hand on his shoulder. We remained that way until the old man finally laid his son's head gently down on the tile floor. Tears from his eyes had rolled down the wrinkled folds of his face, seeming to cut new canyons in the flesh. He didn't look up as he spoke.

"In the thirties it was the Bolsheviks and their *Pogroms*. My father went out with my uncle and my older brother. We never saw them again. In 1944 the Nazi *Einsatzzengruppen* came to our village. They were a flying death squad, looking for Jews. They found my family. My mother hid me in a root cellar. I heard it all as they took them to a place called Babi-Yar. I survived, married, came to America in the fifties. We had two children. Polio took my daughter. The vaccine came too late for her and my wife died soon after. I thought I had no more capacity for grief. My eyes could produce no more tears."

"I'm sorry," I whispered.

He looked up at me, his eyes haunted by a sorrow that reached to the very last dreg of his soul.

"I saw this moment come. I have seen it in my

nightmares since the incident between Zurinov and Sergei."

He stood up slowly with the weariness of an old man who had suddenly added decades to his years. Shirley took his side and we sat on the big couch, Katamay between us.

Anthony came back to the room and took a seat beside us. He had brought four mugs of coffee and distributed them. Katamay didn't touch his.

"How are the kids?" I asked Anthony.

"They'll be fine. Maria is with them and the doctor. He says they inhaled some sort of knock-out gas, same thing used in the other house to put the guards out of action."

"They okay?"

"Yeah, they're good. We got another doctor looking after them. We found one outside, dead. It must have been his turn on guard. Luck of the draw I guess."

Vito Consoli had made a few calls and two doctors had arrived within half an hour along with two private guards and additional people from Bowditch Security. The private guards made sure they all stayed away from the two bodies inside the main house and the one outside.

"They figure out how he got in?" Shirley asked.

Anthony closed his eyes and leaned his head back for a moment. He opened his eyes and sighed before he answered.

"Last night a phony technician from the alarm company came on the pretext of some repair that had to be done. He planted a device that neutralized the system. Zurinov was able to shut it down by remote."

"Anthony," I said, nodding toward the two corpses. "What are we going to do about them, and the one outside?"

"Pop said he'll take care of it. You don't want to know more than that."

Anthony was right. I didn't want to know more than that. A door opened on the far side of the room and Vito Consoli walked in. He stepped up to Katamay as he rose from the couch.

The two old men stood facing each other. There was a

strength and dignity about them as if they were ancient monarchs of some long-gone noble dynasty.

Katamay reached his hand out and Vito took it, wrapping it in both of his.

"I am sorry Mister Consoli," Katamay said. "I have brought violence and death to your home."

"It is I who must apologize," Vito replied. "You were our guest and we failed to protect you properly. Had we done so, your son would be alive. I will bear that responsibility to my own grave."

"There is something else..." Katamay said.

Vito pointed to the two chairs facing the couch. They both sat in front of us.

"We were going to ask you for help, my son and I, before..." and he looked toward the bodies. "Now I ask you for an additional request."

"Name it."

"Will you take care of my boy, make the arrangements? We have a family plot in Calvary Cemetery, in Brooklyn."

"I know the place."

"There is a funeral home in Brighton Beach. It is Russian owned. Will you have them handle it?"

"Yes. I will take care of your son as if he were one of mine."

"Thank you," Katamay said. He bowed his head, wiped his eyes and looked at each one of us in turn. No one said anything. The air conditioning system hummed quietly and there were no other noises. In the stillness we could hear the great clock in the hall, ticking.

"You said there was something you and Sergei were going to ask us?"

Katamay continued looking at the floor for a few more minutes. Then he looked up and his expression changed.

"I am convinced something very bad is going to happen soon. It will be in Delaware, at that new laboratory, and it has something to do with the cold fusion generator demonstration they have set for tomorrow afternoon. Well, today now, since its three thirty in the morning."

"You mean something will happen at that demonstration?"

"I believe so, yes, I'm sure of it. Perhaps if we are there, with what we know, we can prevent it."

Anthony looked at his watch and did some fast calculations in his head.

"Sure, I can get us there. That demonstration doesn't start until four PM. With two refueling stops and the time zone difference, I'll have us there in time. I can phone some people we know in New Jersey and get us some press credentials too."

"I'll go with you," I said.

"Me too," Shirley added. "Someone's got to keep you guys out of trouble."

Up till now Vito Consoli had simply listened, quietly. Anthony and I both knew that his silence meant approval. Now he asked a question:

"Doctor Katamay, why do you believe there will be a problem?"

"I saw it late last night, on the news. I don't know exactly what they are planning, but perhaps if we are there, we may be able to stop it."

"Stop what? What did you see?"

"They showed a brief film clip of the generator being transported out of a particular building, supposedly for calibrations."

Katamay paused, grasped his coffee cup and took a swig of the now cold liquid. He stood and looked at each of us in turn.

"There is no calibration needed on the generator, and if there were, they couldn't do anything in that particular building."

No one said anything as he paused and continued.

"Because they only do one thing in that area."

"What is that?"

"They make nuclear weapons."

CHAPTER 69

Because it was so early in the morning, Special Agent John Ford caught sight of what turned out to be an IRD vehicle. Having just risen, the sun hung low on the horizon, almost in his eyes as he drove the zig-zag road to the Consoli estate. It was that early morning angle that reflected a sunbeam from the IRD car. It had been parked at the side of the road behind some boulders.

Ford continued driving while glancing in his rear view mirror. The IRD vehicle pulled out on the road, following Ford. It was a Landrover, dark green like a military vehicle. IRD used Landrovers, the FBI used Chevy Blazers.

"Company, Sir?" asked Ford's young aide as he looked at the mirror on his side.

"It would appear so. It's kind of strange that they would be waiting here, near the Consoli property."

"Strange but part of the pattern," the aide replied. "IRD, the Consolis, that ATF agent on suspension, those Russians, some unknown gunmen, they're all dancing around each other. It'll be interesting what we'll find when we put this all together."

The vehicle behind Ford accelerated, closing the gap. A red "bubble gum" emergency light on the dash started sending out strobe beams. Ford ignored it.

"They must have some surveillance going on. Maybe we should stop and talk to them, let them know who we are."

"No, they'll find out we're FBI soon enough," Ford replied. "Besides, I want to talk to the Consolis and the people with them first, before IRD."

Ford accelerated into the hairpin turn, the churning wheels keeping the vehicle from sliding in the hard packed dirt. He nailed the gas right after the turn, accelerated furiously for twenty yards, braked before the next bend in the road and repeated the maneuver. He had paid attention during the combat driving classes at Quantico.

The distance between the vehicles increased. The Landrover almost spun out in a cloud of dust. "That should get them pissed off," Ford said.

"Yeah, but, ah, this road dead-ends at the Consoli gates."

"That's okay. We'll talk to them when we get there. Put your ID on."

They both slipped their FBI badges and ID on silver chains around their necks, in plain view.

The gate appeared barely fifty yards around the curve. Ford waited until the last moment, whipped the wheel to the right and hit the brakes. The big sedan fishtailed and came to a stop across the road, parallel to the gate.

"Nice driving, Sir."

Ford grinned and said, "thanks," and they both got out of the car. They stood next to their vehicle, hands held high, palms open. From a corner of his eye, Ford saw two guards wearing Bowditch Security Uniforms looking at them from inside the gate.

The Landrover that had followed them skidded to a stop, raising a cloud of dust that settled around both vehicles and occupants. All the doors of the IRD vehicle opened at once. Four men erupted out of the Landrover. Each one held an automatic pistol. They were big men, everyone over six feet tall. They wore almost identical light sport jackets and open shirt. They had the heavy, muscle packed look of weight lifters. Ford thought there was a good possibility they used steroids. They just had that look.

The first man out, the one from the front passenger seat, screamed at them, "Federal agents. Don't fucking move, keep your hands high."

"How about that?" Ford said calmly. "So are we, FBI."

The man approached them, looked at Ford's ID, and got in closer, nose-to-nose.

"Why didn't you stop back there, jerkoff?"

"Because you have no cause or authority to stop us."

"We're here as part of an anti-terror investigation, asshole. Now take your little buddy here and get back to whatever faggot high-school club you escaped from."

"'Fraid we can't do that. *You* are now interfering with a federal investigation."

"Fuck you."

"Clever," Ford said.

The man looked like he was seconds away from assaulting the two FBI agents. He took a deep breath and seemed to compose himself for a moment. His answer came from behind clenched teeth.

"I am a supervisory grade IRD agent. We are now going to go in that house, question and arrest certain people and seize some documents. You two shit-birds will stay out of the way until we're done, then I don't give a shit if you butt-fuck each other."

Ford held the other man's gaze. He answered quietly, his steady tone in stark contrast to the man's apoplectic outburst.

"I'm afraid we can't allow that, Supervisor. I don't believe your authority exceeds ours in this case. Of course a court of law will sort it out."

The IRD man smiled, stepped back and laughed outright. "I don't think so. Tell me, are you ready to get into an ass-kicking contest with us?"

Neither Ford nor William replied.

"I didn't think so. We're going to cuff your faggot asses until we're done. Got it?"

Ford didn't reply, just looked away as a cloud of dust rose from the road announcing the approach of more vehicles. A

moment later they came into view, four gunmetal-gray, big
Chevy Blazers. The vehicles pulled up to the gate, boxing
in the IRD Landrover and Ford's sedan. Four men got out
of each of the Chevys, sixteen in all. They were dressed in
identical black combat suits with FBI stenciled in back and
HRT in front. They carried stubby military assault rifles
and nine millimeters in belt holsters. A variety of grenades
and canisters were affixed to their Kevlar vests and secured
with Velcro. They looked like a squad of Marines ready for
Special Ops.

A man wearing Sergeant's chevrons approached Ford and
glanced quickly at the ID around his neck. The four IRD
men had gotten quieter and were cautiously backing away.

"Agent Ford? I'm the officer in charge, Hostage Rescue
Team. We're the backup you requested last night. Is there a
problem here?"

"I don't think so Sergeant. These gentlemen were just
leaving."

CHAPTER 70

We took off at Five AM, Katamay, Shirley and I, and Anthony at the controls. It would be a long flight to Felton Delaware. Thankfully Anthony's plane was much more comfortable for the four of us than a jetliner. The seats were plush and reclined completely, not the pitiful three or four inches of airline seats. Even Anthony was able to relax with the state-of-the-art autopilot.

Even though it was not a jet, this high-tech plane flew as fast as any jetliner. Trouble was it didn't have the range. We had to make two re-fueling stops. Still, we were scheduled to arrive near five PM, a little less than an hour after the demonstration started.

We had discussed and argued about involving the authorities. Problem is, we didn't know who would believe us and stick their necks out so fast and so far. After all, there was only vague evidence brought on by one ATF agent on suspension, one out-of-work Arizona sheriff, a scientist whose records had been expunged and the rich son of a famous mobster. We might eventually convince somebody to look into it, but it wouldn't happen quickly.

We were all pretty tired and slept most of the way, except for Katamay. He sat next to me and at one point I woke up and saw him staring out the window.

"You okay, Doctor?"

The old scientist looked away from the glass and sighed. He frowned as if contemplating a number of answers.

"Am I okay? No, I will never be "okay." Not until I join the ghosts that have gone before me. But I will function, that I will do."

"He was a good man, your son. I was privileged to know him, if only briefly."

"Thank you," he whispered. Then he looked around as if the spirits of his past were somehow embedded in the fuselage of the aircraft.

"I feel him, you know. I feel his presence. I know what he wants me to do, I know by intuition, and intuition is the true voice of God."

I said nothing. There were no answers that made sense. In the seat behind me I heard Shirley's soft snoring. The plane hit an air pocket, bounced a little and Shirley mumbled something. Katamay held my eyes as he continued.

"What I must do, Mister Duval, is prevent the death of many innocent people. I know something will happen and we must prevent it. That is the true meaning of my son's death."

He grasped my hand with his. It felt cold, tough and fragile at the same time. "Thank you," he said, and returned to staring out the window. I felt the plane shudder as Anthony began his descent.

CHAPTER 71

———◆———

Special Agent John Ford sat in the kitchen of the big house at the Consoli estate. Across the table from him LaToya Billings put her head down between her arms and closed her eyes.

"Are you alright, Miss Billings?"

She raised her head, opened her eyes and sighed. "Yeah, I'm good. I just feel like a truck ran me over and I haven't slept in a week."

"The doctor said it's the result of some drug you inhaled while sleeping. You got a lighter dose. The men in the smaller house are just starting to come to now."

"Oh God. Come on, tell me what happened here last night. Don't keep bullshitting me, you a brother, come on dawg."

"You won't need the Ebonics, Miss Billings. I know your position with ATF, and you know mine as an FBI Special Agent. We both have Masters Degrees. The truth is we really don't know at this point exactly what happened, so I'm not bullshitting you…"

"Dawg…" he added with a smile.

"Thanks, I believe you. You know I told you everything, gave you all the documents of my own little private investigation into IRD and these murders."

"And I believe you, Miss Billings," he replied.

From the wide kitchen windows Ford could see the HRT men standing in small groups talking. He had requested them in case he encountered resistance from the Consolis. Routing the IRD goons had been a timely bonus.

Something violent had happened in this house last night, of that, he was sure. There was an oddly placed throw rug in the main room and when he looked under it, there were the remains of a stain that he would bet would turn out to be blood. There were people who had arrived at the house just before him and obviously had done some cleanup work. They were in addition to the two doctors tending the victims of this mysterious knock-out agent. Of course Vito Consoli had suddenly lost his memory along with the ability to speak English.

Ford wasn't very concerned about conflict that had occurred here. It was probably mob-related somehow. Someone else could check that out. Like his grandmother would say, he had bigger fish to fry.

"Miss Billings, I'm going to hold you in protective custody as a material witness."

"What? I don't need no protection."

"I believe you do, Miss Billings. What you have discovered helps a great deal in my investigation but you do not have a clear picture. I have more pieces of this puzzle. Eventually, I will have them all. It's very ugly and reaches into high places. Your death would greatly help these people, and I won't let that happen."

LaToya sighed. "Can I stay here? You can have a couple of your agents watch over me. They do it like that at ATF sometimes."

"Possibly. I would have to discuss it with Mister Consoli. Right now he seems to be able to speak only Italian."

"I'll talk to him," LaToya grinned. "And Anthony. They'll agree."

"Speaking of which, Miss LaToya, they seem to have disappeared along with Mister Duval, Miss Case and two or more of our mysterious Russians."

"Yeah, well I told you where they went. You just ain't listening."

"Oh I'm listening, Miss Billings. Tell me again."

"They went to that new Felton National Laboratory in Delaware. The Department of Energy is supposed to hold a demonstration of that cold fusion generator." Then LaToya told him all the things they had discussed last night before she went to bed and was drugged in the middle of the night.

Ford thought she was being truthful. Anthony's wife, Maria, had corroborated that they left for Delaware in Anthony's plane. The question in Ford's mind was straightforward. Should he chase down what happened here, hoping that it would lead to answers, or should he traipse across the country after Anthony and the others?

"So you're convinced that some destructive event will occur at Felton Lab during this cold fusion demonstration? You're sure that's where they went?"

"Yes, I'm sure. Come on, you probably checked on their destination already."

Actually he had. Information from flight control centers had placed Anthony's destination and confirmed what LaToya told him. LaToya started to speak again. She looked in the doorway behind Ford and stopped mid-sentence.

Vito Consoli stood in the doorway. He stepped inside, his cane making hollow clicking noises on the tile.

"She is telling you the truth," Vito said. He had obviously regained his command of the language. He sounded like an Italian scholar giving a lecture in slightly accented English.

"My son and the people with him are trying to head off something dangerous over there. They don't know exactly what, but there is enough evidence to suggest it may harm many people. They will need your help. You should go to them."

"Shit," LaToya said. "You're going to need a rocket ship to get there in time."

Twelve minutes later an FBI helicopter picked up Ford and his aide at the estate. It took a half hour to get to Luke

Air Force Base near Phoenix. By that time calls had been
made to the Director of the FBI who in turn called his
friend, Senator Weill. Connections with the Senate Armed
Forces Committee didn't hurt either.

Twenty minutes later they were in the back seats of an F-
16 Strike Eagle. After two mid-air refueling stops, they
landed at Dover Air Force Base an hour and a half before
Anthony's plane touched down at Felton Regional airport.

CHAPTER 72

Felton Regional is a small, private airport. Apparently it caters mostly to those having business in nearby Felton National Laboratory. Big planes didn't use the airport. By the time Anthony brought the plane to a stop, there was barely enough runway left. He taxied over to a group of hangars. A man wearing blue overalls told him where to secure the aircraft.

We got off to a cold dampness. An icy drizzle immediately chilled us to the bone. Having come from the heat of a Midwest desert, we had very thin skin even though we all had originated from cold climates. We put on the hodge-podge of sweaters and jackets we had scrounged from the Consolis before taking off.

A red, four-door Mercury pulled up. A man got out of the car. He walked over to us and spoke to Anthony just as he finished securing the plane. He handed him a thick envelope and walked away. Anthony turned to us and said, "Okay, we're good to go, bro."

"What was that about?" I asked him.

"I had Franco call ahead to some people he knows."

Anthony reached in the envelope, pulled out a set of keys and nodded toward the sedan the man had left.

"Ours."

"What'd he do, boost it?" asked Shirley.

Anthony rolled his eyes. "Jeez, cops," he said. "No wonder you get along with my wife, always suspicious. It's rented, legit."

He reached into the envelope and distributed the contents between us. "Press credentials," he explained. "It'll get us in."

Shirley turned to me and smiled sweetly. "Rented also?"

"Misdemeanor," I replied, "Gotta cut some corners."

We got in the sedan. Anthony took the wheel since he had the keys. The drive to Felton National Laboratory was less than ten minutes, barely around the block.

Felton National Lab is completely new, operational for just two years. They tried to give it an ultra-modern, futuristic look. To me it looked garish. Thin spires rose above flat buildings whose exterior was painted to make them look like steel construction. Transparent tubing's flashing with electronic lights lit up the buildings and spires. I suppose the designers had intended it to represent the communication systems of tomorrow. I thought it looked like a schizophrenic's version of Christmas decorations.

Security however, was the old fashioned kind. A brick guard-station straddled the center of the road, operating the gates controlling the flow of traffic on either side with plenty of armed guards on duty. The entire laboratory was surrounded by the standard ten -foot security fence topped with razor-concertina wire bearing the usual alarm devices.

Anthony stopped the car in front of the hydraulically operated barrier next to the security station. Two guards came out and Anthony lowered the driver's window.

"New York Newsday. We're here for the cold fusion demonstration."

"You guys are late," the guard said as he took our credentials. "It started an hour ago."

"Yeah, we know. They decided to send us at the last minute."

The guard nodded and took the credentials inside. He

scanned them into a computer and waited. A few minutes later he came out.

"You know there're two people from New York Newsday already here?"

"Yeah, we know. Like I said, they decided to send us at the last minute."

"Okay, we need to get you guys special passes. Pull up inside that parking area next to that trailer. They'll bring them out."

"Fine, just make it fast."

"Oh it'll be fast, alright," the guard replied and activated a remote control. The barrier lifted. Anthony drove through, turned into the parking area and stopped the car where the guard had pointed.

We sat quietly as the drizzle turned into a light rain. Five minutes passed and nothing happened.

"Typical government shit," Shirley muttered.

But it wasn't. Two big SUV's roared out from behind the trailer. Before any of us could react, the vehicles neatly blocked us in, one in the front the other in back, inches from our bumpers.

Four men and two women jumped out of the SUV's. They wore dark windbreakers with FBI stenciled in white. They carried stubby machine pistols. The woman near the driver's door pointed the muzzle of her weapon at us and screamed:

"Step out of the vehicle. Now. Hands behind your heads, right now."

CHAPTER 73

Once they were out of the vehicle and cuffed, the takedown-team had them face toward where Special Agent John Ford and his aide watched from a parked sedan. Ford recognized the ATF man, Gaston Duval, Anthony Consoli and Shirley Case from their file photos. The fourth prisoner, an old man with a shock of white hair and bushy eyebrows, he had never seen before. Ford guessed him to be Yakov Katamay, the missing scientist from Los Alamos. Up to this point Ford had not been sure the man even existed. All he had was certain documents and information from LaToya Billings.

He watched as the FBI team took the prisoners into the double-wide security trailer. He gave them five minutes then left the sedan and went into the building. Several agents stood around and one of them nodded to a door marked "Conference." Another agent stood outside the door and he opened it for him.

Ford stepped into the conference room. There were no decorations of any kind. The walls were made of the cheapest green plastic covering. The only furniture in the room was a government-issue table and six folding chairs. The prisoners occupied four of those chairs with their cuffed hands resting on the steel surface of the table. Two agents stood on either of the far corners watching them with stony faces.

"Take off their handcuffs and leave us," Ford said.

The agents did as told. Ford took a seat at the table. His aide continued to stand.

"I am Special Agent John Ford," he said. "Let's see if I have this right. Gaston Duval, ATF Lieutenant, Anthony Consoli, Arizona businessman and entrepreneur, Shirley Case, former Boston PD and Sheriff," he continued, pointing to each one in turn until he came to Katamay.

"You Sir, I have never seen, but I believe you are Doctor Yakov Katamay. Am I correct?"

"Yes. So you know who I am? They have not succeeded in totally destroying my records?"

"I have reconstructed a part of them. Enough to lead me to believe there is a conspiracy actively suppressing some form of activities at Los Alamos."

"The activity," Shirley cut in, "is going on right now, just a few yards away."

"Miss Case, holding a globally televised demonstration of an emerging technology doesn't strike me as suppression."

Now it was Gast's turn to cut in. "They're going to do something in there. We have information on some plan they call the Tinian Protocol. It's to be activated now, during this four-hour demonstration. It's already going on for an hour so we don't have much time."

"I'm aware of that Mister Duval. I spoke to Miss LaToya Billings this morning."

"You were at my house this morning?" Anthony said. "How…"

"F-16 Mister Consoli. Much faster than your plane."

"Well then you know. Do something. Stop this conference. Let Doctor Katamay look inside that thing. He designed and built it."

"It's not that easy. The entire world is out there, live. Every TV station is tuned in from Al-Jezeira to CNN and Fox News. I can't just step in, supersede the Department of

Energy and cancel everything in front of the whole world without something substantial. All I have is vague intercepted messages and allegations. Have you something more substantial, Doctor Katamay?"

"Yes, if you accept who I am."

"Supposing I do?"

"Well then, here it is. Has your investigation reached Brookhaven National Lab on Long Island and Doctor Jawaharla Bhindra?"

"I have two agents outside his office now but we have not questioned him yet. They are awaiting my instructions."

"Very well then, let me give you the basics. I built only two cold fusion generators. One was installed in a demonstration vehicle that we managed to smuggle out of the lab before they started killing us and I was forced to flee. They have the other one. They're using it for that demonstration right now. Here's the problem: the generator is complete and operational. There are no calibrations or adjustments required. It is run by Nano-Bots servers endowed with Artificial Intelligence, and plasma conduits. It repairs itself. Even destroying it is not easy and it cannot breakdown nor can it be adjusted. So the question is, why did they bring it to Brookhaven Lab? What did they do to it over there?"

"What do you think they did, Doctor?"

"I think they planted something inside that will cause a violent malfunction with loss of lives. Their intent is to discredit the process. Get your agents to link up Doctor Bhindra with me by speakerphone. I know him. We used to work together in that Lab a decade ago. We'll get answers."

Ford nodded and activated a speaker cell phone.

"Johnston, Franklin?"

"Yes Sir."

"Is Doctor Bhindra there?"

"He's in his administrative office, right outside the security perimeter. We have the building under surveillance and he hasn't left."

"Go in, get him on this phone."

"Alright, standby."

They heard the noise of movements, doors opening, and walking, then knocking and silence.

"Doctor Bhindra?" came over the speakerphone several times with no reply to be heard.

"Are you sure he's in his office?" Ford asked.

"Positive," came the reply. "We saw him go in, there's only one way out and his car is still parked there. Do we have your authorization to break down the door?"

"Do it."

The speaker carried the booming sound of heavy blows followed by the splintering of wood. Then, curses, exclamations and a muffled "Oh God."

"What's going on there, Franklin?"

"Sir, he's dead, killed himself."

"What? Are you sure?"

"I've been doing this a long time, Sir. I don't need a CSI team. He shot himself in the head with a small caliber pistol. Between the small caliber and heavy sound insulation, we didn't hear the shot. We're notifying the local authorities and we'll work with them."

Ford disconnected the phone. Katamay held his head in his hands. No one said anything. Katamay raised his head and spoke. His face held the tortured look of one confronting unending agony. He seemed to have aged a decade overnight. His voice was thin, reedy.

"Agent Ford, if you have the authority, you must let me examine that generator. Whatever has been done is so terrible that Bhindra killed himself rather than bear the burden of guilt."

Ford knew he had arrived at a career-changing moment. Whatever he decided or failed to act upon, would define the rest of his life. It also might end the lives of many others.

Contrary to his placid appearance and calm demeanor, Ford had the volcanic quality of a born leader. Like the most effective CEO or military commander, he didn't falter when tough decisions had to be made.

"Let's do it. Right now," he said as he rose from the table.

CHAPTER 74

One thing you could say about FBI Special Agent John Ford: Once he made up his mind, he didn't diddle around. My initial impression was that he had come out of Nerd Central with that sidekick of his. Now I saw his command side and had to reevaluate what I thought of him.

The aide called for the agents who had been waiting in the other room. Ford barked out instructions and orders at light speed. We were all hustled into one of the Chevy Blazers and joined a little convoy of FBI vehicles. Moments later we stopped in front of the building where the demonstration was being held. It was a scene of barely controlled chaos.

The cold fusion generator demonstration was held in a large auditorium named after some scientist I never heard of. Two wide front doors were being held open with brick doorstops. People streamed out of the building, hustled out by a variety of uniformed Laboratory guards, Department of Energy personnel and FBI agents. The people being removed from the building were all members of the press. They spoke excitedly into microphones and cameras held by technicians in various states of bewilderment. They carried everything from tiny, unobtrusive digital audio recorders to six-foot television cameras on mobile carts manned by two or three people. FBI agents and Laboratory guards fended off questions and protests and channeled the crowds toward a field that served as a parking lot. The rain added an element of discomfort and increased the confusion as everyone tried to cover their equipment and themselves.

Two agents shouldered a path inside for us among the crowds being pushed out. By the time we reached the demonstration stage in the auditorium, the last of the press had been routed outside. The people who had been running the demonstration were rounded up in a far corner of the auditorium and kept there by two agents.

Katamay asked for a tool set and someone ran out to get it. The old man climbed the stage to where the generator stood on a stainless steel table. He disconnected a heavy cable from the outlet built into the side of the device. The generator itself was a twin of the one I had found under the hood of the Hummer, two days ago. We surrounded the trunk-size machine.

Ford looked pretty calm considering the risk he was taking. In front of the entire nation and the world, he had stopped this demonstration and evacuated the auditorium. If this turned out to be a bust, he would be made permanent gopher at the Dunghole, North Dakota FBI office—for life.

"They tampered with it. There's no doubt," Katamay said.

"How do you know?" Ford asked.

"An end cap has been added to give it more room. They put something in there."

Now a lab technician appeared wheeling a Craftsman toolbox, the kind auto mechanics use, but so clean it was probably sterilized. Katamay opened a drawer, took out a small ratchet kit and began removing small fasteners recessed in the surface. Ford took another tool and helped him. Moments later Katamay jiggled the metal and the end section of the generator came off. We all leaned forward to get a look at the insides.

The generator looked like nothing I had ever seen. It was so strange, it seemed unreal. It reminded me of some sort of

Science Fiction movie set depicting a graphic artist's view of what alien machinery would look like. At the end where Katamay had removed the cover, a thick cylinder the size and shape of a large fire extinguisher, occupied the space. It was the only thing that had even a vague resemblance to anything I was familiar with. Solid state circuitry connected it to the rest of the generator. Three digital readout gauges were imbedded in the center of the cylinder. One gauge read 44, the one next to it was 03 and dropped one number each second and the last one must be timing tenths of a second because the numbers blurred incomprehensibly as they changed. The middle gauge hit 0 and restarted at 60. The gauge on the left dropped to 43. Whatever this thing was it counted down toward zero.

Katamay reached over and ran his hand over the cylinder. A mixture of shock and anger ran across his face. He said something in Russian that sounded like a nasty curse.

"These vicious, vicious fools," he continued in English. "They deserve to burn in hell for this."

"What is that Doctor?" Ford asked. "It's an explosive device of some kind isn't it?"

"Oh yes, it most certainly is an explosive device, the most dangerous kind in the world. What you would commonly call an atomic bomb."

CHAPTER 75

Katamay's words hung in the air, grabbing us like a malignancy. We looked at him and no one said anything. Some things are so outrageous they stunt your reactions as if dealing with the most banal of affairs. It was Anthony who broke the silence first.

"You gotta be kidding me, doc. Aren't nuclear bombs supposed to be big?"

"That's what they work on in that building in Brookhaven Lab, out on Long Island. Miniaturization of nuclear weapons. You've heard of suitcase bombs?"

We nodded yes. No one spoke and Katamay continued.

"This thing is the next generation of weapons, probably somewhere between twenty and forty kilotons. A bit larger than the Hiroshima bomb."

"Wait a minute," Ford said. "Aren't you supposed to have a certain amount of Plutonium to reach critical mass? That thing is too small to hold all that plutonium plus the triggering devices, right?"

"Wrong. It's a common misconception. Gathering a critical mass of plutonium is not necessary to make an atom bomb. You can take a much smaller piece and subject it to a neutron density equivalent to that found at the temperatures and pressure inside plutonium at critical mass.

When I worked there, they were very close to making a condensed type of plutonium called PL-9. With the advent of supercomputers to do calculations that were previously impossible and metallurgical and chemical advances, we can reach critical mass with small amounts of PL-9 using new alloys and explosives."

Now I understood what went on, what all this had been about. I didn't know exactly who, but I understood the why of it.

"Don't you see?" I said. "First they tried to suppress it, but too many people got involved and it was all going to come out. Now they're going to discredit it. That's the Tinian Protocol they're talking about in those dispatches we intercepted. Look, Chernobyl was a pretty deadly incident. It scared the American public, but they attributed it to Russian incompetence. Sorry, doctor."

"You're quite right."

"Then Three Mile Island came along, and although only a couple of technicians lost their lives, it scared the hell out of the American public and killed the nuclear industry. There hasn't been a new nuclear plant built in over thirty years. Now picture this: Right in the middle of a cold fusion demonstration, with the whole world watching, the generator goes up in a mushroom cloud and vaporizes a million people. That's the end of cold fusion research forever."

No one said anything. As we watched, the minutes gauge dropped to 42.

"We'll get a bomb squad here fast. You can help us, Doctor."

"No."

"No?"

"I will help you, but you cannot disarm it. This is not some movie where a bomb squad person comes in and cuts a wire and everything is good. This is cutting-edge, solid state circuitry. If you tamper with it, it goes off. There's a seismic sensor attached to it. If you jar it too heavily it goes off. When that timer reaches zero, it will detonate. That is its purpose and nothing can stop it."

Agent Ford pulled out his cell phone. His hand shook, almost imperceptibly, but it shook. Shirley's complexion had paled a few degrees and I was as scared as I'd ever been in my life.

Ford hit a button on his cell phone, identified himself and spoke.

"Red Zone One Alert. Imminent nuclear detonation within the continental United States." Some squawking came through the phone and he severed the connection.

"I have a Blackhawk on standby at the Milton office. They'll be here in twenty minutes. We'll load it on there and…"

"And do what?" Anthony cut in. "I know the Blackhawk: top speed 165 miles per hour. The bomb will go off twenty miles from here. It might as well go off right here. Population density in either direction is the same."

"We'll fly it to Dover Air Force base."

"You'll get there just when it's about to go off. If you have a few minutes to spare, you'll have to find a suicide jockey with a ready jet, and you got to do it in under forty two minutes. It'll never happen."

Ford looked sick, until Anthony spoke again.

"But I have a way to do it."

The digital read out dropped another number. 41 minutes to detonation.

CHAPTER 76

"Five minutes from here," Anthony said, "You've got available the fastest production turbo-prop plane in the world: mine. It's an American-Lear ALX-11 with a top speed of 435 knots. That's a little over 500 miles per hour. If we move right now, we can have that thing 150 miles out at sea, drop it and be 100 miles away when it goes off."

We all looked at him. Ford stared at the generator with its open cover. The glow of the blinking digital readout washed the interior of the device in a dim green light as if mocking us. At that moment I think it began to really sink in on all of us that we were most likely doomed.

Ford turned away from the generator and looked at Anthony.

"Will it really go that fast?"

"Actually a bit faster."

"Let's haul ass. We'll work out the details on the way."

It did my heart good to see Ford and his aide swing into action again. The two agents acted as if they were possessed.

Four FBI men carried the generator from the demonstration hall to the outside door. Someone had driven an SUV right up the steps and opened the vehicle's sliding side doors. We all piled into another SUV and rocketed to

Felton Regional Airport. A phalanx of FBI and local police squad cars cleared every corner and intersection for our approach.

William drove the vehicle we rode in. Ford sat in the passenger seat. He had turned around to face us. We sat in the two back seats, Anthony on my left, Shirley to my right, Katamay in the second back seat.

"You know," Katamay said. "You cannot just drop the generator out of the plane."

"Why not?"

"There is a seismic sensor connected to the bomb. If it registers a shock greater than normal handling jolts, it will detonate the device."

"I have four sport parachutes on board. We'll rig it so it floats down on a chute."

"I'm coming with you, Anthony," I spoke up.

"Man, am I glad you said that. I was having trouble figuring out how to do this alone."

"I'm coming too," Shirley said.

"No," Katamay said. "I'm an old man, I will go."

"Hold it, hold it," Ford said from the front. "I am the only one who will go. It's my job, my duty."

"Whoa, whoa! Hold your horses boys and girls," Anthony said. "The only ones coming are me and Gast. We got a fuel problem. We'll make it back to the coast on fumes. Those engines take JP3 fuel and they don't have it at that little airport."

"That is not acceptable," Ford said. "Mister Duval is not going. I am."

"Not acceptable my ass," Anthony replied. "Gast and I are both jump qualified. We're former Airborne Rangers. If it comes down to it, we can bail out. I don't need your untrained ass dragging me down. Got it?"

Anthony's a good guy but sometimes he can be a bit pushy. I held my breath and waited for Ford's reply. The FBI man just nodded and turned away.

I admired Ford for that. Even in life or death situation I've seen leaders allow their egos to guide their decisions, sometimes with disastrous results. Ford had made the right choice.

The aide had phoned ahead and airport personnel had already moved Anthony's plane to the runway and started the engines. Air traffic control and the Coast Guard had been alerted. All planes were diverted out of the area while the Coast Guard ordered nearby ships to port.

We drove right to the end of the runway and got out of the vehicles. Anthony opened the plane while the FBI agents loaded the generator in the cargo area.

I felt a tug on my side and turned. Shirley stood there, her hands about my arm. The airport lights reflected in the moistness of her eyes.

"Be careful," she said. "Come back to me. I love you, you know."

"I love you, Shirley," I said, and I kissed her trying to convey my love in that one brief touch. It was all the time we had. When we took off, less than five minutes had elapsed.

The digital gauge on the bomb read 37 minutes to detonation.

CHAPTER 77

Anthony didn't waste a solitary second. Soon as his rear hit the pilot's seat he cranked the throttles to maximum. I had barely sat down when the acceleration pushed me into the plush seat. Sure, plush as a coffin, I thought. Twenty seconds later we were airborne.

The plane climbed through a low ceiling of rain clouds. Night had fallen and the darkness was absolute until we broke above the clouds. A full moon and panoply of stars littered the sky like an omen of success–I hoped.

Anthony climbed to fifteen thousand feet, set the autopilot and went back to help me rig the generator to the parachute. The air was still and the flying smooth. The plane was designed for comfort as well as speed so vibrations were dampened. There were no sensations indicating the velocity of the machine, yet we flew at over five hundred miles per hour.

We cut the straps designed to tie a human body to the parachute and secured them on the four carrying loops built in the body of the generator. While Anthony double-checked the fasteners, I rigged the parachute's ripcord to an eyehook fixed in the interior fuselage. Soon as we pushed the generator out the door, the ripcord would pull out and the parachute open.

We stood back and double-checked the rigging we had just completed.

"Fucking Rube Goldberg all the way," Anthony muttered.

I wondered what it would be like if we screwed up and the bomb went off under our noses. Would we feel anything as our bodies dispersed into component atoms and electrons at the speed of light?

"Don't worry about it, Anthony. If it doesn't work nobody's going to sue us."

"Cute," he said. Then we both returned to the cockpit.

The digital read 27 minutes. That gave us eight minutes of flying, one minute to kick it out the door and eighteen minutes to put a hundred miles between us and ground zero.

CHAPTER 78

Shirley Case sat in the control tower of Felton Regional Airport and bit her fingernails. It was a nasty habit she had developed in the tension-laced environment of Boston PD. It had taken her years to ditch the habit, and now it had returned.

She hadn't exaggerated when she told Gast she loved him. She had found something in the ATF agent. She admired his casual attitude that didn't take anything away from his drive for justice. There was a strength to him that she yearned for. More than anything else, she wanted him back. He had come along and become her future at a time when she believed she didn't have any.

The FBI had taken over the control tower as a temporary command post. It was only three stories off the ground, but held all the communication equipment needed. She sat with Katamay on hard, barely cushioned seats holding cups of vending machine coffee. Ford and his aide were seated at the communication consoles and two other agents stood by, ready to do anything Ford needed. They caught each other continuously glancing at the digital clocks, counting the passing seconds. A constant stream of radio chatter passed through the speakers, most of it from aircrafts and their controllers. Occasionally Ford would direct some question at a distant control center and receive an answer. Mostly, they waited.

Shirley felt the time stretch out before her, impossibly slow, yet paradoxically fast. She stood and walked to the communication console where Ford sat. He looked up and smiled at her.

"They'll make it, Miss Case. Those are two competent guys out there."

"Thanks, I know," she replied, and drifted toward the wide plate-glass window. It was dark outside, and the night held that dreariness unique to a New England late-fall, rainy evening.

She heard some chatter from the radio and Ford responded. She didn't distinguish the words until the FBI agent said, "shit!"

Shirley stepped back to the console. Ford looked up at her and she knew something was wrong.

"What?"

The FBI man shook his head and said nothing.

"What, Godamnit? What the hell's wrong "

"It's the Constellation," he whispered.

"What Constellation? What the hell are you talking about?"

Ford looked up at her and she saw the frustration in his eyes.

"The Southern Constellation, newest flagship of Atlantic Cruise Lines. It's less than five miles from where they're going to drop that thing and there're four thousand people on board."

CHAPTER 79

Somewhere in the Atlantic, off the Delaware coast.

Captain Dimitri Costa made a final adjustment to his bowtie and checked himself out once again. At age sixty he looked positively grand in the tuxedo-type uniform. This was captain's night on board the Southern Constellation cruise ship. The passengers would be in formal dress, expecting to meet the captain and he would not disappoint them. A regal bearing and social skills were almost as important to the master of a big, modern cruise vessel, as seamanship.

Satisfied with his appearance, Captain Costa stepped toward the door of his suite when the buzzing of the communicator at his waist interrupted him.

"Captain here."

"Sir, this is Lieutenant Davis, Officer of the Day. You better come up to the bridge fast, sir. We have a situation here."

"On my way."

Costa frowned as he rushed down the hallway. To call a Captain to the bridge on Captain's night required a real-life emergency. In calm weather with all ship systems functioning at top efficiency, he couldn't think what that might be. He wasn't particularly worried. The Southern

Constellation wasn't just the largest cruise ship built since the Queen Elizabeth II. It was the most modern and luxurious. In the age of terrorism, it was also the safest. Even though the Southern Constellation was on its maiden cruise, it had undergone a month-long shakedown voyage. The crew comprised the best picks from twenty-two countries. They were well trained and more than just competent: the best ship, the best crew and perfect weather. Captain Costa was supremely confident that no situation could arise that this superb crew and ship could not handle.

Yet, as he made his way toward the bridge, the captain had a disturbing thought:

They had said that about the Titanic.

CHAPTER 80

I looked at the digital timer and it read 20 minutes to detonation. I had two minutes to open the door and shove the generator out. That left us 18 minutes to get the hell out of town.

Anthony and I had both put on the flight suits he kept on board. I hooked up the built-in oxygen mask and Anthony depressurized the cabin. Fifteen thousand feet was high enough to risk some kind of altitude-caused physical problem. The oxygen masks would prevent that.

I triggered the manual override that would allow the cargo door to be opened in flight. I turned the lever and pulled the door open. The roar of the air stream filled the cabin like a living force. I felt the 500-plus miles per hour windstorm trying to suck my body out the door and the safety harness restrained me. The temperature instantly dropped to what I guessed was somewhere below zero.

Outside, the moon reflected a silver glow from the clouds below. The plane shook and vibrated in every inch of steel as the open door upset the aerodynamic equilibrium, cranking the decibel level still higher.

I held the stanchion with one hand, my feet braced against the raised lip of the exit floor. The generator was set up on two steel boxes that were inches higher than the exit.

All I had to do was push it out and make sure that the rigging didn't snag anywhere. Sounded easy but in reality it was a bit difficult.

The generator was heavy and the case didn't slide well against the surface of the steel boxes supporting it. I pushed, it moved a foot and the rigging snagged. I freed it up, pushed again and it was almost out the door into the black void of the waiting jet stream.

All my instincts screamed to get rid of that infernal thing. Push it out of the plane as if by just being out of sight it would lose its power to turn me back into the basic building blocks of the universe. I tasted the rubber of the mask, smelled the chemicals producing the oxygen. In spite of the high-altitude artic cold permeating the cabin, I was sweating in the flight suit.

I braced myself to give the final push when I was grabbed by the waist and pulled away. I stumbled back and leaned against the bulkhead. Anthony let go of me, grabbed the straps holding the generator and pulled it back inside. I screamed at him, trying to override the din of the jet stream from the open cargo door.

"Stop, are you crazy? We got less than eighteen minutes."

He shook his head, strained against the weight of the generator and brought it back fully inside. I grabbed his arm and he pushed me away so hard I stumbled and fell back. By the time I got up, Anthony had closed the door. The cabin was quiet again.

"What the hell's wrong with you, Anthony? We got to get that thing out of this plane."

"No, no, we can't."

"We can't? If we don't, we're going to die, motherfucker. You understand?"

"There's a cruise ship right below us. There're four thousand people on board."

Anthony's eyes were wild, filled with rage, frustration and fear. He took a deep breath closed his eyes, calming himself before speaking.

"We can't do it, Gast. I set a course farther out into the ocean. We have enough time to save these people."

The whole thing raced through my mind. Anthony was right. We couldn't kill four thousand innocents just to save our miserable asses. Yet, there had to be a way, I sensed it.

Katamay's words came back to me: *Intuition is the voice of God.* A psychologist would say it's your subconscious working overtime and providing an answer into your brain. I would rather think Katamay is right.

Wherever it came from, the answer popped into my head. I had a way out, our only chance.

CHAPTER 81

On board the Summer Constellation.

Like any good sea captain, Dimitri Costa was sensitive to any movements or changes in the progress of his ship. He sensed it through the soles of his feet on the deck and the very metal of the walls. As he made his way down the hall and up the stairs to the bridge, he felt the almost imperceptible changes indicating both an increase in speed and course heading. Whatever the emergency was, the Bridge Officer had deemed it sufficiently serious and urgent to warrant such changes without the captain's prior approval.

Captain Costa entered the bridge and a junior officer immediately announced, "Captain on bridge."

Costa had graduated from Kings Park Merchant Marine Academy in the sixties and promptly enlisted in the navy. He spent four years in various US Navy ships but never saw combat. He didn't consider a tour of duty off the coast of North Vietnam as combat. No one ever shot at him as they hurled tons of high explosive shells into the distant shores where unseen enemies lurked.

In the wartime navy he saw firsthand the value of discipline. Now at the peak of his career as master of one of the world's largest passenger ship, he had instilled in his crew a discipline and courtesy akin to that found in the military.

"Carry on," he replied as his first officer greeted him.

"Good evening, sir. We have a serious problem. We received an urgent message from Norfolk Coast Guard of an impending event in our area. They ordered us away on a course heading. I ordered the course change immediately at full speed."

"What kind of event, Number One?"

"Sir, they said possible nuclear detonation."

"Good God! Have you authenticated this? It could be a hoax."

"Yes, sir, I have. I called back Norfolk via closed link satellite. It's as real as can be."

"When? How close?"

"They're not sure, but they estimated less than a half hour. They basically told us to get the hell out of the area fast as we could. I summoned all officers to the bridge for instructions."

"Good work. You did right. Now order emergency speed."

Emergency speed would stop any power drain not essential to propelling the ship. By shutting down those systems, the vessel would reach a speed somewhere around 34 Knots–about 40 miles per hour.

Costa filled his mind with the myriad tasks needed to secure his ship and thousands of passengers. He didn't want to dwell on the unthinkable event approaching his command. That would all come later–if there would be a later for any of them.

CHAPTER 82

Above the Atlantic, on board Anthony Consoli's aircraft.

"HALO," I said.

"What?"

"HALO, don't you remember Fort Benning, the Rangers?"

Anthony frowned. I could see his brain working as the solution came for him. HALO stands for High Altitude Low Opening. This is a unique jump strategy used by Special Forces to insert teams rapidly into difficult areas without being detected. Basically, you jump and open your chute at the last possible moment, just a few hundred feet above ground. Anthony and I had done one of those jumps at Fort Benning, Georgia, at the Special Warfare School.

Of course when they say High Altitude, they're talking about thirty thousand feet or better. Still, 15,000 did the trick for me.

"Here's how we do it, Anthony. Can you set the autopilot to fly at sea level?"

"I can make that mother sing and dance if I want to."

"Okay, we leave the bomb in the plane. We do a HALO so we're in the water in a few minutes. You set autopilot to continue at full speed for a couple of minutes, then descend to sea level and hold it there so it flies just above the wave.

It's either going to run out of gas and crash and the bomb goes off, or the timer reaches zero and boom!"

"Why sea level?"

"To avoid an aerial burst. That would be worse. Meanwhile we're in the water. There should be enough time for the plane to put sufficient distance between us and the blast."

Anthony's face lit up. "Yeah, yeah, it'll work." He dashed to the rear compartment where he kept the chutes. He pulled out two and tossed one at me. While I strapped on the chute he ran to the flight station and programmed the autopilot. Meanwhile, I had almost finished putting on my chute. I helped Anthony with his and we checked each other's rigging. Anthony held up a device and strapped it to his arm.

"We gotta hook up. I only have one altimeter." He took a strap and linked us together. Next, he pinned another device the size of a water glass to his suit and gave me one for mine. It was made out of sturdy sealed plastic with a big bulb on top encased in a transparent hard material.

"EPIRBS," he said. "I forgot what it stands for, but contact with water activates it. There's a strobe light on top for visual contact and it emits a signal so the Coast Guard can find us."

Anthony took a bundle that looked like a wrapped-up sleeping bag and attached it to his leg with a three-foot strap.

"Life raft," he explained. "Inflates automatically when it comes in contact with water."

"Damn, Anthony. For somebody who flies over the desert all the time, you're pretty well equipped for water survival."

"Learn your geography, Gast. Arizona is next to California, the West Coast, Catalina Island, Hawaii. I fly over the Pacific all the time."

One final check and we were good to go. "Ready, bro?" I asked Anthony. He nodded and opened the door. The roaring, icy jet stream filled the cabin again.

I reached out and grasped Anthony's hand and we jumped into the black maelstrom outside the aircraft.

My last view of the interior of the cabin was the glow of the timer in the generator.

It read 9 minutes.

CHAPTER 83

On board the Southern Constellation.

Seven minutes had passed since Captain Dimitri Costa had started issuing emergency orders to his officers. During that time they had begun the task of moving all passengers to secure areas. In this case the word "secure" didn't apply in its full meaning.

Officers and crew spread out throughout the ship, herding passengers into the Grand Ballroom, the Central Dining Room, the Neptune Theater and other large areas that had no windows.

Costa ordered one drink served per guest and the rest soft drinks and juice. He didn't want some drunk stirring a panic. The kitchens were ordered to serve sandwiches and snacks. The ovens and burners were electric and all power had been diverted to the engines.

Throughout the ship, the chimes sound of the intercom sounded, alerting all that the captain was about to make an announcement. Gradually the controlled din of several thousand people hustled into places they had not expected to be in, began to die down. Everyone strained to hear the captain's explanation for this unusual turn of events.

"Good evening ladies and gentlemen, this is Captain Dimitri Costa. Tonight, I had hoped to be among you enjoying this magnificent evening at sea. Unfortunately, just ten minutes ago we received a warning from the United States Coast Guard station at Norfolk, Virginia. They warned us that an explosion of some sort is imminent to our south. We are steaming away at maximum speed and expect to be safe when and if this event occurs. On the Southern Constellation as with every American Cruise Lines ship, your safety is our first concern. While we expect no serious damage or injuries from this explosion, there is the possibility of flying debris. This is why we have ordered everyone to assembly areas that have no outside exposure. We regret this unexpected turn of event and hope the emergency will soon be over. In the meantime, refreshments and food will be served throughout the length of this event. We have some great performers on board for this cruise. They will be putting on impromptu entertainment for your pleasure. If there is anything you desire or need, please speak to one of our personnel and we will make every effort to accommodate you within the bounds of safety. Thank you."

The captain put down the microphone and wiped his brow. In spite of the perfect temperature maintained on the bridge, he was sweating heavily.

Reports now began to filter through the ship's intercom system to the captain on the bridge. All doors to the decks and external areas, secure. All window storm shutters closed. Deck equipment had been secured and all fire and emergency teams were on station. Even the steel hurricane shutters had been lowered hydraulically to protect the wide bridge viewing windows. The ship was as ready as possible.

Captain Costa looked at the ocean through the panoramic view of the full color monitors. The monitors were linked to six cameras placed at strategic angles around the ship.

The sea was flat, placid as an artist's rendering of the stillest of waters. The bow cut effortlessly through the calm ocean and the ship's progress appeared deceptively slow. Behind the vessel, a wake stretched out until it vanished in the gloom of the overcast night. It held a slight glow as the four giant propellers churned up tons of microscopic plankton, giving the disturbed water a pale luminescence.

Captain Costa couldn't help but think of a clichéd phrase: the calm before the storm.

CHAPTER 84

A 500 MPH plus air stream sucked us out of the airplane the moment we let go of the stanchions. The wind hit us like an invisible living force, tumbling us over and over until we finally got in a head-down attitude.

The first few thousand feet rushed through in seconds. The nylon strap kept us linked as we plummeted, head-first, arms at our side for the least air-resistance and fastest downward velocity.

Moonlight reflected from the clouds rushing up at us and the very sight of their wispy presence gave us a bearing, calmed us. Then we plunged through the cloud layer and it was like being flung through a fog headfirst at hundred of miles per hour. All visibility vanished and a primordial survival instinct screamed in my mind.

Moments later we passed through the cloud layer and emerged into the absolute darkness of the atmosphere below. Moon and starlight failed to penetrate the cloud layer above, leaving us suspended in Stygian empty darkness where the only sensations were the violent rushing of air around our bodies and the emptiness in the pits of our stomachs.

We fell head first, arms at our side like Superman flying in the movies. I imagined the sea rushing up at us with blood-boiling speed, ready to kill us instantly for the most minute of error.

All the what-ifs ran through my mind. What if the altimeter was off and we crashed into the ocean? At those speeds the water was like a wall and would obliterate our bodies. Would we have time to feel the pain? Would it be a moment of excruciating agony followed by the nothingness of instant death? Would the bomb go off prematurely, maybe far enough away that we wouldn't be instantly vaporized, but instead agonizingly roasted alive while we plummeted as screaming, living cinders?

I tried not to think, attempting to fantasize. I was Superman on a mission to save Earth. Then Anthony yanked on our link and gave a thumbs-up. We broke away and I pulled my ripcord. I felt a giant hand snap my body as the parachute opened and I drifted down in the darkness. Seconds later the water appeared below. I splashed down.

Even before it penetrated the flight suit, the icy water of the Atlantic chilled me to the quick. For a moment the shock of it took my breath away. I tore off my helmet and oxygen mask and swam away from the parachute that was now falling gently to the surface. It would be too ironic to have come all this way to drown, dragged under by billowing silk and entangling straps.

The life jacket built into the suit inflated automatically via a CO_2 cartridge. The EPIRB pinned to my shoulder started sending out blinding strobes every four seconds. Both had been activated by contact with the water.

The surface of the sea was still as a pond. It was one of those nights where no breeze stirs the air, as if the ocean wants to lull its victims into feeling safe before destroying them in a violent storm.

I looked around and saw a flash from a nearby strobe: Anthony's EPIRB. I swam toward it. When I got to him, the life raft had already inflated and he had climbed inside. He held out his hand. I grabbed it. He pulled me in.

The raft was a fully inflatable model made for compact storage in a small airplane. Unlike the ones on ships that

Patrick Astre

often had hard surface flooring, this one had a tough plastic base that inflated automatically with the rest of the craft. It was an octagon with air-filled sides five feet high. Having been designed to hold four adults, it left us with room to spare. The raft had a roof on it that consisted of opaque plastic hung on flexible struts that composed a dome of sorts. It was sturdy enough to keep us out of the water, at least under normal conditions.

"Welcome to club Med," Anthony said.

I leaned my head back against the inflated wall and didn't reply.

"You think we'll make it?"

I had thought about that a lot and told Anthony, "Depends on three things: First, how far away your plane gets. Second, how close to sea level it descends before the thing goes off, and last, how powerful it actually is. Katamay said twenty to fifty kilotons. That's a big spread. If it comes in on the lower end, we got a chance."

"Hey, you remember CBR training?"

I remembered. Ranger training included CBR, Chemical–Biological–Radiological. I also remembered what the instructors at Fort Bragg had said to do if you find yourself too close to a tactical nuclear weapon blast: Squat down on the ground, put your head between your legs and kiss your ass goodbye.

"Yeah, I remember, Anthony. The three stages of a nuclear detonation."

First stage was the intense, radiation-packed light of the explosion. To look at it without protection was like looking at the sun, blindness, possibly permanent would result. The second stage was the noise, much slower than the light, like seeing summer lightning in the distance and not hearing the thunder for several seconds. The noise by itself was harmless, except it presaged the coming of the real destruction. The third stage–the blast wave, a wall of superheated air moving out in all directions with enough power to set wood on fire instantly, obliterate buildings and uproot trees. The power dissipated with distance.

The original plan had been to put over a hundred miles between us and the detonation. A misplaced cruise ship had changed all that. We probably wouldn't even have fifty miles so the real survival factor was the strength of the device.

I looked out the opening in the plastic dome of the raft. Something splashed nearby and a phosphorescent streak ran under the raft from some unknown sea creature's passing. There was a crisp, briny tang to the air that smelled clean and natural. In different circumstances I would have enjoyed it.

"Better look inside and down to the floor," Anthony said. "You don't want to be looking out there when that thing goes off."

"What if it doesn't go off?"

"I'll buy you a beer, okay? Besides, we got another thing to worry about that they didn't have to deal with in CBR land training."

"What?"

"The Tsunami effect. When that bomb goes off at sea level, it's going to make one hell of a wave."

I started to reply, but at that moment the sky lit up brighter than anything I had ever experienced. I silently thanked Anthony for telling me to look down on the floor. I closed my eyes but the light was a living presence. It was as if my eyelids were translucent membranes. I felt the heat of it through the thin plastic raft and feared for a moment that it could even melt it. A tiny portion of the sun had been created here on Earth, so close that it might yet turn us to cinders.

CHAPTER 85

———◆———

Onboard the Southern Constellation.

It was still and silent on the bridge of the big cruise ship. It was as if Captain Costa and his officers could stave off disaster by merely being quiet, like children hiding under the covers could make imaginary monsters disappear. All eyes were on the rear monitor, the one whose camera was on the stern, toward where the detonation would take place.

As they watched, a sudden glow appeared on the horizon. The light rebounded from the cloud cover, lighting it in blazing white, expanding as rapidly as if a giant flashbulb had gone off nearby. There was a quality of fantasy about it, as if someone had inserted a science fiction video with really good special effects into the monitor.

The rear camera, unable to transmit the massive amount of light, blanked the monitor in stark white. Gradually, seconds later, the brilliant light reverted to a glow as darkness crept in, reclaiming the night again.

"Range?" Captain Costa said.

The bridge technician hesitated a moment as he ran the computer program that would approximate the distance from the source of light to the ship.

"Forty-seven miles, sir."

Costa let out an explosive sigh. He hadn't even been

aware he had been holding his breath. He didn't know very much about nuclear explosions. They just didn't teach that kind of stuff to cruise ship captains, but it seemed to him that that kind of distance would impart a measure of safety to his ship and passengers.

No one said anything. The bridge was so well insulated that the only sound was a low whisper from the hot-air heating system.

A rushing hiss of static came through the ship's communications systems as the electromagnetic energy of the blast washed over the antennas and electronic components. The rumbling of the explosion passed through the ship. Passengers and crews stopped whatever they were doing as the noise resonated through the great rooms and chambers. It had barely diminished when the blast wave hit.

CHAPTER 86

It seemed an eternity, but only had been a couple of seconds before the light subsided. It went out slowly, not like turning out a lamp, but as if a rheostat had been turned down so the light dimmed gradually until it darkness returned.

"Guess it exploded after all," Anthony said.

"You think?"

There was a new quality to the air, a sort of psychic anticipation, the kind I imagine people feel just before a big earthquake or volcanic eruptions. Animals are sensitive to it. There are hundreds of stories about animals running away and dogs barking as if to warn their owners of the impending catastrophe. I swear, I felt some of that now and before I could say anything to Anthony, the noise came.

The rendering of the nuclear structure of the universe doesn't occur silently. It creates a primal roar like a thousand jetliners taking off, but deeper, so deep it jolted us on a gut level. I had an overwhelming urge to run, to flee this unnatural event as if the impossible act of running could banish it. But there was nowhere to run to, not even a ground to run on. We floated in the vastness of the Atlantic Ocean on what amounted to some glorified, inflated Hefty bags.

The noise diminished, but didn't quite go away. It settled to a kind of low rumble like the growl of a distant, giant carnivore. Anthony looped a nylon line around the plastic stanchions of the raft, clipped it to his wrist and handed me the other end.

"If this thing tumbles ass over end, we want to stay in it."

I clipped the open end to my flight suit.

"Hey, you know what we forgot to do, knucklehead?" I asked him.

"What?"

"Pray. We're Catholics, man. It should work."

"That's all I been doing since I seen this thing. Hey, listen…"

It started as a susurration, a whisper growing in volume until it filled every molecule of space. A wave of superheated air carrying vaporized steam from the ocean and a variety of assorted debris headed our way. It cooled and lost its explosive power gradually as it traveled through the cold air and over the surface of the water. I kept seeing those newsreels in my mind, the ones that were filmed close to the Trinity bomb in Nevada in the forties. Houses, telephone poles, trees, all smashed, torn away by the force of the blast wave.

The noise reached a crescendo and the blast hit the little raft. I was facing the side that got hit first. The plastic wall collapsed around me like butcher paper around a piece of meat. For a split second I couldn't draw breath, the thin material was forced over my entire face. Then a giant hand slammed us and the raft lifted in the air. The floor tore from one section of the wall. Something struck me hard on the shoulder and I felt the sudden scorching heat of the air. Anthony rolled over me, then the raft lifted again and I slammed into him. A wave crashed over us, and another slammed us down again. The water surged with choppy waves of varying heights raised by the force of the passing blast wave.

The violence of the blast seemed as if it would only end with our oblivion. But gradually, the air stilled again and returned to a semblance of normalcy. The sea remained choppy, buffeting us in what remained of our sea shelter.

Only two walls had remained inflated, bobbing on the waves and still attached to the tattered floor. The dome roof had totally blown away. We remained tethered to the plastic loop that had once held the eight walls of the raft. Now it was the only thing that linked us to the shredded remains of the survival craft. Immersed three-quarter in the water, we clung to the plastic tatters as the cold began to seep though our flight suits.

In those few moments our entire surroundings had changed. Toward the North a dim glow persisted on the horizon. Somewhere above that, in a roiling tempest, a mushroom cloud rose. I thought I could see its outlines like a monstrous gargoyle in the night, but I knew it must be my imagination.

The surface of the sea didn't return to its previous calm. It remained choppy with no particular direction to the waves, as if the ocean itself was boiling. Wisps of vapor floated above the surface and the clean briny smell had been replaced by a vaguely sulfuric smell of burning. I looked over at Anthony. Something had hit him on the lower part of his face. Blood came out of his mouth, mingling with that from a cut higher up on his forehead. He looked like someone had stuffed him into a giant washer and put him through the spin cycle.

"You alright, buddy?" I asked him.

"Yeah, okay."

"You look like shit."

"Still look better than you. That's what the ladies always said."

"Well, anyway, we made it."

"Not yet we didn't."

"What?"

"The Tsunami, remember? It's on its way."

CHAPTER 87

After the fury of the blast wave, the Tsunami was almost anti-climactic. Still, it managed to make things worse for us. Suddenly we felt ourselves rising, at least a hundred feet as the wave passed. It broke at the top and we tumbled again. After the mountain of water passed we were left barely clinging to one inflated wall and the trailing plastic sheets that were all that remained of the raft. The sea didn't resume its previous calm, but settled down enough so we didn't have to fight it constantly.

Our EPIRBS had remained fastened to our flight suits and the strobes continued sending out signals every ten seconds. That meant the electronics had survived and somewhere, rescuers were hopefully picking up the homing signal.

Our biggest enemy now was the cold water. This was the Atlantic in November. I didn't know what the statistics were, but I didn't think survival time was very elevated for us. We shook violently, uncontrollably as our bodies desperately tried to create heat through shivering. It was hard to talk, but I knew that if we were to survive, we had to fight it together.

"A..An..Anthony…"

"Huh?"

"You re..re..remember..Ca..Canarsie Pier?"

His teeth chattered so hard I could hear them clicking. I could tell he remembered as he managed to answer.

"Ye…Yeah…you…Pu…Pussy."

"N..No..Sm..Smart..cause that's..what…we…wo…would…have…lo…Looked   like. Like…w…we…do…now."

We had been ten years old doing one of those stupid boy stunts on a dare that occasionally ends very badly. It was during Christmas recess and we had taken the El to Canarsie and the new piers they had built on the edge of Sheepshead Bay in Brooklyn. We had brought two towels smuggled out of the house in a paper shopping bag from the A&P. The dare was to jump in on one end and swim back in the freezing water to the ladder at the foot of the pier. There were two ladders there. Whoever got out on the first ladder was officially a pussy. The real tough guy would make it to the farther, second ladder. I got out on the first ladder. Anthony made it to the second one. That night the doctor had two emergency home visits and we spent the next three days of holiday recess in bed.

I couldn't feel my limbs now, but the cold seemed less painful somehow. I dimly remembered that was one of the symptoms of hypothermia. Anthony's eyes held a glaze to them and he shook his head as if that would be enough to warm us. He had stopped shivering also. I didn't think it was a good sign.

"Gast…Dinowitz…You remember Dinowitz?"

"Yeah…Stupid little bastards," I said and I made a noise that started as a laugh and ended as a gurgling cough.

It had happened two years later. We were then twelve, but evidently not much smarter. Dinowitz' was a junkyard that specialized in trucks. An entire half-acre of old wrecked trucks, that for two boys, was an attraction even more powerful than the fabled FAO Schwartz toy store in Manhattan. Old man Dinowitz locked his junkyard every night at five. The gate surrounding it was low, easy to climb for a couple of Brooklyn kids, but there were the dogs. Every night, Dinowitz let loose five dogs on the property. These animals took the term junkyard dogs to a whole new level. We had leaned a ten-foot plank against the fence and climbed to the top. Then we lifted the plank and placed it between the top of the fence and the roof of the nearest truck. By moving the plank from the roof of one truck to another, we were able to explore the yard. Below us the dogs jumped and barked at our plank-walking act, just waiting for one of us to fall like morsels of meat to be torn to bloody shreds.

We didn't fall. The plank did, leaving us stranded on top of a truck through a cold winter night. When old man Dinowitz opened his yard the next morning he called us a couple of stupid little bastards before phoning the cops. He didn't bring in the dogs until the police arrived. He must have been surprised at the number of officers and squad cars that appeared. When we went missing that night, Vito Consoli and Franco stirred the NYPD in Brooklyn like an overturned anthill. We were brought back to our families for tears, hugs, smacks in the head and weeks of punishment.

"We gotta hang on, Anthony, just like at Dinowitz."

Time passed and it began to get warmer. I thought about taking off the flight suit, even tried it, but the zippers and fastenings had become impossibly difficult. My fingers didn't work right and the sensations of heat felt like torture. I found out later that this is not uncommon. Hypothermia causes confusion of not only logic, but sensory perceptions. Cold becomes hot. Victims often remove protective clothing to ward off imaginary heat.

Now an intense light washed over us, and for a moment I believed another device had somehow gone off. I whispered "Hang in there, don't look," to Anthony, but the words didn't get out and I know he didn't hear me.

A raging wind swept over us directly from overhead. I tried to raise my head and look, but couldn't find the strength. I heard splashes on either side of me and felt hands pulling me from the remains of the raft. There were people in the water. They hollered things I didn't understand. Whatever weak response I managed was torn away by the hurricane washing over us from above.

I was dragged through the churning waves into a cage hovering in the water, suspended by a wire. Anthony was already there, curled into a ball as if all his bones had become elastic. I felt myself lifted into the air and looked up, blinded by a tremendous light. For a moment I thought I died and that was the light people were supposed to see when they passed on. Then the roaring noise got louder. We approached the bottom of a huge orange-colored machine and I could read the words on the side.

United States Coast Guard.

CHAPTER 88

Three days later–Bethesda Naval Hospital, MD.

Michael's little face peered up at me from the lower edge of the door. I opened my mouth and made a monster head. He giggled and retreated out of sight and stuck his head out again. His sister Gina appeared and pulled him away. She had that exasperated look only a nine-year old girl dealing with her immature six-year old brother, could have. I winked at her and she smiled. Anthony's kids had been playing sneak attacks to my bed all afternoon. They were all there in Anthony's room next door, Michael, Gina, and Maria.

I turned to Shirley, sitting next to me, between the bed and the window.

"How come he's getting out a day before me?" I asked for the umpteenth time. "That ain't fair."

"Life's not fair. Besides, you're probably more fragile."

"Fragile? Fragile this!"

"Oh my."

I grinned at her. It felt unbelievable great to be alive, recuperating, and Shirley here waiting for me.

"Seriously," she said. "You have a medical history with that previous wound. They want an extra day of observations. Don't you pay attention when the doctors talk to you?"

"You can't always trust doctors."

"As opposed to ATF agents?"

"Or sheriffs."

"Ex."

"Once, always."

Right then, Anthony came into the room. He was fully dressed and ready to go. Two bandages adorned his face where he had suffered bruises and lacerations during our altercation with the nuclear device. Both his kids hung on him like little tree ornaments, pulling at his arms and the folds of his jacket. Maria followed behind them, carrying the armful of video games, toys and books necessary to keep two rambunctious kids reasonably quiet during a hospital visit.

"Daddy, how come Uncle Gast doesn't have bandages on his face like you?" Michael asked while his sister rolled her eyes.

"Cause your Uncle Gast is much cuter than your daddy," I replied.

"Nice going, corrupt my children," Anthony said. "Anyway, we have a suite at the Marriott Courtyard. We're going to be staying there for a couple of weeks."

"How come?"

"Got no choice. That FBI agent Ford wants to debrief us. Translate that to a week of questioning. That includes you and Shirley."

"That's alright. Didn't have anything better to do anyway."

"We got you a room for you too, buddy. For you and your nurse," Maria said.

"Can't wait to take his temperature," Shirley replied.

"Ouch."

"I made reservations at the hotel restaurant for tonight. Will you join us, Shirley?" Maria asked her.

"Hey, what about me?"

"Tomorrow night. You have to stay here another day, remember?"

"Bummer."

"Don't worry, they won't run out of food, big guy."

After they left Shirley stood, leaned over and gave me quick kiss.

"I'm leaving too. I'll be back at ten, tomorrow morning to pick you up. Doctor says he'll have you checked out by then."

"Hey, bring me a pizza. I can't stand that hospital stuff."

"Okay. What do you want on it?"

"Pepperoni and garlic."

"Yuk. For once, I'm glad I'm not sleeping with you tonight."

After she left, I turned on the little TV over my bed. I clicked it to CNN. The three top stories seemed to have crowded out every other shred of news around.

I tuned in to the FBI mass-raids story. During the last twelve hours the Bureau had moved in force into the Los Alamos area and Oklahoma City, home of Investigative Research Division. There were still more raids in Long Island and Delaware. It seemed as if the Justice Department acting under Presidential Directive had shut down IRD and revoked its charter as a federal law enforcement agency. Video clips came on with IRD agents taken away in FBI vans. I recognized some of them including the one who had damned near stopped my heart with that punch when they held me at Los Alamos. Barely a week had passed since then, yet it seemed almost a lifetime. So many things had taken place. I also recognized Dallas Wilson, head of the now defunct IRD. There were some pretty serious charges arrayed against them: murder, conspiracy, falsification of government documents, with more pending.

The next story was the aborted cold fusion demonstration at Felton National Laboratory. No one seemed to have much information about it and the Energy Department refused to grant any interviews or answer questions. I suspect Agent Ford and the FBI must have had something to do with that.

I was disappointed at how fast they ran that segment. I'd been there. I thought that maybe I'd see myself on TV. No such luck. Seems like they wanted to get to the story of the century; The nuclear blast off the shore of Delaware. They didn't realize yet that the events were related. I wondered how long it would be before the conspiracy theorists rightfully blew apart the developing cover. I hoped the government would have the sense to tell the truth, soon as they figured it out that is.

The Department of Homeland Defense and the FBI were as tight lipped as I'd ever seen them. The newscasters didn't really have any kind of coherent story or videos about the nuclear blast. They kept running the same thing over and over, stock footage of FBI agents and the Coast Guard. Interviews with passengers on the Southern Constellation and the arrival of the big cruise ship in Norfolk Harbor.

The rear of the ship appeared a little battered, but not heavily so. Blown-out windows—those that did not have storm shutter protection—bent poles and metal struts, that kind of thing. The debris had been cleaned up by the crew before putting into port, including any damaged deck chairs that had not been swept overboard by the blast wave.

The captain had taken exactly the right measures. There were about two dozen injuries among crew and passengers, all relatively minor. They were caused when the Tsunami wave hit the stern of the ship and sent it into a thirty-degree downward angle. Many who had the misfortune to be caught standing when the wave hit were knocked off their feet. Only two with broken bones were deemed serious enough to require hospitalization.

I thought for a moment on how close all these people had come to oblivion, to being incinerated in the nuclear furnace. Sometimes you're going about your life, doing normal things, when death passes so close that you can almost feel dark wings brush against you.

If I had pushed a little harder on that generator as it hung out the cargo hatch of Anthony's airplane, if the radio message had been delayed a few seconds. That's all it takes. The most minute of events may carry the power to remove you from earth. That's the luck of the draw.

I felt a surge of pride. We had done it, Anthony and I, we had saved perhaps millions in Delaware, most certainly the passengers and crew of the Southern Constellation, all four thousand of them.

I guess that should count for something come judgment day, when we would be called to account for all the shit we'd done.

EPILOGUE

Ronald Reagan International Airport, Washington, D.C.

I looked out the big windows of the airport at the bustle of moving airplanes, vehicles and workers dressed in shorts and tank tops. It's hot as hell out there. Washington gets that way in June, sometimes. Thank heaven for AC in airports.

Anthony and I sat at the bar right outside his gate, knocking down a draft beer each before they called his flight. He had just finished testifying, for the third time, this one before a congressional sub-committee. The times before that had been for the special prosecutor. The events of the previous November had eclipsed anything that passed before it, even, 9/11. The details were slowly being pieced together by tenacious prosecutors and FBI investigators. We were gratified to see that there was a candor to the events being revealed. The public was being informed while the press had a field day.

I had wanted to drive Anthony to the airport and he had been pretty quiet all the way. He opened up now—probably the brewskis.

"You and Shirley, you're pretty tight now?" he asked.

"Yeah, I think she's the one. She hasn't quite figured out what she's going to do now, I mean the sub-committee gig is temporary."

I had been fully re-instated with ATF, even given a promotion. I was Captain-grade now, temporarily assigned to the DC office to assist in the investigation. I was also a prime witness and participant, so it worked out.

"Well bro, I tell you one thing you owe us—A nice peaceful visit. We'd love to have you and Shirl over for a few weeks when you get your shit together."

"We will, Anthony, guaranteed."

"So how many did they snag so far?"

Good question—two Senators and three members of the House of Representatives and about another twenty or so from various branches of government. Although they had been charged with a litany of things, in a sense it was heartening that they had been clueless as to the Tinian Protocol. I like to think they had only fallen prey to basic greed and power-lust and would never have participated if they had known the extent of the evil their actions would facilitate. I told Anthony as much. He didn't sound convinced.

"You know, they talk about my father and the other crime families. How bad they are, but you know what? They have a code, some semblance of honor. These other mutts don't even have that, they just wear better suits."

"Not even that," I replied.

"At least I'm glad to see that IRD bunch get nailed."

"Yeah, they're the real evil ones. They knew what would happen, they set it up. They deserve their sentence, capital punishment. Think they'll ever get it?"

"Dear old Dallas Wilson, and a few others, I think they probably will, eventually. I mean they still haven't executed that Zachariah Moussai for 9/11 yet."

"Did you read about the Russian, that Petrovsky guy from Petrovskaya Petroleum? He's on the Committee of Five. They should rename it, there's only three left now."

About three months ago the story of the Committee of Five had broken out. Interpol had turned a key member of Sir Hubert Montrose's staff. Petrovsky had been implicated.

He had protested his innocence, but the evidence had been pretty strong. Yet with the money and influence behind him, the affair could have dragged on for years. Others in positions of power throughout Russia and the old Soviet Republics would undoubtedly have been dragged in. They had settled it the same way other embarrassments had been settled in that part of the world. Somewhere, somehow, Petrovsky had taken a dose of "Russian vitamins." They'd found him dead the next morning. Of course everyone was investigating, but nothing would be found, just like that other Russian dissident in late 06.

Sylvie Papadopoulos remained safely ensconced in Greece, protected by her deep roots within the Greek government. There were four international warrants for her and although they would never be served, her globetrotting days were over. She would remain in Greece, watching her power slowly dwindle and bearing the condemnation of the world. Doesn't seem like much punishment for participating in a scheme that could have killed so many people. Sometimes justice can be limited.

Richard Vandermere, the recluse billionaire CEO and shareholder of Energy Sources LTD was a different story. Holed up in Malaya, he was spending a sizable chunk of the fortune he had been able to bring overseas simply to avoid extradition. It wasn't working. A Malayan court had just denied his appeal. Mister Vandermere would face a jury of twelve in the state of Delaware, then a battery of federal charges.

And the last member, Sir Hubert Montrose III had recently been arrested by a joint task force of Scotland Yard and Interpol. He would spend the rest of his life and fortune in jail, trying to avoid extradition to the US and a lethal injection—perhaps unsuccessfully. Yeah, it was a pretty grubby story. It sickened me to think about it and I changed the subject.

"Hey, Anthony, see old Doc Katamay around?"

"You wouldn't believe it," Anthony replied with a grin. "He's at the estate every weekend. The old man flies him in on Friday and flies him back to Los Alamos Sunday nights."

"Get outta here."

"No, for real. Him and Vito are best buddies. I guess with Katamay losing Sergei and Vito taking care of him, they kinda bonded. Now they sit by the pool, talk philosophy, the human condition, whatever. It's a pisser, they drink Espresso and eat that Hungarian ghoulash shit every day."

"You're kidding?"

"No way. Never thought I'd see an ancient Sicilian like my old man eating that stuff. What's the world coming to, eh?"

"So he's got that cold fusion thing back on track again?"

Anthony nodded as he answered. "Yeah, but you know, there's lots of different stuff to think about with that. I mean you can't just throw it out overnight. The petroleum industry is huge and it's not just big-shots either. Lots of ordinary people have their 401K's and IRA's in it. You destroy that overnight, you've got chaos. They're in the process of bringing those companies into it, replacing petroleum, gas, coal, all of it with cold fusion. Katamay says within five years the US will be completely energy self-reliant. Inside of a decade all forms of petroleum will be as obsolete as whale oil."

"Makes sense."

At that moment we heard Anthony's flight being called. We finished our beers and I walked him to the gate. We shook hands at first then I pulled him into a hug.

"You take care now, bro. Hug Maria and the kids for me. Pay my respects to the old man."

"Yeah, I will, Gast. Give my love to Shirley and come to see us, alright?"

I said we would, and I meant it. I watched Anthony walk through the gate to his plane until he disappeared.

THE
APOCALYPSE SERIES

———◆———

The Boomer Protocols
Cold Fusion
Sylvans
The Devil's Caldera

Also by Patrick Astre
<u>Remnants of War Series</u>
The Last Operation
The Doppelganger Protocol
The Devil's Eye
Twilight of Demons

Turn the page for an

excerpt from

SYLVANS

The Apocalypse Series
Book Three

Patrick Astre

Doctor Pravin Prabinwah thought Duncan Wesley was like an overheated pressure cooker with undercurrents of violence leaking out the edges like wisps of steam. Dr. Prabinwah's colleague sat next to him with bulging eyes peering out under thick glasses like a frightened owl. Although the two scientists sitting across from Wesley represented the best minds in the world of physics, they seemed nothing more then timid mice before a lurking hungry tomcat.

Duncan Wesley rose from his seat. He placed his hands on the table and leaned forward from the waist until his face was less then two feet from the scientists. They both craned their heads back as Wesley swung his gaze from one to the other.

"I don't give a damn about your protocols and procedures or any other academic bullshit," Wesley said, "You may be on the Government tit, but right now I control the flow of milk. In other words gentlemen your ass is mine. I want that test run in forty-eight hours. Do you understand that? Am I clear enough?"

Dr. Prabinwah glanced at his colleague who blinked furiously as he licked his lips with little cat-like furtive movements of his tongue. Prabinwah realized he would have to be the one to make this volatile man understand, if that was at all possible.

"Uh, Mr. Wesley," he said, "these are not military exercises we can run on demand. Our protocols and procedures are not the problem. Even eliminating all safety concerns, we must still deal with laws of physics. Five days would be the absolute minimum."

"Why?"

Dr. Prabinwah sighed. This was not the first time he had explained this. He felt as if he was being interrogated, as if the man was trying to trip him up somehow. He also knew he had no choice but to play along and comply. In the last two weeks the Physics Science Department had been hostage to Duncan Wesley and his National Security Agency mandate. Since the arrival of the Artifact from Israel, all operating time of the Ion Collider and the new Phased Pulse Array Nuclear Aligner were locked in by the Agency. All other projects had been placed on hold.

"Well, uh," replied Prabinwah, "without Dr. Wu…"

Both scientists jumped as Wesley slammed his hand on the table, the noise violent and alien against the muted whisperings of the computers lining the opposing wall of the room.

"Screw Dr. Wu. He's already facing Federal charges for his disappearing stunt. You can bet his ass is in a major sling when we catch him, and that won't be very long."

"Yes, I understand," replied Prabinwah, "But that leaves only Dr. Hashimo and myself to interpret the data and set the Frequency Arrays. The Artifact's ionic pulses must be correctly interpreted and the alignment frequencies properly set before the Collider and the Phased Pulse Array Nuclear Aligner can be effective. Any error would not only negate the experiment but possibly ruin the Artifact for further tests."

"How about I get you a couple dozen NSA computer techs or a couple more physicists?" Wesley asked.

Dr. Prabinwah smiled for the first time as he replied.

"That would be like getting a clerk-typist to do a dissertation on surgery because she knows how to use a keyboard. Dr. Hashimo, Dr Wu and myself, invented the theory and the machinery that is the Phased Pulse Array Nuclear Aligner. This is a brand new science, even to us. Bringing in outsiders would mean at least a year of training."

Wesley leaned back, his eyes never leaving the scientists. He sat for what seemed endless moments before he replied.

"Five days, five fucking days maximum."

Dr. Prabinwah nodded. The undercurrent of threats and possible violence, the intensity of the man, even the profanity had shaken the academic's gentle soul. He wanted out, away from this man.

After the two scientists left, Wesley raised his face toward the ceiling and rotated his head like someone trying to get rid of a crick in his neck. It always began this way, that unpleasant buzzing in his head like a bee loose in his cranium. The noise settled to a sort of background hum as he felt the presence of the Sylvan.

It was late evening when Duncan Wesley stepped outside the main Physics lab. He could recall how he got there, where his feet went for each step, the feel of the handrail as he descended the stairs. But he was not in control. He felt as if he was tied on the front seat of a car while someone else drove. They might take your directions, or they might not. He felt the force, the push and pull of the alien presence. He didn't sense any threats, but still wondered what would happen if he tried to push it out.

Five days from now it wouldn't matter.

The grounds of Brookhaven National Laboratory form a U the size of a small town. The top of the U abuts William Floyd Parkway and the U itself is a band of pine barren forest about two miles wide. The Lab is nestled inside the U. The Physics Lab and adjoining buildings housing the Ion Collider and Nuclear Aligner are at the edge of those woods.

Where the Sylvan waited.

image:flourish.png

COLD FUSION
available in print and ebook

Award-winning author Patrick Astre served in the US Army Infantry, stationed in Germany during the height of the Cold War. Rising to the rank of Sergeant E-5, Astre finished his last year of service as a Drill Instructor at Fort Benning, Georgia.

Now, Patrick Astre, CFP, EA, RFC is a recognized tax and financial expert specializing on the economic issues of longevity. Patrick is independent and has been advising individuals and corporations since 1969.

Patrick's second financial book was released in mid-August 2007 by Entrepreneur Media Publishing. It is Entrepreneur's "cornerstone" retirement book. *This is Not Your Parents' Retirement* is one of the top sellers in its field, addressing the convergence of the longevity revolution and the aging baby-boomers, woefully unprepared for retirement.

In addition to his financial books, Patrick is the author of numerous articles as well as fiction thrillers. His novel *The Artifact* won the Salvo Press Mystery Thriller of the year Award in 2005.

Patrick is a professional public speaker and member of the National Speakers Association. His seminars, speeches and keynotes are a lively, enthusiastic mix of entertainment, motivation, humor and unique insights.

Some of his clients include Celebrity Cruises, John Hancock, Princess Cruises, LIBOR (Long Island Board of Realtors) Passaic Board of Realtors, and many others.

Patrick lives in Long Island, New York with his wife Lynn. The couple has two children and two grandchildren and enjoy traveling throughout the country in their motor home.